Destined to Get This Cash

D1557155

DEDICATION

This book is dedicated to my late grandfather James C. Jimmy Brown. Our birthdays are on the same day, August 17th. I love you and miss you grandpa.

I want to send a shout out to my family which consists of my lovely mother Bert, my pop Samuel Sr., lil bro's Sherwin, Tank, Foba and Jaime. Sisters Carolyn, Kena, Regan and Mosheika. My cousin lil Bruce. My special kids lil Sam III, Ashley, Samari, and Sadarian. My grandsons both named Samuel Austin IV LoL! My beautiful granddaughter Miracle, the Princess. Aren't I lucky! If I ain't include you, you know why!

It ain't no secret that I've been locked up over 15 years. I wrote this book while in confinement for getting caught with a cellphone. My motivation came from my homegirl "Mae," I love you chic.

I can never forget my biggest fan, RoRo. Thank you so much. This book could not have been created without you, my baby. The real "Chrishonna" your support was priceless. Pooh, my soulmate no matter what, you still continue to love and support me. Thank you.

Last but not least, I want to shout out to all the cats in the pen: Rick, Wise, Freddie, Pakistan, Mike, Head, Nut, Pat, Teflon, Pooh, Sweat, my roommate who I drove crazy, Nose. It's talent in here ya'll! **Peace!**

$ El Capo $

Samuel Austin

CHAPTER 1

Stars Are Born

St Joseph's Hospital, Tampa, Fl 1976

"Push baby push," yells Cameron C-Money Jones. "I can see our son's head." "Oh God, baby," yells Tonya Jones.

It's her first baby and he is giving her pure hell. She's hitting C-Money hard with her fist.

"One more push," yells the doctor as he pulls out a handsome 6lb 7oz baby boy. Clapping, C-Money says, "I'm naming him Cashmere R.R. Jones." "R.R.?" yells Tonya. "Rolls Royce!" laughs C-Money.

"Doctor, we have another one!" yells the screaming nurse, running towards the hallway.

Two minutes later...

"Shiiit," yells Eldrena Drena Jenkins-Jackson. "I swear to God, I'm getting my tubes tied. Having these babies are so painful and you sit your crazy ass up there looking like you ain't got a worry in the world." "Fuck you!" Screams Deshean D Jackson Sr. "All the hell you take me through, the mental pain has to account for something. Now stop crying and push out my beautiful baby girl." "Kiss my ass!" Replies Drena while pushing with all her might. "There we go, ma'am." Dr. Smith says while pulling out a beautiful, 6lb 3oz, baby girl. "Ooh God, she's gorgeous!" Yells Drena with excitement. "You named our other two bad ass kids so I'm naming her." Drena rolls her eyes at D. "Destiny Mercedes Jackson." "The same Mercedes you promised me 8 years ago when you took my virginity in my seniior year of high school?

m still living in College Hill Projects with a ten-year-old Ford Taurus." "I love you too," replies D.

Deshean was a star athlete at Middleton High School. He was the school hero, excelling at baseball, football, basketball, and track. All the girls chased behind him every day. They were always denied because since he was seven years old, running around College Hill, he was always head over hills about Eldrena Jenkins. They are two months and two days apart. Their moms were drinking buddies and grew up together. Eldrena is all that; five-foot eleven, slim, fine, long good hair and a fat lil' plump ass. More than that, she was smart. She loved to read and dreamed to own her own restaurant; she loves to cook.

That was eight years ago. Now Drena is a gossiping stay-at-home mother who treats her nose to cocaine. On section eight with three kids, no job history and hangs with a bunch of sorry ass gossiping friends just like her.

Deshean had the skills, but no ambition. He is now the owner of the 22nd Street Car Wash. In the back of the shop, him and all the jits in the projects gamble by shooting dice and playing cards all day.

****

Tonya is from West Tampa. An area called up-top. She was raised in a two-parent home and was basically a good girl until age fifteen when she met Cameron aka C-Money.

They met at Prince Grocery Store on Boulevard and Columbus Drive. He was outside selling nickel bags of weed. At fifteen, he was already doing his thing on the hustle tip. He even had his own Cadillac Seville with white walls and a child. He begged to take her home when she came out of the store.

Now, eight years later, he's the strongest young nigga in town. Selling three to five kilos a week for his Cuban connect, Carlos.

Tonya owns the biggest beauty salon in Tampa called Super T's. She launders her husband's money. She also sells stolen clothes that she buys for the low from all boosters.

They have a mini-mansion in Lutz but mainly live at another home they own in Tampa Heights where C-Money was born and raised.

****

Destiny came home from the hospital to a roach-infested 3-bedroom apartment in College Hill Projects. Buy here pay here, Buddy Bi-Rite furniture. Tore down end tables, dirty walls. She has to share a bed with her older sister Cherell, who is now five. Her brother DJ, Deshean Jr., is seven and the oldest. She grows up on WIC, which includes King Vitamin cereal, Kaboom's, free cheese, free lunch at the big park and bootleg cable on a black-and-white T.V. She had daily fights with her brother and older sister over kool-aid and peanut butter and jelly sandwiches. Her mother and father were always gone.

****

Cashmere had it all growing up. He goes home to two rooms of his own. One at each house. Both rooms were laid out in Batman. Nice color cable T.V. He also had a nanny. His parents took him to all the theme parks and Malibu Grand Prix. He was able to do all what he wanted. He was a spoiled-brat and didn't want for nothing. He wore all the name brand shoes and clothes. A true hustler's son.

CHAPTER 2

My First Love Cashmere, Fifteen Years Later

"What do ya'll boys want to do tonight?" Cashmere says.

By now, everybody has nicknamed him Cash because he always looks like money. Being the only son of a kingpin has its advantages.

Cash and his two BFF's are walking around Eastlake Mall in Tampa, off 56th St. and Hillsborough Avenue.

Cool Al is his right-hand man. A straight-up pretty boy. Long dreads, light brown skin and eyes. His mom works at Super T's and his dad is one of C-Money's top lieutenants, so of course he's soiled too.

Fat Dre is the killer of the crew. He's big and ugly but stays fly because his father is C-Money's muscle and BFF. Fat Dre will take a bullet for Cash. The three of them go everywhere together.

"Man, I'm trying to fuck somebody's daughter," says Cool Al. "That's what I'm talking about!" Yells Fat Dre.

Being with two fly cats, he always gets the leftover pussy.

"How about we go to the party my girl Angela is throwing in Hyde Park?" says Cash. "How you claiming a little bitch you ain't fucked yet?" Laughs Cool Al. "You been kicking it with that chic for two months and ain't got the pussy?" Fat Dre asked. "Tonight, her ass is grass and I'm the lawn mower," Cash says. "Her mother is out of town and I'm sending her up and through there after the party, whether we go to the party or not."

At fifteen, Cash is that dude. He's 5'10, has four gold teeth to the top and four at the bottom. He keeps his hair cut in a "Craig Mack." Weighing 165lbs but all muscles. His pop bought him a 1991 Nissan Maxima for his fifteenth birthday. It has rims and music.

He's fucking whores like mad crazy, but he's crazy about Angela. In his mind, she is gonna be his wife and the mother of his kids.

"In that case," Cool Al says, "her party is where it is. I'm trying to fuck her home girl Rosie anyways. I ain't never had no Spanish pussy." Fat Dre laughs, while mocking a Spanish chic's accent, "ooh Papi, a train?" Dre says Referring to him and Cool Al both fucking Rosie. "Naw, my man. It's too many whores gonna be in the spot. Get your own pussy tonight." "That's fucked up, bro." Fat Dre laughs.

Later that night, "Dance all Night" by Poison Clan is jammin' from the speakers and everyone is dancing, drinking, smoking weed and having a good time.

"You having fun?" Angela asks, in Cash's ear. She is grinding on him. "Not as much fun as we are about to have tonight," he says while squeezing her soft, round ass. "I'm scared, Cash. Please don't hurt me." "I got you ma," he assures her.

An hour later, Cash is on his knees. They are on the floor in Angela's room. He's about to suck her small, firm, titties. "Damn baby you have a nice body," Cash says while admiring Angela's beautiful body.

She is the twin of Jada Pickett, the star of the movie, Set It Off.

"Ooh shit," moans Angela. She's never had her tits sucked. Reaching his hand down, Cash is also rubbing Angela's hairy, wet pussy. "You ready baby?" Cash says trying to stick a finger inside Angela's tight pussy. "Put it in, Cash." Moans Angela. "Oooh God," she yells as Cash puts the head of his 8' dick inside her tight walls. He's slow grinding her, "oooh Cash, it feels so good." About to cum, Cash speeds up his pace and is now fucking Angela something serious. "Fuuuuck Cash, it feels like you're in my stomach!" "Oooh shit ma, I'm about to cum!" Cash shouts while cumming inside of her.

DESTINY

"No, I'm not going with you to the skating rink, Meme." Says Destiny. "Why?" Meme whines. "I'm tired of Stardust and them same old boys trying to talk and dance on us every week. One called me a stuck-up, virgin bitch last week. DJ heard him and stole him in his jaw. I ain't with all this mess. How about we go to the movies? Boyz In the Hood just came out. I heard it's good." "Bitch, I want me a boy in the hood," Meme says.

Jomesha Carter, aka Meme is Destiny's BFF, even though mentally they are nothing alike. Meme is wild. Been fucking since she was twelve. She is one year older than Destiny but in the same grade due to failing a grade. She's from the projects too (College Hill). Her mother Tracey is one of Drena's snorting and gossiping partners. She loves the dope boys and loves to party.

"Meme, do you ever dream of getting out of this place?" Questions Destiny. "Yeah, I do. I need to catch Mike Tyson, L.L. Cool J, or a rich nigga and I'm gone. Other than that, I'm good. I hate school. Don't even like to clean our apartment. I dream to be a hustler's or rich nigga's wife so I can just lay back and spend his money," Destiny hates that her friend is so simple minded, but loves her to death, so she deals with it. "Well, I want more," Destiny says. "Look at my big sister Cherell. She's only 20 years old and pregnant with her third child. She has her own apartment right here in these dirty-ass projects we were raised in. She's with a woman beater who works at checkers. DJ is still staying with us. Him, his baby and their bad ass baby.

He's supposed to be a hustler, but ain't never got no money. Gold digging ass baby momma spends the lil change he does make. I want to go to school for Criminal Justice. I want to be a detective." "Bitch, I know you ain't talking about being the police!" Meme shouts. "Yes, and right here in College Hill. I'm going to put an end to all the violence and drug dealing that's keeping our hood down." "Bitch, please!" Meme rolls her eyes. "One, you can't stop it and two, hell it's a police department next to the projects and people are hustling and killing every day." "You'll see. I'm going be the first black female detective working our hood." "I'll see you tomorrow. I'm going be the first bad bitch in Stardust Skating Rink tonight." Meme says walking off, swinging her fat ass.

Destiny lays back on her bed and begins to daydream. She wants it all. A career. A good husband who will go hard and treat her right. A nice home with two kids, a girl and a boy and to uplift her neighborhood.

She falls asleep.

CHAPTER 3

When It Rains, It Pours – Adversity

DESTINY

"Happy Birthday, lil sis!" Cherell says, hugging Destiny. "Thank you, why do you have on them big, ugly glasses?" Destiny says. "Shh, stop talking so loud. It wasn't Coop's fault I played. I came in the house at 4:00 am last night. I went to the Zoo and lost track of time, went to Gyro's afterwards. Coop was up all night with the new baby. As soon as I hit the door, he hit me in the eye." "How is that not his fault? A man ain't got no business hitting on no woman." Destiny says. "Girl, I was dead-ass wrong. He should have really beat my ass. Anyways, happy sweet sixteenth. Let me go before daddy or DJ see me." Meme is walking up crying as Cherell is leaving. "What is wrong?" shouts Destiny. "I'm scared. I ain't seen my mother in two days." "What? Let's go ask my momma if she seen her." Destiny says walking up the stairs to knock on her mom's bedroom door. "The fuck you want. I know it's your birthday. I got you later on today." "I ain't even worried about that, ma. Meme is here crying. She hasn't seen her mom in two days. Have you seen her?" "She hasn't been fucking with me since last week, when she started fucking with that nigga CB from Ponce de Leon projects. He sells heroin on eighteenth. Check by there, Meme." Drena says shutting her door.

Not even a minute later, a cop car pulls up to Meme's door. An old white lady gets out with the cop. Destiny walks over to the apartment with her BFF.

"Which one of you pretty girls are Jomesha Carter?" The cop says. "Me." Meme says. "You need to go pack your things and come with us. This is Mrs. Wilks; she is a social worker." "Where is my momma?" Yells Meme. "I'm sorry baby." Mrs. Wilks says trying to console Meme. She's gone." "Gone?" Meme yells. "I'm so sorry." The nice white lady, Mrs. Wilks says. "She was rushed to Tampa General Hospital three hours ago. She died of a drug overdose."

Meme faints.

CASH

"Happy Birthday, son!" C-Money says hugging his son. He rented the American Legion to host his son's sixteenth birthday party. Him and his wife Tonya showed their ass. They have ice sculptures, catered seafood, a photographer, Rock It Rod DJ's. They even brought one thousand bottles of Boones Farm for him and his friends to sip on. He ain't seen his main gift yet. They brought him a Range Rover Sport, fully equipped, all black with black rims.

Cash does not know it, but this is also a retirement party for his pop. He's about to give the keys to the city to Cash and his crew.

Angela comes up to Cash, looking stunning in a Cavalli dress that Mrs. Tonya gave her, especially for tonight.

"Hey babe, Happy birthday!" She says giving him a big kiss. "Thanks" he says grabbing her ass. "You staying with me tonight?" He whispers in her ear. "I can't do nothing if I do, why?" "Your period finally came on?"

Her period didn't come on last month and they were both scared; well, she was. Cash secretly wanted her to be pregnant. He also wants a boy and a girl.

"No, Cash! I'm sorry! I had an abortion yesterday!" "You what?" Cash yells. "How could you kill my baby? And without even telling me?" Cash is furious. He has tears in his eyes. Angela does too because she only got the abortion because she was fucking an older hustler out of West Tampa projects named Wewe.

He caught her walking to the store on Main Street one day and she was mesmerized by his Chevy Vert' and big jewelry.

The same night she snuck out and let him beat her back out raw at the Motel 6. When she told him she was pregnant, he made her get an abortion. He paid her $3,000.00. He couldn't take the chance of the police or his main chic finding out he had a minor pregnant.

Cash looked at her with pure disgust in his eyes and says, "You need to leave and please don't ever attempt to contact me." "Cash please, I can explain..." "What's understood doesn't need to be explained," Cash says, turning to walk off in the other direction. This same night is when he met Seleena, a half-black, half Asian beauty with a drop-dead gorgeous body. She was the caterer's daughter.

Cash parties and enjoys the night but deep down inside, his heart is broken. He takes the news of being the new Don in stride. Cool Al and Fat Dre are happier than him.

Show time

DESTINY

"Daddy, can I please go to my auntie Felecia's house?"

Felecia Jackson, Fee is Destiny's favorite aunt. She stays in Jackson Heights apartments on Lake Avenue side. She is Deshean's baby sister. "I ain't taking you," D says. He's outside of his car wash smoking a Newport. "I'll ride my bike. It's 4:30pm. I promise I'll be back home by 8:00pm." "7:30," says D. "Here" he says handing her $20.00. "Happy Birthday. Tell my sister I said not to make me have to come down there. I heard that nigga Ren she fucking with keeping his foot in her ass." "Okay Pop, I'm gone." Destiny says riding on her bike.

Ten minutes later, "Hey auntie," Destiny says hugging her favorite aunt. "Hey baby girl, what's up?" Fee says hugging her back. "Nothing. I came by to spend some time with you. Oh yeah, and get my hair done." Fee is one of the best hair stylists in Tampa. Just too lazy to get her license so she does hair in her kitchen. "Come on in. My last customer just left. I'm so tired of this crazy nigga Ren. He is so jealous; he swears I'm fucking everybody I speak to. I ain't living like that. I ain't never cheated on him or any other nigga I've been with. When I'm with you, I'm all in." Says Fee. "That's what I'm talking about, auntie. That's why I'm still a virgin. I ain't letting a dude get my stuff. Just to add me to his hit list." "Okay!" Screams Fee. She loved her niece. She sees so much potential in her.

So many nights she cried and prayed, wishing she had made better choices. Although she has no kids, at twenty-seven, she's still nowhere in life. Just doing hair, going to the clubs 24/7 and fucking with an abusive nigga that is corner hustling.

A couple of hours later, Destiny says her good-byes and heads home.

Later that night she is awakened by her mother screaming into the telephone at 3:30 am. "We're on our way down there now. It's your sister, Fee," yells Drena. "I'm going too!" Destiny says, piling into D's Ford Explorer.

Pulling up, they see yellow tape all around Fee's apartment. Destiny's heart drops. "Stay in the car," D yells to her.

Five minutes later, Destiny finds out Fee came home early from the 400 Club to find Ren fucking a lil young girl in her apartment.

She used one of his guns and shot him five times. He died on the scene.

Real hood shit!!!

CHAPTER 4

Meet the Connect

"Where are you, son?" C-Money is talking to Cash on his car phone. "I'm pulling up to Seleena mom's house about to drop her off. We just left from eating at Di Pierro's." "Okay, meet me in Central Court Apartments in twenty minutes." "For show Pop," Cash says while disconnecting the call. He immediately calls Cool Al on his car phone.

Cool Al has a black 535 BMW his pop got for him three months ago on his sixteenth birthday.

"It's on, baby boy. Call Fat Dre and tell him I said be on point. My pop just called me. I think he's about to give us our first bomb."

"That's what the fuck I'm talking about," screams Cool Al. You can't tell him he and Cash ain't Nino & G-Money, the two gangsters off the hit movie New Jack City.

They have watched the movie one thousand times with Cool Al vowing to never let money or no bitch to come between them. He respects the game; he knows Cash is "Nino."

"What's up?" Pop Cash says, getting out of his Range Rover. C-Money daps his son up all day. "You ready?" "All day Pop. I got everything you told me I needed. Stash spots for the money, work, a hungry team of hustlers, two trap houses with the steel doors and cameras installed. Oh, and three gunmen. Fat Dre is a beast with his tool. He's gonna be with me every time I move.

Cool Al is in charge of keeping the traps supplied and bringing me the money." "I hope you got some whores on your team." C-Money says. "I told you, bitches are loyal, and you can control them with money." "I got it Pop. All the stash spots and traps have whores. I trust in them." "Okay, come on and ride with me. You can leave your truck here."

C-Money is in an all-black Chevy SS. "What about these?" C-Money says, pushing the a/c button, reaching behind the passenger seat, showing Cash a stash spot. "I'm giving this car to you, but you need to get Cool Al and Fat Dre something like this and all of your whores. You feel me?" "All day, Pop." Ten minutes later, they pull up to a small dingy-looking house in Ybor City. To Cash, the house almost looks like a baser's house.

No cars in the yard but has old washer and dryers in the yard. The grass needs to be mowed.

Knocking on the door, C-Money laughs to himself, remembering almost twenty years ago coming to this same house, thinking the same thing.

"Gracias Amigo." Carlos says in broken English. "Si." C-Money says. "This is my son Cash." Shaking the old cuban's hand. Cash says, "Hello sir."

Carlos looks about eighty years old. He has on no jewelry, some dirty blue jeans and a work shirt. This the connect? Cash thinks to himself looking at Carlos. "Come inside," Carlos says, inviting them in. "So, you are finally done, C-Money." Says Carlos. "I ain't never done hustling, my friend. I'm just laying down my gloves and passing the torch to my son. It's a new generation. My days are now going to be spent fishing, hunting, and traveling with his crazy-ass momma." Looking Cash in the eyes, Carlos says "Are you ready to run an empire?" "Yes sir." Cash confidently replies. "On your father's face I'm giving you ten kilos of fish-scale cocaine and fifty pounds of high-grade weed. Remember, it's all about speed. I've got this stuff by the boat loads. Here is a pager; after you pay for this load, I'll page you when to meet me here. Always come by yourself; you and your trusted gunman. Until further notice you will give the money to your mother."

Looking at his pop for an answer. C-Money says, "I said I was done." Laughing, "I look forward to making a lot of money with you."

They all shake hands. Carlos goes into the backyard and comes back with two big black duffel bags. Cash get an erection, he's so excited. He adores his Pop, but he always had dreams of being his own man and running his own team. He just doesn't plan on doing this as long as Mr. Carlos or his dad. His goals are to get married, have kids and open up some successful businesses.

Money has a way of taking over people's minds.

DESTINY

"Ma, I'll be back. I'm about to walk over to Lee Davis Clinic to see aunt Donna."
"Okay. Tell that tired whore I said to call me."

Donna Jenkins is Eldrena's only sibling; her eldest sister by two years, they are as different as night and day. Donna is a social worker at Lee Davis Clinic on 22nd Street, between College Hill and Ponce de Leon Projects. She works with young girls who get pregnant and diseases by the age of 18. She graduated from FAMU located in Tallahassee. She came back home to her hood to make a difference. Destiny idolizes her. Donna always has good advice and is the motive behind her pursuing her dreams. "Hey auntie" "Hey there, sweetie," Donna says, hugging her niece.

"Did you get my message?"
Donna says, "No ma'am." I told that bad-ass DJ to tell you to come and see me yesterday. I talked to the administrator at FAMU, he said he's gonna do everything he can to get you in their Criminal Justice class. "Oh my God auntie, are you serious?" "Yes, all you have to do is make all A's and B's next year as a senior and you are in. That's all." "I got that, auntie." Destiny says confidently. She is so happy; she can't wait to get to Tallahassee to start her mission.

"My sorority sisters are hoping you'll pledge A.K.A. like us." "I got you auntie. I promise you I won't let you down." "Okay, I'll call you later.

"I have an appointment with a thirteen-year-old who's pregnant with twins." "Twins?" yells Destiny. "Yeah, and the dad who is seventeen, just went to jail last week for three strong- armed robberies." "God help us." Donna sighs. "Love you baby." She screams at Destiny. "Love you too, auntie. Oh, my mother says call her." "Okay," yells Donna. She watches Destiny walk down the hallway. She says a silent prayer that her niece remains strong.

CHAPTER 5

Paid in Full

CASH

"Cash Money in the building." Cool Al screams at the top of his lungs. The past ten months they have been getting paid in full. They have five traps now: one on each side of Tampa Heights, one in Robles Park, one in Oakhurst apartments and one in Palm River. The whole city is fucking with them. They are running through forty bricks a month and two-hundred pounds of weed. The whole crew is eating and tonight for Cash's seventeenth birthday, they are showing their asses in Level II. Cool Al and Fat Dre is throwing Cash a party in VIP.

Cash is sitting in his king size chair with Seleena sitting on his lap. They are both super-fitted in matching Gucci outfits.

Both are iced out from their wrists to their neck.

Cash stands up with a bottle of VSOP Remy Martin in his hand. He feels like Nino, everybody is calling his name. All the women are licking their tongues and winking at him.

At seventeen years old, he's sitting on $200,000.00. His entire crew is eating. He got a super-bad bitch and a connect that gives him all the coke and weed he wants on consignment.

"I'm rich, bitch!" He yells while taking a fat knot of money out of his pocket.

He begins to throw $20.00 after $20.00 in the air. Cool Al starts doing the same thing; it's raining money. Fat Dre, on the other hand, has his hands in his MCM sweater, gripping his 9mm Ruger. His eyes are on the hating nigga's watching his main men stunt. Thirty minutes later, Cool Al and Cash have the parking lot jumping with their Chevy Verts, both on all gold Dayton's. Cash's is money green with tan insides and a tan top. Cool Al has the candy apple red with the grey top and grey insides.

They both have all sixteen switches, hydraulics and eight 12-inch speakers. They show their asses with the trailers painted the same color of their cars pulling high boosted bikes.

But tonight, Fat Dre not stunting. He's in a black Lexus ES300 with a Mac II on the seat, he's about to follow Cash to the condo that him and Seleena have in Brandon.

Twenty minutes later...

"Oh shit!" Cash screams. "Damn baby, this pussy feels good!" Seleena is riding his dick reverse cowgirl in their King size canopy bed. "Smack my ass, Cash!"

She yells. Seleena is a straight up freak. She's two years older than Cash.

About to nut, Cash screams, "turn around and get this cum outta your dick." All happy to oblige, Seleena spins around, grabs Cash's thick pole and sucks him dry. He starts to scream and try to pull his dick outta her mouth.

"Damn," he says looking at her stunning body.

DESTINY

"Meme, how could you slip like that?" Yells Destiny.

"T-House is on every young girl's head in the projects. He's tried to get me million times. Now let alone you sleep with Raw. Now you're saying you're pregnant by him after all you have been through. You should be trying to get out of these projects. Damn, I'm disappointed in you. How many kids does T-House already have?" "Three that I know about," Meme responds. Talking all low, "It is what it is. I will always help you. I love you girl." Destiny says, giving her BFF a comforting hug.

"What a birthday gift you gave me. At least go with me to my auntie Fee's trial. It starts today.

An hour later, "Your honor, we have reached a plea deal with the defendant," the state says. "Are you under any medications, Mrs. Jackson?"

"No sir."

"Did anyone force you to take this plea?"

"No sir."

"Okay, I accept the terms of this plea and sentence you to fifteen years in the Department of Corrections for count one, manslaughter, to be ran concurrent with count two, possession of a firearm. Bailiff, you may take Mrs. Jackson's prints."

"Wait!" Destiny screams. "Can I please hug my favorite auntie, Mr. Judge?" "Yes ma'am. Go ahead." She gives her aunt a big hug. Fee and Destiny are crying. "It's gonna be alright, baby. With a third off for gain time, I'll be out in less than six years."

"Alright ladies" the bailiff shouts. "Bye Destiny. Finish school and get that degree, baby." "I'll be praying for you," shouts Fee.

Destiny is more determined than ever to be a detective. She blames Ren for having the guns in her aunt's house. Drugs and violence are ruining her life and the people around her. She's gonna go hard this senior year to make all A's-

Motivation!

CHAPTER 6

Grown Folks Night

CASH

"Hey ma," Cash yells while walking into Super T's. He is on point as usual; he has on a pair of all white Air Max tennis shoes, a blue and white striped Polo shirt, a pair of navy-blue Polo cargo shorts, a big bracelet with "Cash" in diamonds. He has on his iced-out Cartier watch, fresh haircut, wearing dark blue Gucci shades. Cash strolls in like he owns the place. All eyes are on him as he gives his mother a big hug. "I need to get my nails done. Is my big sister in today?"

Camille Jones is the daughter C-Money had by an older chic a year before he met Tonya.

Paulina seduced young C-Money at age fourteen. She was twenty-eight. He hates her guts, but being the standup dude he was, he took great care of Camille and made sure she had the best of everything.

To this day, she's still spoiled. She does nails at her stepmother's shop, when she wants to. She's a wild child- just like her mother- loves to club and fuck- she has two kids from two different niggas. Rashidi; a spoiled powdered head nigga whose folks have money. They own a few 7-11 stores and plenty of real-estate. They share a beautiful baby girl named Brooklyn. She's six.
Camille also has a bad ass little boy, who's four from a petty weed seller named Flat Top. The boy's name is Supreme. She's not with neither one, but still fucks them both from time to time.

Cash came to the shop to give her the news their Pop told him to give her, which was: she's twenty-six and it's time for her to woman up. She has a house in Brandon, C-Money bought and furnished, and drives a new GS-300 Lexus that C-Money bought three months ago.

"What?" She yells, hearing the news. Standing at 5'3, 135lbs, Camille is a dime piece. Tan skin, green eyes, nice thighs, and a fat round ass.

"The good news," Cash says in a cool voice, "is that I," pointing at himself, "have a great paying job for my big sister." "Doing what?" She snaps. "All you have to do is, starting today after you leave here, or at 6pm everyday… is go to all the trap spots and pick up my money. When you are done, you will meet Cool Al, or he will take it from you at your house. Before I continue and tell you your pay, let me make you understand something. I love you. You're my heart, but business is business. Any mistakes will come with repercussions. I'm not threatening you; I'm letting you know what it is. This game is way bigger than me. You were raised in this life just like me, so you already know what it is." "Cash…" She tries to speak. "Hold up!" he yells," a gunman will follow you to the traps, then to your home. After you get the money to Cool Al, you can do as you choose. I don't want no niggas at your house while my money is there, or in the car with you on the pick-ups, no exceptions!"

"How much do I get paid?" She snaps. "Three thousand a week."

"Oh shit." She smiles, "hell to the yeah, I call that."

"Listen, big sis. I'm giving you this advice from the heart. Save your money. The game ain't forever. Always remember, it could end any day. Here is for one week." Cash says going into his pocket, pulling out a fat knot of money. He counts out three stacks and hands it to her. "Let me get my nails done and a manicure." "Slick." He laughs. "Put Cool Al's and Black Isaac number in your phone. Am I my sister's keeper?" He says, laughing. "All day," Camille says, putting the three stacks in her purse. "C.M.F." Shouts Cash. "Cash Money Family!

DESTINY

10 months later…

"Oh my God, Destiny; you did it!" Screams Donna. Destiny is having a double day; she's graduating from Hillsborough High School and it's her eighteenth birthday.

Her entire family is here at the fairgrounds on MLK Boulevard.
"I wish auntie Fee was here," Donna says, "She is baby. Trust me, all of our prayers are being answered. So, are you ready for FAMU?" Donna screams.

"Baby, we are so proud of you!" Meme is crying, she dropped out two years ago. DJ and his crazy baby momma are present. Cherell sporting a fresh fat lip, she is crying tears of joy. She has her G.E.D. but haven't even thought of college.

Her favorite uncle, Melvin Jackson, is there cheering on. He owns a gas station on Nebraska and 26th St (Coastal) and has always spoiled her.

"Let's head to Red Lobster on Busch Boulevard. Everything is on me!" Uncle Melvin shouts. Destiny loves seafood, she grew up so poor, this will only be her third time eating at Red Lobster. The other two times were Uncle Melvin taking her for her sixteenth and seventeenth birthday.

"I have a surprise!" D shouts, handing Destiny the keys to a 1989 Toyota Corolla. "Oh God; daddy, Thank you!" Destiny shouts, grabbing the keys to the car. Come on Meme, she yells, getting behind the wheel. It's her first car.

D brought it last week from a hustler down on his luck, for seven hundred dollars.

"Happy birthday and graduation from me and your ugly momma!"

"Fuck you!" yells Drena, laughing.

CASH

This Is How We Do It by "Montrell Jordan" is on. The club is going mad "The Party's here on the West side" Cool Al mimics they are at Club ATL on Freemont. It's Cash's 18th Birthday. "Cash," the napkins, and glasses have C.M.F. printed on them.

Their whole crew is on deck. Mr. & Mrs. Jones are even in the VIP, in the cut. Looking like a million dollars. Cash is dressed casual tonight in an Armani, all black, tailored suit. Square bottom Alligator Ferragamo hard bottom shoes. The entire Rolex watch set, chain, bracelet and pinky ring. His Queen, Selina is in all black Chanel dress with a split coming all the way up her thigh with some black Hermes wrap around heels.

Just like her man, she too has on a matching Rolex watch set glistering. Her hair and nails are flawless.

Cool Al is in black Cavalli two-piece suit, Ferragamo shoes, with heavy jewels on.

Fat Dre is casual as well, in a black Prada suit and black Prada boots; jewelry blinging heavy.

Camille is straight stuntin' in a Dolce and Gabbana body suit hugging her sexy body, red bottoms on her feet, ice in her ears and on her neck and wrist. Major niggas are drooling, watching her dance. "C.M.F." she is yelling.

"I'm about to turn up bruh," Cash says to Cool Al over the music.

"Because in 5 years, I'm getting out of the game and going legit."

Cool Al loves everything about the game, especially the money and whores. He responds, "bruh, you are bugging, it's C.M.F. for life for me. I want $1M and 1M whores," he laughs. Cash is dead serious. He's already been reading books like Rich Dad, Poor Dad and Think and Grow Rich. He's seen so many niggas get killed or get football numbers in the fed and state prisons. His dream is to retire on top like his Pop did, but better because he will have a better life to leave his generation. Selina grabbing his dick, breaks his daydream, "You ain't hear your dad? Cash ain't even notice the music had stopped.

"I want to propose a toast," C-Money says. Tonya is standing next to him.

"To my son, Cash," he says holding up his glass of Dom P. "The world is yours, son. At age 16, I put a lot on your plate, two years later, you're running your team like a true champion. We love you son, Happy Birthday." Cash grabs his parents and hug them tight. Selina and Camille come join with Cool Al and Fat Dre right behind. "C.M.F," they shout, and they all begin to throw money. Mrs. Tonya, Camille and Selina too.

DESTINY

Six weeks later… "OMG auntie, I'm headed to college! Me, broke college Hill born "Destiny," I'm so excited. I've already talked to my roommate, her name is Chrishonna, she's from Jacksonville. She's majoring in Drama and Production. She yearns to be a play writer and producer. She comes from a good family."

"We will be in Tallahassee in another hour. I remember my first time making this drive." Donna says. "I was so nervous. You'll be home in two weeks. Tallahassee is small. It only has two malls. Tallahassee Mall and Governor's Square. "I ain't got no mall money. I just want to concentrate on my grades so I can get on with my career.

Little did Destiny know; Donna thought the same thing 20 years ago. "Just stay prayed up and focused. I'm gonna be right with you every step of the way. "Destiny look at me," Donna seriously says. "Don't you hesitate to call me for anything. You hear me?" "Yes mam," responds Destiny, "I love you baby girl," Donna says. "I love you too, auntie." Destiny loves school and just like Donna said, two weeks Destiny was back home. Her and Chrishonna clicked right away and became BFF's.

CHAPTER 7

Women Lie Men Lie

CASH

"Sup Cuzzo," shouts Veronica Williams AKA Baby Doll. She is the only cousin Cash has. "What it do chic?" Cash responds. Baby Doll is a straight up hustler. She's two years older than Cash but been hustling way before him due to her mother, Roxy Williams, AKA Roxy. Cash's favorite aunt was addicted to crack cocaine since the 80's. She is also an only child but had it rough growing up with a crack head mother. Baby Doll runs Cash's most profitable trap house. The one on Keys and Ola in Tampa Heights.

"Where is auntie?" Cash says walking into the spot. "Her crazy butt around here somewhere. Probably on Florida Ave, at the Good Samaritan. She's been doing her little thing, catching the day labors, spending their money. You want me to call her? I got her a phone last week." Naw, I actually came by to holler at you," Cash says. "Oh, what's up cuzzo?" Cash doesn't know if Baby Doll is gay or what? She fucks with niggas here and there, but she dresses in tennis shoes and white t shirts every day. She must have every pair of Air Max Nike has made and she never keeps a dude for more than 2 months. "Listen I'm about to turn it up next week because of two things. One, I'm giving up the game at 23, to go legit. Two, I'm buying this house next week for Selina and me in Hunter's Green. Ain't a bunch of money, but I like it." "What's the tab?" "160,000.00." "Damn, big timer!" Screams Baby Doll. "It ain't nothing cuzzo, homeownership opens so many doors for people and I want it.

I got a house for myself- maybe I can give it to Lil Cash and his wife as a wedding gift one day." "I hear you. What's up with this retirement talk?" says Baby Doll. "Hopefully you will stack your chips and roll with me. I'm talking real estate, promoting, buying some franchises. Imagine us owning our own Burger King Franchise?" Bringing Jay-Z to concert in Tampa? Buying Central Court Apartments?" I am definitely feeling that cuzzo." Responds Baby Doll. "A scheme beats a dream baby girl. Be ready, starting next week. I'm going to double your supply." "I got you cuzzo, count me all the way in." Baby Doll says giving Cash a big hug.

DESTINY

"Girl we are almost sophomores and all we do is go to school and sit around in the dorm. It's Wednesday and we are going to grown folks night at the Moon," Chrishonna says. "Okaaaay" shouts Destiny laughing. "My uncle Melvin sent me $600 last week. Let's go to the mall and get our hair done. You buying your own clothes chic. But I got us with the hair do's." "Alright, I'll pay our way in and buy us a drink." "I don't drink," Destiny laughs. "Well you are about to start tonight. Chic, we are about to hang out and enjoy ourselves." "Alright chic, I'm with you!" Destiny says grabbing her car keys.

Later that night~

"Damn this is a big ass club," shouts Destiny. "It looks like the white house!"

"Doesn't it?" Replies Chrishonna. They're both looking fabulous. Destiny has on a pair of DKNY tight fitting stretch pants, a black DKNY shirt with glitter on it. Her hair and nails are on point. Chrishonna has on a red Chanel dress, hugging her petite frame and a pair of black Chanel heels with Chanel accessories. Her hair and nails are also stunning.

"Ladies are free, pretty ladies," the bouncers tell them at the door. As soon as they walk in, it's going down. People are dancing, drinking and having a good time. Mr. Cheeks "Lights, Camera, Action" is playing. Come on let's get us a drink," Chrishonna says, pulling Destiny to one of the six bars that the Moon has.

"I'll have a Peach snap and an orange juice." Chrishonna says, "No give me a Long Island Iced Tea, two of them please." "That will be $8." "Damn," Chrishonna says, giving the girl a $10 bill. "Keep the change," she says, handing Destiny her drink. "Let's walk, chic," Chrishonna says, heading towards the dance floor.

"Oh shit, girl this is my song," Chrishonna says, moving to the beat of Lauryn Hill's song, "That Thing," come on. The dance floor goes wild, Meme used to teach Destiny all the new dances. She knows a little something and the liquor has got her feeling good. She spreads her legs, drops her head and starts shaking her ass. Chrishonna is surprised. A crowd is forming around, watching her and Destiny.

Well mainly Destiny because she is cutting up. As soon as that song goes off, Tootsie Roll comes on. Destiny goes to dropping and waving her hands in the air "The butterfly uh uh that's old, let me see you Tootsie Roll." Chrishonna is trying to keep up, but Destiny is off the chain. As the song is finishing, a guy walks up to Destiny and says, "may I please buy you a drink? I owe you for making my night a pleasure." Looking at the guy, he's looking good in a pull over green Polo shirt with a blue horse, navy blue jeans, all white Air Force Ones, a nice size Cuban link chain, looking nice around his neck and a Movado watch on his wrist. "I don't accept gifts from strangers," Destiny replies. "My name is Wugga, I'm 24 years old and I grew up right here in Tallahassee.

I own a barbershop on Saxton Street. Now Ms...." "Destiny," Destiny says. "May I buy you a drink?" I will take an orange juice please, she says laughing. "And your friend?" Wugga asks, looking at Chrishonna. "Get me a Long Island Iced Tea," Chrishonna says. "The Moon will be closing in 40 minutes," the DJ announces over the speaker. "Come on chic, we got to take us some photos." "Ya'll go ahead, I'll bring your drinks over to you. "We'll wait," Destiny says. Aunt Donna warned her about dudes putting stuff in people's drinks. Wugga pays for their drinks and photos and then asks Destiny can him and his little brother, Gabe, take her and Chrishonna to get some breakfast. Before she can answer, Chrishonna goofy self says,

"Yes, we want to go to Village Inn." Okay, we will follow ya'll, meet us at the bookstore across the street.

Destiny is impressed when Wugga pulls up in a tan colored Ford F-150, sidestep truck on nice chrome 22" wheels. After eating and having a good time, Wugga takes Destiny outside and they talk in the parking lot for almost an hour before Gabe and Chrishonna starts complaining. Well, Gabe because Chrishonna ain't talking about fucking tonight. Chrishonna complains because she's tired, full and ready to lay down. Wugga gives Destiny a hug before she walks off and asks her to put his number in her phone, and to please call him when she makes it home, so he knows she made it safely. He then says, "Red Lobster tomorrow?" She told him about her favorite food and about Uncle Mel being her savior, about her family and her goals.

"You better believe it," Destiny says getting into her car smiling. You like dude? Chrishonna says. "He's nice," Destiny responds. But really feeling Wugga in her mind.

CASH

"You on my dick or what?" Cash says to Selina. They are standing inside their new 5 bedroom, 3 ½ bath home with a 3-car garage, pool, 4 seat jacuzzi, vaulted ceilings and marble flooring. I want everything new in this bitch, you have a $40,000.00 limit for now. "Let me show you how happy I am," Seleena says, dropping to her knees. She unzip's Cash's Polo shorts and pulls out his semi erect penis, and skillfully wraps her mouth around his dick. Seleena slurps and gags as she bobs her head up and down like a woman possessed. Cash's eyes roll back in his head "God damn baby," Cash moans through clenched teeth, "ummmm."

Slurp, slurp, slurp, um…um, gag, slurp, is all that is heard as Seleena continues her oral assault. "Oh, shit Seleena," Cash let's out a pleasurable cry as his entire body stiffens, "AAAHHGHH," Cash screams as he shoots load after load down her greedy little throat. Seleena still didn't stop until Cash's entire body goes limp.

Cash had plans to talk to Seleena about doing something positive with her time and life, like maybe opening a boutique or a hair store, but after the show she just put on, he could only stare at her dumb founded. There is power in the head. LOL!

DESTINY

"It's our third date, Chrishonna do you think it's time I give him some?" "As much as you talk about him, I thought you already did chic." Chrishonna responds, laughing. "Forget you," Destiny says laughing. "I'm just scared, I've never done it." "Once you start, you can't stop." Chrishonna says. Having lost her virginity 5 months ago.

Later that night…

"That was a funny movie," Wugga says. They just left from seeing Next Friday. "Yeah, I liked the 1st one better though." Destiny says. "You hungry?" Wugga asks. "Not really but I could eat some curly fries from What-A-Burger and a strawberry shake." That's what it is for my Queen," Wugga says, heading towards Lake Bradford.

I'm staying with you tonight," Destiny blurts out. Wugga smiles and asks, "are you sure?" He knows Destiny is a virgin. He's fucking a few little whores, so he doesn't mind waiting for Destiny, whom he wants for the long haul. "I'm scared, but I'm ready." "I got you baby; I promise I will treat you like the Queen you are." Destiny panties get moist every time Wugga calls her a Queen. After they leave What-A-Burger they head to Wugga's apartment on Capital Circle.

Destiny been here before, so when she walks in, she immediately goes into the bathroom and takes a bubble bath. When she comes out, she's shocked because Wugga has turned all the lights off and candles are burning throughout the apartment.

He has the stereo playing, H-Town's Knocking the Boots. He grabs her and begin to kiss her soft lips. Kissing him back, Destiny is on fire. She only has on a pair of red lace Victoria Secret panties. Wugga has on a pair of black silk boxers.

Wugga eagerly cups Destiny's breasts in his hands and gently massages them. He starts kissing each one of them and circling her nipples with his tongue. Both nipples were erected. Wugga continues to suck and nibble on her breast. Destiny moans, "Oh Wugga, that feels so good." Wugga picks Destiny up and carries her to his bed. Emotions by H-Town comes on as Wugga pulls down Destiny's wet panties. He pulls her to the edge of the bed and kneels. He reaches his hands between her thighs and spread them

Destiny begins to shudder and shake as Wugga lowers his face to her lovely cunt. He kisses and runs his tongue between her pussy lips. "Oh, mmm...um..." Destiny yells as she pushes her cunt into Wugga's face. He licks her gash harder and deeper. He then withdraws his tongue and searches for her clitoris, which he found swollen as the size of a fiery, red pencil. He tongues it softly; Destiny is going crazy. She begins convulsing so violently that Wugga thinks he's hurting her. Destiny begins to orgasm. She groans so loud, Wugga can't hear the music, "Oh my god!" Destiny shouts. Wugga asks, "Are you ready?" Taking off his boxers. He leans her back on the bed and gently inserts the head of his penis inside of her warm wet spot. "Oh shit!" she screams.

Wugga begins to get a little groove and starts to give Destiny the business. "Damn bae," she cries out. Not in discomfort, but in joy. "Oh baby, I'm feeling it again." Destiny screams, about to climax again. "Oh, shit baby, your pussy is so good!" Wugga screams while pulling his dick out, shooting his hot load over Destiny's stomach.

CHAPTER 8

It's A Hard Knock Life for Us

CASH

What can I do for you nephew?
Jaheim Jones is C-Money's older brother
by 5 years. C-Money bought him a used
car lot 10 years ago, to launder some of
his money through. Jaheim is Cash's
real idol. He's smart, having attended
Morehouse College in ATL, and always
doing something positive. Rather it's
giving away back packs with school
supplies to under privileged kids or
rallying for an injustice done to black
people. He's the one who taught Cash
how to hunt and fish in addition to
giving him all the business books he
has.

"Can you take me the auction with you
next week Unc?"

"Yeah, no problem nephew. I'm going on Thursday. The auction is on 40th street. You looking for something in particular?" "Yes, I want me something nice, but real low key." "I see, I guess you're finally starting to get what I've been trying to show you. The key to the game nephew, is being out here. You don't have to live with the Joneses to be one of the Joneses. All of them fancy cars and exotic bling, brings too much attention. Attention brings the feds, robbers, murderers, thot hoes and home invaders; you get it? Save your money, invest your money into things that will increase in value, like real estate. The minute you leave out the door of a jewelry shop, you have lost 30% of what you paid for the piece. Unless you invest in exotic diamonds or collector's items.

When your father gave me a shot, I was fresh out of a bad marriage- dead ass broke. I gave her everything in the divorce. Your pop needed a way to clean up some money, I came up with this idea that changed my life. I've been a single man since and getting plenty pussy, you know." He winks at Cash. "I also now own 3 houses, not including my own. I drive my same 8-year-old Dodge Dakota. I have a high-speed boat; jet skis and I travel like I want to. This came from making wise decisions with my money, nephew. You're smart, you have magnetism. Take your traits and make something positive out of them. Get your money by all means, but don't get stuck. Don't ever get comfortable, have an end game. Always have a vision, a mission.

I'll help you with anything you choose to do. Just please don't wait until it's too late. The last thing I'm going to say before I let you go, you have to have people on your team, that's on what you're on, it's called networking. Because birds of a feather really do flock together.

Destiny

"I've got it," Melvin says to the young kid, Tony, who works at his store part-time, 5 days a week. They are closing the store for the night. Tony was about to lock up the front door so he can begin cleaning up and wiping down the windows. "Okay, Mr. Melvin," Tony shouts while sweeping by the coffee machine. Soon as Melvin is about to turn the lock, a big black ugly dude pushes his way into the store. "I'm sorry, but we're closed," says Melvin. "I know!" The dude says, pulling out a rusty .38 revolver. Instantly, putting his hands up; Melvin says, "please don't shoot. The money is in the register, you can have it." "I know," replies the robber. Pushing Melvin towards the counter. "You get over here!" The robber shouts at Tony. "Get down on the floor and don't you fucking move."

As Melvin is opening the register, the guy hits Tony upside the head with the gun. "I said don't move!" He yells as he turns to Melvin. Melvin hits him with a hard jab, right on the chin. The robber stumbles backwards, raises the gun and fires two shots at Melvin. The first one misses, but the second one catches him in the chest, right below his heart, killing him instantly. "Oh shit!" The robber yells before turning and running out of the store.

Later that night…

"Hello." Destiny says, groggily into the phone. It's her favorite auntie, Donna. Everybody knowing how close Destiny is to her uncle Melvin, they did not have courage to call and tell her what happened. Donna decided to do it. "Please sit down," Donna says. "What happened auntie?" Destiny asks, already about to cry.

"It's your uncle Melvin, he's dead. Someone shot him trying to rob his store tonight." "Noooo!" Destiny screams to the top of her lungs. "Please tell me I'm dreaming!" She yells, falling to the floor, sobbing uncontrollably. "Oh God, why?" Chrishonna grabs Destiny and consoles her. "What's going on?" "My uncle Melvin is dead. Some robber shot him attempting to rob his store." Chrishonna begins to cry too. Feeling the pain of her friend. "I need to call Wugga and let him know what has happened. I'm leaving for Tampa tonight."' "I'm going with you." Chrishonna says, still consoling her friend.

CHAPTER 9

It Cost to Floss

COOL AL

"I'm gone call you back bro, I've made it to the auction," Cool Al says. He was having a conversation with Cash about going to the club the next night. It's a new spot on Fletcher called Sandals Bay Club. Cool Al is picking up the car that he bought last night. It's his birthday present to himself, a 500 Benz Sedan. It's gray and black with leather seats, wood grain everywhere on the insides. "How many niggas can say they owned a Benz by their 20th b-day?" He shouts to himself.

Getting inside the whip, Cool Al feels like G-Money for show now. Fuck a house, Cool Al says thinking back on the convo him and Cash had last week when he told Cash what he was buying himself for his birthday. I'm young, I don't have any kids and I'm the only child. I keep my stuff at my parent's crib, and I live in hotels and with my hoes, he stated. We are getting so much money, hell I'll buy a house too, he said laughing. What's the use of having money and not enjoying it? Breaking his thought, his main chic, Tiana says, "baby you want me to follow you to the rim shop or are you good?" "Naw, follow me. Dwight may be with the bullshit. I'm hungry and need to get my hair cut. I may just leave it with Dwight and ride with you." "Okay baby," Tiana responds.

DESTINY

"God, I don't know why you do certain things. I apologize for questioning you. I ask that you watch over my uncle Melvin, as I know he's in heaven with you. Amen." Destiny is at her uncle Melvin's funeral. She's standing next to his casket, alone. Everybody is watching but giving her her space. She grabs his hand and bends down to kiss his forehead, like he always used to do her. "Uncle Melvin, I'm not going to let you down, my grades are good. I'm focused and more determined than ever. Thank you for always believing in me, for always supporting me. My loyalty will remain to you, even in death. I love you, Uncle Melvin and miss you already."

Destiny walks off and heads towards a waiting limo.

She refuses to see them put her favorite uncle into the ground. Her aunt Donna is ten steps behind her. "Destiny, I can't say that I know how you feel, because I don't. I will say that I feel your pain and that I'm here with you and I love you." "I'm leaving after the re-pass. I'm going back to Tallahassee. I'm going to study even harder. I'm going to make Detective, auntie. I'm gonna find this animal who killed Uncle Melvin and put him away for life." "That's right baby." Auntie Donna hugs Destiny, "that's how you win- success is the best revenge."

COOL AL

"You killing em baby boy," Cash says looking at Cool Al's new 500 SL Benz. "I like them rims. You did ya thang." Cash says giving his main man some dap, "you rolling with me tonight?" Cool Al says. "It's my main man's 20th b-day." "You already know, Cash responds. Cool Al doesn't know it yet, but Cash and Fat Dre have Sandals docked out for Cool Al. They even have a super bad stripper, Jordan McKnight, to jump out of a huge cake for him. "Pick me up at Camille's house at 11:00pm." Cash says. "I'm allowing Seleena to come but I'm riding with you. What are you wearing bruh," Cash asks, "A shit load of diamonds?" Cool Al laughs and respond, I'm going casual, you?" "The same," Cash replies.

Later that night Cash steps out of Camille's house looking like a model in a grey Polo linen two piece, no collar suit. Hard bottoms, black Alexander boots. A black Derby hat, black Movado watch, black diamond chain and bracelet. "Oooh wee," Cool Al shouts while he gets out, giving his main man a hug. Cool Al is straight stunting. He has on two chains, a big diamond bracelet, his presidential Rolex iced out. He has on cream colored Luis Vuitton suit (no collar) and some brown and cream Loui Bo shoes. "You ain't looking bad yourself," Cash states while looking at his main man looking like a rapper. Camille comes out of the house in an all-black Bebe body suit, iced out, red bottoms on, ass swanging. "Can I ride with y'all?" "Hell to the no!" Cash and Cool Al shout in union, LOL, while getting inside the Benz.

They drive off laughing. "Fuck both of y'all," Camille shouts, getting inside her Lexus.

15 minutes later…

"Happy birthday!" Everybody shouts as Cool Al enters the club. It's so packed. Him and Cash are having a hard time making it to the dock outside where his party is at. The Lost Boys are blaring through the speakers: *I'm in love with these two chics. I don't know which one to pick.*

Freaky Ty is rapping. Seeing his whole crew and about ten of his hoes, Cool Al is smiling from ear to ear. Big bouncers are everywhere. Fat Dre rolls a cake over to him and says, "Happy b-day my dude." The music switches up and plays, *It's Your Birthday by Uncle Luke.* Jordan McKnight jumps out of the cake and goes to shaking her ass. Everybody points to Cool Al. She pushes him on a chair and begins to give him a lap dance. She's licking inside his ear; they are damn near fucking. Luke screams "go Leos it's your birthday." Tiana joins the show and starts dancing on her man. She secretly wants all his jump offs to know she's his main lady. "This is what the fuck I'm talking about." Cool Al shouts over the music. "And you talking about retiring from this shit?" He screams looking at Cash. "C.M.F." Shouts Cool Al and the club goes wild. A sexy slim dime piece walks up and hands Cool Al a bottle of Remy VSOP (gold). "Damn," he says, "who are you lil mama?" "You can call me SENSATION, because tonight I want to make every part of your body feel the sensation of my tongue." She says licking her long tongue out. Cool Al looks at the camel toe poking outta her Bebe shorts and his dick instantly gets hard.

"Meet me at Denny's on 30th and Bush at 3:15am," she says walking off. Her ass is perfectly round, she has a gap you can fit a pole through.

An hour later… Cash says, "I'm about to head out. I'm heading home so I can send Seleena's ass up and through there. Be careful bro and call me when you get to where you're going. I love you. Bro," Cash says giving him a farewell hug. Fat Dre says, "later player." Giving Cool Al a hug also. He has to follow Cash home and go get him some pussy too. "I'm right behind y'all," Cool Al says walking behind them, looking at his watch, it's 2:45am. "I'm about to go to the 24 hours McDonalds on Fowler and grab me some chicken nuggets, ditch all my hoes and go smash sexy ass Sensation," Cool Al thinks to himself. Pulling up to Denny's, "I wonder what kind of car this lil bad bitch drives."

Soon as he pulls in the parking lot, he notices an Acura sitting, backed in, parked beside the entrance doors. Lizanne flashes her lights and says to herself, "this is going to be easier than I thought." Being that I see Cool Al alone, with no trail car. These Florida niggas got shit sweet.

Lizanne is from Memphis, Tennessee where slipping doesn't count. She and two of her home girls, Shayla and Elise, go all over the United States hitting licks. They almost got killed in New Orleans at the Mardi Gras six months ago trying hit a lick on Max and Tear. Their lives were spared in agreement to set up licks just like this one.

"Sup mami?" Cool AL says walking up to the driver's window of Lizanne's car. "Hey good looking," Lizanne responds. "You trying to eat or are you ready to get ate?" She says sexually, looking at

Cool Al's crotch. "Follow me." Cool Al states while heading back to his Benz. He is heading to the Quality Inn Suites off 30th and Bush. After getting the room, Cool Al waves his hand for Lizanne to follow him to the back. He likes parking in the back because it has a wall and you can't see his car from 30th. He's not trying to get caught up with none of his many women. As Cool Al push his key to lock his door and activate his alarm, a nigga (Tear) is climbing from out the backseat of the Acura with his 9mm Ruger. "You ready ma?" Cool Al says watching Lizanne exit her car. "I'm ready," Tear says pointing the heat at Cool Al. "Run them jewels and empty ya pockets nigga!" Lizanne shouts, pulling out a chrome .380. "Y'all got that," Cool Al says, putting his hands in the air.

He is livid. He's slipped and allowed a total stranger with a fat pussy print and some sweet talk, allow him to get caught slipping. "Put your hands down and start taking off them jewels nigga!" Tear yells through a black ski mask. After taking off all his jewels and handing them to Lizanne. Cool Al takes his money out of his pockets and throws it on the ground, hoping they fall for his trick. Lizanne does and as she is reaching for it, Cool Al reaches for his 9mm Beretta on his waistline. Tear is on point and fires… Boom! Boom! Cool AL falls to the ground, dropping his pistol. "I should kill both of y'all!" Tear screams. "Get the money and let's go!" He yells at Lizanne, mad that she slipped. Tear picks up Cool Al's gun, get in the driver's seat of Lizanne's car and drives off.

CASH

"Hello!" Cash says. He's half asleep, tired as hell from a good fucking session with freaky ass Seleena. "What?" He yells, "I'm on my way." "Where are you on your way to?" Seleena says, looking at the time on the T.V. 4:27am. "Somebody just signed their death wish by shooting my nigga, Cool Al!" He shouts. "He's alive, he's at Tampa General. That was my pop, they are all on their way to the hospital now."

Twenty minutes later, Cash is pulling up at the same time as Fat Dre. Cash says, "I want the word out, I got $50,000.00 on the nigga's head who shot my nigga."

"You may as well give it to me," Fat Dre says, "because I'm going to kill whoever had a hand in this shit!"

Walking into Cool Al's room. Cash is relieved his main man is okay.

He's flirting with the young pretty nurse. "Hey unc, auntie, mom and dad." Cash says, speaking to everyone. "May I please have a word with Cool Al and Fat Dre alone?" "We'll be outside." All the parents and the nurse say leaving. "What the fuck happened?" Cash says through clinched teeth. "I played bro. I went to meet this lil bitch I met at the party and the bitch and a nigga she had with her robbed and shot me." Cool Al tells Fat Dre and Cash play by play on what happened. All the way to him being shot twice, once in the arm and once in the left thigh. "You are lucky, considering how close the nigga was."

"It's like the nigga knew me bruh, because he didn't fire any head shots and he had a chance to finish me. But he didn't and he wore a mask." "I'm gonna kill that bitch and the nigga!" Yells Cool Al.

"The nigga took my gun bro." "I want somebody following you from now on." Cash says. Fat Dre just shakes his head.

DESTINY

"Cherell, it looks like you're pregnant."
"Duh! I am," she says laughing at her
baby sister. She's trying to put a smile
on her face. They are at Uncle Melvin's
house at the repass. "How can you keep
having babies by a guy who keeps you
with black eyes and busted lips?" "I ask
myself the same thing. I guess I've
gotten so comfortable and he's a good
father. I don't want my kids growing up
without their father." "Well if he keeps
beating you, one day it could go too far.
They will both grow up without y'all
because you could be dead, and I will
arrest him and put him away for life."
"You're right baby sis. I had a serious
talk with my baby daddy and told him
all the fighting has to stop, he agreed.

I'm also trying to go back to school next year. I plan to sign up at Erwin in August for childcare.

I would like to open a nursery." "That's great, Cherell. I will help you in any way possible." "Hey, can I get some time with my baby sis?" DJ interrupts. "What's up with you baby girl? Ma told me you got a lil boyfriend now." "She talks too much," Destiny smiles. "His name is Wugga. Next time I come home to visit; I'm going to ask him to come. How are you, big brother?" "I've got a new chic and she's pregnant." "Wow!" Destiny says. "I got me one this time. She's a nurse at St Joseph's Hospital and she got me a job working with her dad, doing roofing. I start Monday." While hugging her big brother, Destiny says, "that's great DJ. I'm so proud of you.

Please stay focused and whoever this woman is, please do right by her and stay on track. I love you." "I love you back lil sis."

"Everybody, I'm about to leave." Destiny shouts. "Chrishonna, you ready?" They talk about life all the way back to Tallahassee. "I may have to leave Wugga alone," Destiny says. "Why chic? I thought you were sooo in love?" "I do love him, but I think he's a hustler." "Whattt?" Yells Chrishonna. "That lil barber shop in the hood doesn't afford him the lifestyle he lives. Seeing my uncle in that casket made me realize life is too short to be taken for granted. I'm going to ask him to stop whatever he's doing or to leave me alone. I'm going to school for criminal justice and plan to be a detective. How can I be involved with a criminal? I've prayed about it.

When I get out of class tomorrow, I'm going to his apartment to confront him."

"You're doing the right thing chic," Chrishonna says. "Even though you're gonna be dickless," she laughs. "Dick is not my integrity....

CHAPTER 10

Game Over

CASH

These lil pretty boy, daddy's boys are gonna start paying dues Mad Max a.k.a. Maxwell Roberts, 28 and fresh out of DOC. He was released from Sumter 10 months ago. He's from West Tampa Projects and very known. He went to prison at age 17 for attempted murder. He tried to kill his stepdad because he kept his foot in his mom's ass and treated him and his lil brother, Terrell Roberts (Tear), like shit. Mad Max shot him six times but somehow, he survived. Fucked up his life and walks with a cane. His pussy ass testified, and Mad Max caught 20 years. He did 11 years with the 3rd off.

When he got out, a few major players from West Tampa broke him off and took him shopping, he has his own plans. His lil bro 23 years old, Tear, is crazy. He will bust his gun in a minute and Mad Max has a vendetta against pretty boys because he grew up poor and is super ugly. Dark skinned, 5'6" and 180 lbs. All muscle. He worked out seven days a week in prison. He is so institutionalized; he still does his lil prison work out every day.

By Tear doing petty robberies, that is what kept his books straight and looked out for their mom.

Their plan was to go to all the major events. The Classic, Freaknik in Atlanta, The Goombay in Miami, The Mardi Gras in N.O.L.A., etc. They robbed big dope boys, rappers and ball players until Mad Max was almost robbed by Lizanne and her crew.

Looking back on that night makes Mad Max laugh. He and Tear were on a steak out, watching two niggas with heavy jewels, mack on some bad hoes. That's when Lizanne approached Mad Max and asked him, if he was horny. Looking at the bad sexy slim bitch, Mad Max was like hell to the yeah; me too, she said pulling his hand towards her hotel room. "What you want me to do Bro?" Tear shouted. Mad Max winked at him which was the signal to be on point. "What is the tab, baby?" Mad Max says, watching Lizanne's ass jiggle in the Bebe tight shorts she's wearing. "One hundred," she yells. Entering the room two minutes later, Lizanne doesn't even play, she pushes Mad Max on the bed and straddles him. "You look like you have a big dick. I want to ride it. Take off these shorts," she says trying to help him out of his Gucci shorts and shirt.

She lifts his shirt to make sure he ain't scrapped. She yells, "you have a condom?" Which is a signal for Shayla and Elise to come out of the closet with their .380 drawn.

"What the fuck!" Yells Mad Max. Laughing while looking at the two bad hoes holding guns aimed at him. Elise is high yellow, almost to the point she looks mixed. She's 5'2" 120 lbs with a sexy petite body, with long black hair. Shayla is the thick one of the crew. She's light brown, 5'1" 170lbs with thick thighs and a buffy ass. She has a beautiful baby face and tantalizing hazel eyes. "Fuck you laughing at, nigga?" Shayla says, picking up Mad Max's shorts. "Get that big bracelet too girl," Elise tells Lizanne. Mad Max has on a 200-gram Cuban Link bracelet. He robbed a nigga from N.Y.

Him and Tear caught the Bama nigga's stunting, entering the Rolex in Miami last week. "I'm laughing at you sexy,"

Mad Max smiles. "This is real cute," he says. "Bitch! This nigga ain't got but $1,700!" Shayla says, throwing Mad Max's shorts down. Mad Max is laughing because he knows Tear is waiting outside to flip these hoes. Shit, their plan was to rob her. They figured she may have tripped up on a few stacks. "Let's go!" Lizanne shouts as she walks to the door. As soon as she gets her head out of the door, Tear, has his hand around her throat and pistol in her face. "Bitch! Get back in here." He catches Elise and Shayla off guard. They had already put their guns in their purses and was right behind Lizanne. "Oh shit!" Screams Elise.

Mad Max and Tear had a rule, only one of them holds both guns until they are actually ready to hit a lick.

The reason is if the police ever get on them, the one that's clean will take off running and cause a diversion so the actual dirty one can escape. In his boxers, Mad Max grabs his .45 from Tear's waistline. He bluntly states, "sit ya'll asses down! Y'all weak ass hoes tried a real gangster this time. Who wants to die first?? Mad Max says, walking up to Shayla. He slaps the dog shit out of her with the hand that didn't have the gun in it. He's gonna rob them and scare the shit out of them. "Give me my $1,700 and all of your money. Don't make me have to do a strip search to get it. I just did 11 years in prison for murder. I like to kill people. Shayla is terrified, so is Lizanne and Elise.

"Please don't kill us," Lizanne says. "Let us work it off. We'll set niggas up for y'all the rest of the weekend." This made sense.

Mad Max had heard so many whore stories in prison. Niggas with bread love to floss and trick with bad hoes. I call "How about we all get money together and split 50/50? We could get rich." Glad to be living another day, Elise and Shayla readily agrees before Lizanne could even speak. They get money all weekend and got to know one another. Snapping back to reality... Mad Max says, "how much money did the nigga have on him?" "$13,000." Lizanne says. "But at least $100,000 worth of jewelry on." "That's what's up," Mad Max responds. "This is just the beginning. I want to start moving a lil work too, in order to keep niggas out of our game." He says to Tear.

"Y'all keep doing what y'all are doing, but only out of town. This nigga Cash will be looking for Lizanne.

We don't want him on point before we get at his soft ass again. What's the info on this nigga, Fat Dre?" "He is official, big Bruh. The nigga is a beast. When we get Cash, we are gonna have to kill him." Mad Max laughs and replies, "we are taking over. Fuck them pussies. If it ain't you, ma and our three wifey's right here, they can get it."

DESTINY

"Hello? Yes baby, this is me," Destiny says, "What's up Ma? Wugga responds. "I need to talk to you about something baby," Destiny says. "Where are you at? "I'm at school. I'm about to leave." "Okay, go to my place. I'll be there in less than an hour. I'm at the barber shop. I have to handle a few things; you got your key?" "Yes, Wugga. I'll be there." "Are you hungry? Because I'll stop and get something to cook." "That sounds good." "I want you Queen for dessert." I've got to get the dick at least one more time. Destiny thinks, instantly getting wet. "Okay baby, I'll see you soon." Destiny says hanging up the phone. "Damn!" she shouts. She really is fucked up about Wugga.

For the past 16 months he has shown her nothing but love and respect. She says a quick prayer that Wugga will choose her over the game.

CASH

"It's been two weeks since my man got shot and ain't nobody said nothing?" Cash screams.

Cash, Baby Doll, Cool Al, and Fat Dre are in Calderon's eating on 7th Avenue. "Maybe they were from out of town," Baby Doll states. "Yeah, I was thinking the same thing." Cash replies. "Until I thought about the ski mask and how the chic made it her business to get Cool Al." "Well he was the man of the party with all that ice on." Baby Doll says. "They may have just seen a lick." "I ain't feeling it," says Cash. "Put word out the reward is now $100,000. We have to make an example out of these chumps! Shit ain't sweet," Cool Al says. "I'm almost sure the broad was from out of town. Texas or Tennessee." Fat Dre have a nigga shoot the cat Wayles out of Central Park. "Me and him had an argument last week." "Make an example. I'm gonna kill him then!" Fat Dre says. "Our example is gonna be…you fuck with C.M.F, your momma is going to be crying at your funeral." "That's what it is then." Cash says smiling. "C.M.F." Says Baby Doll.

DESTINY

"Oooh Fuck, Wugga eat this pussy. Ooh yeah that's my spot," yells Destiny. "You ready to give daddy this pussy?" moans Wugga. "Get your pussy Daddy," Destiny yells having an intense orgasm. Wugga puts Destiny on all fours and enters her from the back. "Ooohh shit Wugga," Destiny yells. Wugga slaps Destiny hard on her ass as he pumps her. "You miss this dick? Wugga yells. "Oh yes baby!" Destiny screams. "Damn ma," Wugga says rolling over panting. "I'll be right back." Destiny says jumping up out of the bed. Ten minutes later she returns with a warm soapy rag and a cold beer for Wugga. After wiping him off, Destiny says, "baby, I'm all the way in love with you and you men so much to me.

You're my first boyfriend and I would like to spend my life with you, but…you're gonna have to make a sacrifice for me." "What's that?" Wugga asks. "I need you to stop hustling. Anything illegal." "What!" Wugga yells. He thought Destiny had no idea he was in the game. "Don't I spoil you and treat you like the queen that you are?" "Yes, you do. You have made my life so much brighter on every level. But…for everything I am and what I believe in, I cannot be with a criminal. Baby I'm going to school for criminal justice. My goal is to be a detective and put people who break the law in jail or prison." "I feel you ma and I fully respect your mind, but…I'm in no position to give up the game. Nor do I want too. I'm sorry baby but this is all I know."

"Well, I guess it's good-bye," Destiny says kissing Wugga one last time before getting up to get dressed to leave. She has tears running down her face. Uncle Melvin's words are driving her. *Destiny, it's not always about right or wrong in our decision-making process, it's about doing what your heart tells you,* he quoted. Destiny is on a mission and nothing is more important.

We in This Bitch

CASH

"This is the life!" Cash shouts. Him and Seleena are pulling up to the Fountain Blue Hotel in Miami. Cool Al and Tiana are behind them in his Benz. They are about to spend some money, relax and get all the pussy and head that they can. Little do Seleena and Tiana know, Cash and Cool Al plan on hitting up Miami Night's Coco's, The Rolex, and South Miami Beach while they are there. "Baby, I want to go shopping today," Seleena says. Cash is secretly starting to lose interest in Seleena. She's cute, has a banging body and is super freaky, but that's it. The book closes there. Outside of helping her father with the catering business, she has no work history. She never talks about any goals and has no ambition.

Cash wants more from his woman; his kids deserve a better mom than that. Here they are barely checking into their hotel and she's whining to go shopping. That shows where her morals are. Cash doesn't want a simple-minded housewife; he wants a partner. A woman with integrity, a purpose, some drive, a big heart, a true go getter in all that she sets her mind to do. He wants love. He's been with Seleena over three years and he's not in love with her. She doesn't even know him. They barely talk about the future. She's never even asked him what he dreams about. Her pussy is the bomb, head is super, she can cook like an old lady and she's a down ass chic. So, for now, Cash is gonna continue to let her be his chic, but in his heart, he's looking for that one.

"Where do you wanna hit first?" Cash asks. "Niemen Marcus. I saw a pair of Christian Louboutin pumps I want, but they didn't have my size in Tampa." "I tell you what," Cash says giving her $8,000, "you and Tiana go hang out in the rental. Me and Cool Al are going to hit up 183rd St Flea Market." "Thank you, baby. You know I love you right?" Asks Seleena. "For show, I love me too." Cash responds. "Alright," Seleena says punching his arm.

Ten minutes later…
"Pop, Pop, Pop that Pussy," by Uncle Luke is screaming out of the speakers. Cash and Cool Al are at Coco's. It's only 7:45pm, but the club is swanging. Hoes are everywhere. "Lou Docs ain't got nothing on this spot," Cool Al shouts.

"Look at lil Red over there." He points to an exotic, high yellow dancer.

She's but naked about to pick up a Budweiser bottle with her pussy. "Damn!" Cash yells, walking over to get a close up of the show.

Lil mama see the two young ballers walking up, jeweled down. She closes her eyes... she uses her pussy muscles to pick up the bottle. Pussy juice is coming down the bottle like she just came. She licks her tongue out and begins to rub her clit. Cash is stuck. Cool Al takes out a big stack of money and starts throwing $20 after $20 at her. She opens her eyes as Cash is pulling a wad of money out his pocket. "Let's go to VIP," she seductively moans.

Picking up all of her tip money that mad niggas had thrown at her.

She pulls Cool Al and Cash towards the VIP room and says, "y'all give m $600 and I'm gonna make both of ya'll cum in 3 minutes all together."

Cool Al couldn't get his money out fast enough. Peeling of six one hundred-dollar bills. Cool Al hands the money to Lil Red, no faster than she sticks the money in her garter belt.

"Head, Head and More Head," by J.T. Money comes on. Lil Red drop to her knees and pull Cool Al's dick out. She spits on the head and goes to pulling and sucking on it. "Oooh shit," he moans. She takes a Magnum condom out of her garter belt, without breaking stride, pulls it down Cool Al's rock-hard dick.

She spins around and bends over. She inserts his dick in her hot, wet pussy. "Umumum," she moans as she reaches for Cash, pulling out his already rock-hard dick. She goes to eating his dick off the bone, "slurp, slurp," and jacking his dick at the same time. She takes her pussy muscles and squeezes tight causing Cool Al, who is fucking her senseless to yell out, "oh shit, I'm cumming." His body starts jerking.

She puts damn near 9 inches of Cash's dick in her mouth and pulls roughly. Moaning, "gimme that cum." Cash damn near falls down as he shoots twins down her throat. Remarkable!!!

DESTINY

"Chic, I'm so horny." Destiny says talking to Chrishonna. "And I miss Wugga sooo much. It took everything in me not to go over to his house last night. He texted me goodnight, Queen, I miss you about 10:00pm last night."

For the past six months, Destiny has been locked in on school. Only place she's been is church. It's a nice church on Saxton Street, called Faith Hill.

"Girl, I am so ready to get back to Tampa," Destiny says. "Not a day goes by that I don't think about what happened to my uncle Melvin. He was my rock. I have to make him proud. I made a promise to myself, I'm gonna find the person who killed him. "So, what are your plans, chic?" Destiny question.

"I think I'm gonna go to California and try to get on at a major studio. Either there or New York. I was thinking about doing something for Showtime at the Apollo. My long-term goal is to do plays or reality black movies. I feel like it's so much to tell about black people. Movies like Set It Off, Boyz In the Hood. I want to write and direct some of my own. My parents have a trust fund for me that I get once I graduate. I'm gonna use that to start my career." "That sounds great. Don't get all distant on me once you get famous chic," Destiny laughs. "Never that. You know I'm gonna dance at your wedding," responds Chrishonna. "Just come, don't dance!" Destiny laughs. "Forget you Janet Jackson."

FAT DRE

"What? Man get out of here! The bitch got both you niggas off in three minutes, all together?" "The bitch was a beast," Cash says. He's on the cell phone with Fat Dre. Him and Cool Al are at USA Flea Market. They have been in Miami tricking for three days now. "What's up with you Fat Boy?" Cash says. He's out of town because he wants Cool Al to be nowhere in sight when Fat Dre kills Wayles. "I'm on point," Fat Dre says. "As a matter of fact, I'm gonna hit you up a lil later. Tell Cool Al I said Happy Belated Birthday. Code for Wayles is dying tonight."

Ten minutes later… Fat Dre is watching Wayles climb into his Acura. He already knows where he's going because he's been following him the past three days observing.

Wayles doesn't go to club or have too many hoes, unless he's fucking around Central Park. He lives in Sulphur Springs with his bitch, off Yukon.

He goes from there to Central Park, where he's at all day selling packs and shooting dice. Wayles stops by the liquor store on Nebraska and Lake. Fat Dre keep going… get on the interstate and get off on Bush. He parks three houses down from Wayles's house and calmly walks down the road. He goes into Wayles's backyard to wait on him but five pit bull begins to bark, that changes his mind.

There're some duplexes across the street. Fat Dre sees a chair in the driveway and sits down. Five minutes later, Wayles pulls up to the house and get out. He grabs the bag of liquor off the seat and shuts the door. He doesn't see Fat Dre, who jogs across the street until it's too late. Boom! Boom!
Fat Dre fires into his chest. The slugs from the .45 knocks skinny as Wayles off his feet. Boom! Boom! Fat Dre shoots two more times, once in the stomach and once in the head. He calmly walks back to the stolen Chrysler Lebaron, get in and drive off… bumping Scarface, "I never seen a man cry, until I seen a man die."

CHAPTER 11

Let's Get It

(4 months later)

DESTINY

"I did it!" Yells Destiny. She just received her degree in Criminal Justice. The whole family in Tallahassee to celebrate. Wugga is even there. Destiny invited him because without his support, she would not have had it easy. He came up to her and gave her a big hug and peck on the lips. Handing her an envelope with $5,000.00 inside of it. It also had a note saying, *good luck- I'll always love you. This the money that the barber shop made, LOL! Signed Wugga.*

"Come here baby," shouts aunt Donna with her arms out. "Oh, thank God! Jesus!"

She yells as Destiny comes into her embrace.

"Baby, I'm so proud of you. I knew you were gonna do it." Crying Destiny says, "I wish Aunt Fee and Uncle Melvin was here and Ms. Tracy. She always treated me and Meme the same." Everybody came to show their love. Destiny was finally able to meet Veda, DJ's new lady. Cheryl and Coop were there as well. Her parents could not stop crying, they were so proud of her. Neither of them, nor their older kids had graduated or even attended college.

Meme came up and gave her a big hug. She too was crying. Everybody was so happy that Destiny had graduated college. "I'm coming home y'all!" Destiny shouted.

Her aunt Donna already had everything set up.

Destiny starts The Tampa Police
Academy in 45 days. She will stay with
her aunt Donna. "I'll be in Tampa on
Monday. Aunt Donna I'm going to clean
out my dorm and I'm going to see Aunt
Fee. She's at Gadsden C.I. up this way."
Destiny went in to go see her at least
once month.

CASH

"Help me finish counting this money," Cash says. He's at the Sheraton Suites off Cypress. Him and Seleena have been counting money so long she's gotten tired. His birthday is next week, and he wants to see what he's worth before turning "21". "I have $600,000.00 right here in front of me says Seleena." "Okay I have $630,000.00 over here. All together this $1.2 million. Yesss!" Cash yells.   He owes Carlos $200,000.00 for his last package, but he still has a couple hundred grand owed to him. "I'm a millionaire," Cash says excitedly. Seeing all the money on the bed turns Seleena's freak light on. She starts playing in her pussy. "Oooh," She moans catching Cash's attention. Cash is blowed. Seleena is lying flat on her back with her legs spread open.

She pulled her purple panties to the side and rubbing her clit with one hand and has two fingers deep inside her pussy with the other. "Umm, umm." She moans. Taking her fingers out of her pussy and sucking on them. Cash walks over to her and replaces her fingers with his super hard dick. Still rubbing her clit, Seleena tries to put the whole 9' down her throat. Her gagging turns Cash on and she knows it, so she continues to choke herself. "Oooh, S… S… Seleena damn," Cash moans. Seleena is now tickling his balls with her tongue. Not able to take it anymore, Cash screams as he cums deep down Seleena's throat.

DESTINY

"Hey auntie," Destiny yells greeting her Aunt Fee. "Destiny, I'm so proud of you. Not a day went by that I was not praying for you. How was the graduation?" "It was great! Everybody was there. I wish you could have been there auntie." "You already know, I'm your biggest fan. I was in here bragging my ass off," laughs Fee. "I do have some good news, I'm headed to work release in Tampa," shouts Fee. "That's great auntie, I'm proud of you too." Fee has completed her cosmetology exam. All she has to do is 100 hours of internship at a beauty shop and she can get her license. "I'm gonna open my own beauty shop baby." Fee starts crying. "I love you, auntie and I'm gonna help you. I promise." "I love you too. I've learned so much during this time. Outside of your crazy dad nobody but you have been to see me. Ya'll are the only ones that kept my books straight. None of them so called friends who I was doing their hair for free and clubbing with sent me a dime! Not even one club photo. This has been a helluva ride. I will never put myself in a position like this again. I'll never deal with a guy like Ren again. I did write his mother and apologized to her. What I did was wrong. I thank God I have another chance. The next man I find will be just that, a man." "I'm with you, auntie. I'm about to head out, I've got to get on this journey. I start the police academy next month. I'm so ready." "Drive safe, baby I love you." "I love you too," Destiny says, hugging her aunt Fee goodbye.

BABY DOLL

"I'm in the spot," Baby Doll says. "Can you meet me at Silver Ring?" Pancho says in the phone. "Let me hit you back," Baby Doll replies- hanging up. "Hey baby," Roxy says walking in the door of the trap. "What's good ma?" She replies, "nothing." "I just left the Good Samaritan. I need 3 packs." A pack in Tampa is 8 big rocks of crack cocaine. They sell for $100.00. "I got $250.00," says Roxy. "If I need to, I'll bring back the other $50.00." "Come on Ma, you already know this is C.M.F. Ain't you family?" She shouts, handing her 3 brick packs. "Here," Roxy says handing Baby Doll the $250.00. "Thank you," Roxy says. "I will be back in a minute, they just got paid at the Labor Pool. I'm about to go flip this and come right back.

Baby Doll likes the fact that Roxy is hustling. It was a time all she did was beg and trick.

Standing on Floribraska, Cash saw her tricking one day and snapped on his whole crew. He told them he better never see his aunt sucking cracker's dicks again for a high when they have 5 traps booming. "Give her a job," he yelled at Baby Doll. That was two years ago. "Alright, ma. Call me if I ain't here." "I love you," Roxy shouts while heading up the block.

Pancho is sweating bullets. He got knocked off an hour ago selling an ounce to an undercover officer. He's trying to set Baby Doll up to free himself. "So, you're telling me," the Sgt. says, "that this woman, Baby Doll, as you call her is your connect?" "Yes sir. As long as you have the money, you can get all the dope and weed you want from her," Snitching ass Pancho says. "Can you get us a buy?" Shouts Sgt Miller. "Yes, I may have to go to her though because she seemed skeptical when I told her to meet me at Silver Ring." "What do you usually cop from her?" "A quarter." Pancho says. Sgt. Miller knowing this, still ask, "what is a quarter?" "9 ounces," replies Pancho. "For how much?" "She charges me $5,500.00."

"This is what we're gonna do. You are gonna go cop a quarter from her spot. Officer Woods is gonna ride with you. You get her to come outside before or after the transaction, you got that?" Sgt Miller needs his officer to identify Baby Doll to be able to get a search warrant so they can bust her house in the future. He has so many snitches, he'll have her birth marks by later tonight.

Thirty minutes later…

" I'm on my way to you," Pancho says into his cell phone, talking to Baby Doll. That's all he says because the streets have a code- no talking on the phone. One of her workers wasn't watching the camera because they would have seen the stranger in the passenger's side of Pancho's car. That breaks all of the trap rules, no strangers, period! Getting out, Pancho is so scared because he knows Baby Doll is C.M.F. and that they have reach. But going to prison is not an option for him. His lil tender roni, 16-year-old Natasha is pregnant, and his main chic Tina just had lil Pancho, 4 months ago. "Sup my dude?" Baby Doll says greeting Pancho on the porch. Another mistake. "Just cooling big sis, trying to get this money. You know me." Replies Pancho. He's been copping from Doll since he's been getting money.

When he was copping a half a pack, it's because of her that he's a quarter key strong. He really hates what he's about to do, but I come before you is his only thought.

"Here," he says handing her the $5,500.00 the popo gave him to cop with. "That's the business," she says heading to the kitchen to grab the 9 pieces of glass. "Just like always," she says handing the dope to Pancho.

"For show! When you gone give a nigga a shot?" Pancho says, starting a convo that he knows Baby Doll will entertain and walk him outside. "I don't mix business with pleasure. Plus, your lil young ass Pancho, 22, ain't ready for this grown woman shit. I ain't them lil girls you be fucking. I like this pussy ate," Baby Doll says laughing.

"I call that." Pancho says, opening his car door. Baby Doll sees the passenger and says, "you played? Who is this?" "My bad Baby Doll, this one of my best customers, his name is Roscoe. He's off 40th." "Whatever, don't bring him or no one else around here again." "You're dead right," Pancho says pulling off.

DESTINY

"I'm here Auntie," Destiny says walking into her auntie's house in Palm River. "I'm in the tub. I'll be out in a minute," Donna screams. Destiny goes to her room and begins to un-pack. Auntie Donna has set the room up nice. Growing up in College Hill, auntie Donna always wanted her own home. So that's the first thing she bought in her 1st year of working. She lives simple. She drives a late model Nissan Altima. She gets her hair done every week. She doesn't have any kids or no man. She dates every now and then, but her vibrator, Chester, is her husband. "Get ready Destiny, I have somebody I want you to meet." Ten minutes later auntie Donna comes out of her room looking fabulous in a Kate Spade dress.

"We are going to Red Lobster." Auntie Donna knows Uncle Melvin would have taken Destiny there for her graduation, so she wants to keep that tradition alive. Destiny is about to cry. She's not upset, she's grateful to have a strong person in her life as her aunt. "Please don't cry baby. I didn't mean no harm." "I know auntie. Thank you."

After a great time at Red Lobster, Auntie Donna stops at a house off Chelsea and 22nd St. "Who stays here?" Destiny asks. "I'm outside," Auntie Donna says into her cell phone. A minute later, a nice-looking man comes out the door. Auntie Donna says, "let's get out." "Hello, Mrs. Donna. This must be Destiny?" Deron Tiger Stuart says as he shakes Destiny's hand. Tiger is 6'0, 190lbs, brown skinned, nicely built, straight teeth, and a low bald fade. Destiny is impressed. "Hello, I'm Tiger."

He says greeting her. "I work for the Tampa Police Department, East Tampa. I'm assigned to the Belmont Heights area. I work out of the precent in the back of Lee Davis. It's nice to meet you." "I asked him to be a mentor to you," Auntie Donna says. "His goals are in line with yours." "Thank you, auntie." Donna says. "You start the academy next month, right?" Ask Tiger. "Yes." "Anything I can help you with? Let me know when you finish the academy. I'm gonna pull some strings and get you assigned to our unit." "Ooh my God! That would be a dream come true," Destiny shouts. They exchanged numbers with Destiny promising to call him soon.

CASH

"Damn Pop! Is this mine?" Cash shouts looking at the cocaine white Rolls Royce Phantom. "Happy 21st birthday son." C-Money hugs him. His mom and Mr. Carlos are standing in the driveway of C-Money's and Tonya's house. "We all put this together for you." C-Money says, pointing at his mom and Carlos. "I know you're gonna show out for your birthday. After tonight, promise me you'll put it up and drive it only when you go out of town." Mr. Carlos says in broken English. Him and Tonya really didn't want C-Money to buy his $200,000 car for Cash. But he was persistent, stating Cash is smart and ever since he named Cash, he wanted to give him this car. "Yes sir, Mr. Carlos. I got the specialties done."

His Uncle Jaheim comes up hugging him. "Thank you all!" Cash says getting in his car pulling out. He calls Cool Al, "sup my dude?" Cool Al answers. "Where are you slick?" "I'm in Central Court shooting dice, what's up?" "Nothing much, just wondering if you wanted to shoot to the mall. I need to hit up Mr. Man to get me something to wear tonight." "Damn, Happy Birthday my nigga. I almost forgot." Cool Al lies. Him and Fat Dre has rented Club Joy to throw him a big birthday bash. "Yeah, come grab me. I need to get fitted up too."

Fifteen minutes later…

"Oooh shit!" Cool Al screams seeing the Rolls Royce pull into Central Court Apartments. All the hoes, niggas and even the little kids are star struck as Cash steps out. He tries to play cool.

"You ready to roll, bruh?" He says giving Cool Al some dap. Before dapping up Willo, Bee Bo, Fu, Red and Big J, "sup my niggas?" Cool Al says, "bruh, we are rolling in this bitch tonight." Taking his hand and running over the hood. "Look at this shit," he says, opening the passenger door. "Everything is cherry oak. It has a cocktail table in the back seat. Looks like a living room. This is Puff Daddy's shit here bruh!" "Here y'all go," Cash says, calling all the kids over. He pulls out a fat knot of money and gives every kid out there a $20 bill. "I'm gonna holla at y'all fella," Cash says getting into his whip. "Damn Bruh, when were you going to tell me you grabbed this?" Cool Al says. "I just got it 30 minutes ago. My Pop, mom, Uncle Jaheim, and Mr. Carlos gave it to me as my birthday present."

"You're a lucky dude. I've got to step up my game! I'm getting the GT Bentley coupe ASAP!" Says Cool AL. "Those joints are banging!" Cash replies.

"I hope you follow my lead; I'm only stuntin' like this when I'm out of town. Tonight,is my last time driving this hot ass car in Tampa." "I feel you. I'm not spending 100 racks to stand out just out of town. I'm going down Main to ChUncy Sunday in St Pete. It's on bruh." "That shit brings heat. We have been lucky and people ain't been on our trail. Thanks to our dads having people on their payroll in high places. We gotta get our money and stay out of the limelight."

"We have been stuntin our whole lives. We are them dudes." "Look at you," Cash says pointing at Cool Al. "You're in the hood in a big Benz with over $80,000 worth of jewelry on, shooting dice!"

"This is where we are from." "Do you know how many shooters I had to duck? "If you were in a plain old Chevy truck with a g-shock on, you wouldn't even have to have no shooters because a robber would walk right past you."

"I feel you bruh," Cool Al says. Seeing Cash has no jewelry and a plain nice Mavado watch on. "Look how you just came through, by the time we turned on Columbus Dr, the whole city knows you just came through in a Rolls-Royce."

"You are right, they are going to think it was the rental for my birthday because they will never see it again," Cash says. Breaking the tension, Cash says, "you're grown my nigga. I'm just trying to give you some brotherly love."

"You already know, I'm with you 100% no matter what." "That's why I love you!" Cool Al shouts.

Later that night...

BABY DOLL

"We are going to have to grab her once she gets where she's going because she ain't been in the spot all day," Sgt. Miller says. "We have two teams ready to go while we are grabbing her. The other team will be raiding her spot. Take everybody to jail, even the dog if they have some. Pancho made another buy today, this time he was wired up and got Baby Doll to incriminate herself. Her exact statement was, you know I keep that butter. They had Poncho purposely short her $300 all on tape. If she beats the sales, she will be stuck with conspiracy."

CASH

"I'm on my way bruh. Have your pretty boy as ready," Cash says to Cool Al. "Fuck you, blame it on God. He made a nigga this fly," Cool Al replies. "Real talk, I am two minutes away from your door," Cash says. "I'm walking outside now," Cool Al says, disconnecting the phone. Cool Al has on an all-black Versace pants suit. Some black alligator Versace hard bottoms, a black Ice Man Diamond watch and a white gold iced out necklace and bracelet. Heading out to greet his main man, Cash is matching his car in a cocaine white Nino Cerruti linen suit, a pair of tan Louboutin soft bottom boots, a gold iced out Jacob the Jeweler watch, a gold diamond necklace with no medallion and a bracelet to match his pinky ring with a "C" in diamonds.

"Where are we headed?" Cash says. "To Club Joy on Hillsborough, it's usually a good crowd tonight." Fat Dre is behind them in a black SS Chevy. He's super fitted too, in a black Prada linen suit. Black Prada hard bottoms, a black iced out Jacob watch and a big white gold Cuban link chain and bracelet. As usual he has a big gun on the seat. "I'm gone park in the front, fuck a ticket!" Cash says parking on the sidewalk in front of the club. All heads turn their way. The club is super swollen, the line is around the corner. They step out looking like a million bucks while heading to the door. Fat Dre is right next to them as they step inside the club, as if in a dream, everybody shouts… "Happy Birthday Cash." He's blowed! The whole team is here. Selena walks up and gives him a big hug. Baby Doll hands him a $1500 bottle of Remi Martin Louis XIII and says, "happy birthday cuzzo."

Everybody is yelling C.M.F. Camille pulls him to the dance floor as Trick and Trina "Nan Nigga" comes on. Cash starts to rap along with Trick, "you don't know nan nigga, that dress fresher than me..." Camille is looking just like Trina in an all-white short Givenchy dress. Some open toe Giuseppe Zanotti heels iced out, hair and nails flawless. "This that dude!" She's yelling while pointing at her lil brother. "They Don't Dance No More" by Goodie Mob comes on and the club goes wild. Niggas don't dance no more all they do is this, Cool Al and Cash are straight stuntin. Dancing with about 20 hoes when all of a sudden, the music stops. "Grab her!" Someone shouts. "It's the police!" The DJ yells. Before she can even throw down her blunt, Baby Doll was roughly thrown to the floor. "Oh shit," Fat Dre says, pushing Cool Al and Cash into the closest restroom. "The fuck is going on?" Yells Cash.

"I don't know bruh, I saw them crackers rush in here about 30 deep and go straight to Baby Doll." Already on point, Cash is pulling out his phone trying to call Aunt Roxy to tell her to shut down shop at the trap.

"I was trying to call Veronica," Auntie shouts. "I was walking up the street and I see 20 crackers with a ram bust down the doors. They are inside the spot now!" "Listen auntie, throw your phone in the river. Go to my mom's beauty salon. Somebody will be there to get you in a minute. Yes auntie, I know it's closed. Just hang by the back where everybody parks." "Damn!" Cash shouts. "They are at the traps in Tampa Heights rounding people up!" "Fuck!" Yells Cool Al. "She must have sold to an undercover." "Had to," says Fat Dre. Camille comes running into the bathroom screaming, "where is my brother?" "I'm good," Cash says hugging her.

One thing C-Money always taught them was to always look out for each other "blood is thicker than water" he quoted. "Are they gone?" Cash ask. "Yes, they grabbed cuzzo and left. They are towing her car now." "Okay, go by ma's shop and pick-up auntie Roxy. Take her to your house. I'll be by to get her. Tell Seleena to drive my car home. Tell her I said to go straight home not Denny's or Gyros but straight home and to make sure no one is following her. Here…" he says handing Camille the keys to the Rolls-Royce. "We are riding with you Fat Dre, let's go!" Cash shouts walking out the restroom.

BABY DOLL

"Hello Veronica." Sgt. Miller says.

"I have nothing to say to you, cracker." Baby Doll states. "Oh, you're tough, huh? Well, I'm gonna see how tough you are once I turn this case over to the Feds; how does that sound? Killer!" "Fuck you sissy!" Baby Doll says. "You know the first one who tells, gets the best deal. Who is your supplier?"

No answer. "Call them and set up a buy and you can help yourself." Nothing. "Will the name Pancho mean something to you?" Baby Doll is hot with herself because she already felt Pancho was behind this. "We also found $16,000 in cash, 900 grams of crack cocaine, 14 pounds of weed and two 9mm. Mandatory minimum with firearms, you're looking at life in prison young lady.

You ready to be somebody's bitch?" "May I please call my lawyer?" Baby Doll says. "Sure, when you get to central booking with the rest of your crew. Take her in," yells Sgt. Miller.

Damn! Baby Doll thinks as she is being escorted to Orient Road Jail. Cash is going to be so disappointed in me. I was supposed to cut Pancho off and shut down shop after he came with that stranger. "Fuuuuuuck," she yells. "Fuck it. I'll have to take a ride." She says to herself. They don't know anything about cuzzo because if they did, they would not have asked me to call my supplier. Cool Al never meets her at the trap to bring her the work and Camille always comes and get the money, so even her few workers don't know where she gets the work from. "Damn my mother," Baby Doll says. "I hope she wasn't there because she knows everything."

Walking into booking, Baby Doll is praying she doesn't see her mom. She sees her gunman, Pookie and her two workers, a girl name Ann and a dude name Rat. 10 minutes later they confirm that her mom was not there. Thank God she says to herself. "Y'all chill, we will be out as soon as we get our bonds."

"We good," they all say in unison.

CASH

"Shut down all shops until we find out the business with cuzzo. Call Eric Kuske and tell him to represent Baby Doll. Get her and her crew out on bond. Whatever it is, tell Big John, C.M.F. he will already know." Cash says.

They are in front of his house sitting in the SS… him, Fat Dre and Cool Al. "Alright bro, I'll sure everything is done," Cool Al says. "All I need you to do, Fat Dre, is to go shut down all the traps." "I'm on it!" Fat Dre replies. "Alright, both y'all meet me at Martha's restaurant on Hillsborough at 9 AM for breakfast. I'm about to get some head and go to bed." Cash says getting out of the car. "C.M.F." Cool Al shouts while climbing into the front seat. "All day!" Cash replies heading towards his door. He sees his R.R in the garage as he opens the side door.

"Take me to my lil freak bitch Ronda's house in Clair Mel." Cool Al says.

"She got a friend?" Fat Dre asks. "She got an ugly, skinny, freaky white roommate." "That'll work." Fat Dre says laughing.

CHAPTER 12

Family Straight

MEME

"You Nasty" by the Notorious BIG and Lil Kim is blasting through the speakers. Meme is walking around Lou Doc's strip club in a pair of boy shorts cut deep in her ass. She has two stickers with stars on her bare breasts. In the club her stage name is "Cinnamon." "You want a dance?" She says to a tall light skinned nigga with long dreads. Seeing Meme's camel toe, dude says, "hell yeah." "Where you wanna go?" Grabbing his hand, Cinnamon leads him pass the pool tables to the back of the club where it's 5 small VIP rooms. Luckily, it's one left empty.

Each room has a small stereo, a small stage with a pole attached and a small couch. Meme puts on "Too Much Booty in Your Pants" on the small stereo and begins to dance. Her and the nigga are on the couch.

Cinnamon is going hard throwing the hell out of her petite frame. "Smack that ass," she tells dude while smacking her own ass. She's putting it on dude so good. He's about to bust in his pants. "Damn lil mama. Do you date outside of the club?" He asks. Lying, Cinnamon says, "no!" She has turned a trick or two but usually it's with a big money nigga that's not from Tampa. She doesn't want to be all out there. Destiny already fusses at her every day for dancing at a strip club. "I'm not trying you on the trick tip, sexy. I said date. I would like to take you on a date, like the movies or out to eat or something.

Meme look at him for a long moment before she say, "what if I tell you that I live in West Tampa Projects, have 2 kids, dropped out of school in the 10th grade and don't have a car. Would you still want to take me on a date?"

"What if I told you, my mother had me when she was 15. Raised me in Jordan Park Projects as a single mom. Broke her back working 2 to 3 jobs to send me to school looking decent and I would love to help you. Would you accept my company?" "What is your name?" Meme asks. "My name is Ricardo Wilson. Everybody calls me Rick. I am 23 years old. I was born and raised in St. Pete. I went to UCF in Central Florida and I have a degree in engineering. I work for Sim's Electrical in St. Pete as an engineer. I have no kids and to be honest with you, me and my high school girlfriend broke up three weeks ago because she wanted to move to Atlanta to be a hair stylist to the stars. I told her I wasn't leaving my mom and my job just on a vision. I asked her to go see what the opportunities were first before she made a move, she told me I was a mama's boy and left for Atlanta the next day.

I only came here because my cousin has a girlfriend who works here and asked me to ride with him to come pick her up. You know Champagne?" "Yeah I know her. That's my partner. We are tight." "Good because that's my cousin's girl. So, when do I get to meet these beautiful kids?" "Their names and ages are Terrence Jr. and Emphany. TJ is five and EMP is a little over two." "That's what's up. Can I take you out to eat tomorrow?" "I get off at 6 PM. That will be nice. Put my number in your phone and call me when you get ready to leave St. Pete." "Can I call you tonight, once I get home?" Rick says. "I hope you do." Smiles Meme. She is so excited. It seems like she's finally met a real man. She can't wait to tell Destiny.

CAMILLE

"I'm headed to get my bad ass kids ma; I'll call you when I get home." Camille is talking to Tonya. She calls her, Ma, because Tonya is really who raised her. She's leaving the shop. "Ok tell my babies grandma loves them. See y'all later." Camille says to all the customers that's still in the shop. Camille is happy that she can go straight to the day care today. She doesn't have to go to the traps because Cash has closed them down temporarily.

Camille has thought about being picked up by the Feds ever since cash told her the Feds picked up Baby Doll's case. Have they ever seen me? Do they know my car? She asked Cash. She even parlayed that into getting the new Denali truck she's driving now. Saying her Lexus was hot. "Damn, I'm hungry."

Camille says to herself pulling into McDonald's on Hillsborough Avenue and 19th St. The drive-thru is so crowded. She parks her truck and goes inside. She's at the counter ordering her and the kids something to eat when somebody taps her on the shoulder. She jumps. "Is that you Camille Jones?" The guy yells. Squinting her eyes, Camille yells, "oh my God Pale Rogers! Boy where have you been?" She gives him a big hug. Pale was her first boyfriend way back in eighth grade when she was still a virgin.

"I just moved back to Tampa. I've been back for 4 months now. I was living in Houston Texas. When I graduated, I went to T.C.U. and got my master's degree in Computer Programming. I worked at a software company in Houston for six years. I got homesick. They have a company here in Tampa and here I am." "Wow! Are you married? Do you have kids?"

"No and no. They actually go hand-in-hand. I was engaged to this nice woman. She's a pharmacist. Same age as us. She told me that she didn't want kids. At first, I was like maybe she's just saying that right now that she doesn't want kids. Well while we were making wedding plans, she asked me if I really wanted to spend my life with her and never having a child. I said no. She told me that I was a nice guy, and I will be a great father, but she doesn't like kids and doesn't want any. We decided to go our separate ways. That was six months ago. How about you?" "No, I am not married. Yes, I have two kids. A boy named Supreme and a daughter 11 named Brooklyn. I work at my mother's beauty salon. I am a nail tech. I am in the process of opening my own nail salon and spa. I've been single forever," Camille says. "Well, I would love to change that," Pale says. "Can I take you out this weekend?" "I don't know, can you?" Camille responds. "Still sassy I see." Pale says laughing. "All day," replies Camille.

CHAPTER 13
When It Rains It Pours

CASH

"They have her on tape saying some incriminating things and they have this Pancho Davido as a state witness saying he bought 9 ounces of crack cocaine from her on two occasions. Lucky for her, they didn't recover not one marked bill in all of the money they found at the house or in her possession when they arrested her," Kuske says. Him and Cash are at Leroy Selmon's restaurant. "So, what's the deal?" "I can get her seven years. I know the prosecutor. It's gonna cost you $25,000. They will throw out the weapons and money laundering charges. She will have to cop to the trafficking charges." "I'll have the money to your office by 5 PM today," Cash says looking at his Ice Tech watch. " What about the other PPC that were in the spot?"

"I can get them three years a piece for an additional $30,000." "Get it done!" Cash says getting up to shake Kuske's hand. "Go see Veronica today and tell her that auntie Roxy is ok, and I will find a way to see her soon. I put $2000 in her account and all the bread she had at her spot is put up. Thank you." "Have a good day," Kuske says walking away.

One hour later...

"Yes, I want them all taken out and have ivory put on all my teeth," Cash says to Dr. Myers, the dentist he grew up going to. "Do you want to keep your golds once I take it out?" "Naw you can have it. "How long is the process?" Cash says. "Well, my assistant will clean your teeth after I take the gold crowns off today you can come back tomorrow, and I'll do the ivory. It will be 7 hours all together. "The price?"

Cash asks. "For you, $11,000." Responds Dr. Myers. "Okay, let's get started today," Cash says. "Mrs. Brewer, can you get the customer ready?" Shouts Dr. Myers.

DESTINY

"Auntie I am physically and mentally drained. I had no idea this police academy was gonna be this rough thank God for you and the guy Tiger you introduced me too. I'm so glad I only have five more weeks before I graduate. "With risks there comes a reward baby," auntie Donna says hugging her niece. "You're that much closer to achieving your goals, Aunt D says using her finger and thumb.

CASH'S MOM, TONYA

"I am so tired. Girl it has been a long day," Tonya says to her last customer of the day. "Pat, I definitely feel you girl. I am a schoolteacher and I sometimes cry tears of joy once that last bad ass student leaves out of my last class of the day." Pat and Tonya laughs. "Girl you are crazy," Tonya says. She's sweeping the floor getting the shop ready to be closed. She has a cleanup crew that comes in at 1:00AM to clean the shop 6 days a week. But she's a neat freak and a busy body. "Let me see," Tonya says as she is pulling up the dryer to feel Pat's hair. "Ten more minutes and I can style it and we can get out of here." Cash has Tony calling Black Isaac to be there when she closes every night and to follow her home some nights.

Tonight, Tonya doesn't feel like going through the hassle and just wants to close up. She keeps her .380 in her purse with the purse open as protection. 20 minutes later she's setting the alarm.

Tonya says, "come on girl. I am ready. Her and Pat go out of the shop. Tonya locks the door behind them. As they are bending the corner to go to the parking lot, a tall nigga in all black screams, "don't y'all fucking move!" Pointing a moose pump at them. Miss Pat screams and is hit in the mouth with the gun. "Bitch shut up!" The gunman says. Seeing this, Tonya hesitates to pull out her gun. Miss Pat falls to the ground holding her mouth. "Get up!" The sound of a van is heard. Another guy jumps out of the van and puts Pat and Tonya in the van. "Strip," he says pointing a .357 at them.

Get down to your bra and panties," he yells closing the door. The first guy with the moose pump gets in the driver's side and drives off. "Don't be looking at them old lady pussies." He says laughing to his accomplice.

"I bet you're lying. Both of these old hoes are sexy, and they have on sexy undergarments. "Damn," Tonya says to herself. Knowing C-Money and Cash is going to be mad at her if she **survives** these fools. "What do y'all want? I have $6000 in the safe." It was a trick Cash and C-Money taught her. They purposely kept six grand in the safe in case a person robbed the salon. It was enough money C-Money said it was enough money for a robber to take and leave happy. Slapping the shit out of Tonya, the gunman says, "shut up and sit down."

As he's searching their purses, he sees the .380, he points it at Ms. Pat and shoots her in the leg. POW! "Aahhh," she yells. "Stop right here!" He tells the driver.

He opens the door, looks both ways, then pushes Ms. Pat out of the van. They are in Seminole Heights. 2 blocks from Hillsborough High School. He has accomplished 3 things by shooting Ms. Pat... 1) he's letting Cash and C-Money know he ain't playing and 2) they know who they have and what she's worth. They know that the flesh wound won't kill Ms. Pat. 3) they want her to tell Cash and C-Money what happened.

DESTINY'S DAD, D

"The car washing is over!' Yells D. He's ready to gamble. It's 7 PM and all the lil jits have been busy all day selling dope or weed. He knows their lil pockets are fat and he's ready to trim them. Last night he received his trick dice game in the mail from Miami. It's a lil shop down south that he's been dealing with for years. They sell all kinds of things to cheat and gamble with. They even have a pair of regular looking dark boy glasses that can see through a certain deck of cards. You get the glasses and 3 decks of the cards for $40. He's got red and white sets of loaded dice. All they will do is 7's. He plans to switch them in and out all night and hit the jits up for a couple grand. The dice are only 2 a pair. "Old nigga close this raggedy ass car wash so we can break yo ass," yell T-Roy, a tall black kid out of Ponce de Leon Projects.

"This the last car here," D says as he points to a box Chevy on 20's. 10 minutes later the dice game is crUnc. it's at least 15 jits screaming, smoking, drinking, and gambling. Every hour D charges everybody $5 apiece. He's the house man. "Come on old man, you aint shot the dice yet!" Yells Reggie, another lil bad ass go-yam jit. "You ain't said shit!" D yells grabbing the dice. He shakes them and rolls an 8. "Who don't like my 6 or 8? Y'all win on 7 or 11 and all craps." He yells.

"Put down nigga," yell about 10 jits. The other 5 all from College Hill and betting with him. In two rolls D hits the 8. "I won, gimme my money." He mimics Smokey off of the movie Friday. "Shoot nigga," Reggie says throwing down $10. They are shooting $10 and $10 more once you get your point. "7!" D Yells while getting another 7.

Reggie is getting hot because he's losing, and his home boys are fussing at him for not catching the dice. "Fuck y'all!" He yells. "I'm in the main. Don't bet nigga because I don't catch dice. They're gonna do what they're gonna do.

D rolls the dice and hits a 10. "I like my 10 or 4, y'all get 7 or 11?" "We straight. 10 in the main." Reggie says dropping $10 more down. As D is putting down his $10, another white dice falls out of his hand. He quickly tries to grab it but it's too late. Reggie already has his gun out. "Open your hand nigga, he screams. D says, "fuck you, I ain't…" That was all he got out before T-Roy had stole him on the side of his head with a .357 pistol. Him and Reggie both pistoled whip D damn near to death Before taking all his and their money back and running off.

CASH

"Ma calm down." I can't fully hear you.
Tonya is telling Cash that these niggas
have her tied up in her panties and bra
in some cheap motel room. "That's
enough!" The robber says snatching the
phone. "Look here nigga, ya moms is
looking good in these lace panties."
"Nigga you," Cash says, "I what?" The
nigga yells. "Nigga you better act like
you know who's got the upper hand
and talk like you want your momma
back!" The robber says checking Cash.
C-Money grabs the phone from Cash;
He's a vet and respect 's the game. He
knows emotions can get you or someone
you love killed. "That's my wife. What's
the tab so I can have my woman back.
Please don't hurt her. Just tell me what
and where to meet you. I respect the
game. Ain't no poor hero shit on my
end." C-Money says.

"Now I like you." The robber says. "I want $500,000. Meet me at Malibu Grand Prix on Nebraska in an hour. Come by yourself and you'll leave with your wife. Keep this phone with you." "OK, I'll be there." C-Money says disconnecting the call. "The fuck is wrong with you?" He yells at Cash. "Acting off emotions, you could have gotten your mother raped or killed. Ain't no emotions from a king," C-Money yells. "A good hunter must be able to think like his prey. These niggas don't want no pussy. They are some broke niggas that capitalized off us not protecting my Queen. They want some money, so we are going to give them some money, get her back and when they slip… we'll make them pay." "I'm sorry Pop," Cash responds. Knowing his dad is right.

DESTINY

"Oh God Auntie, I hope he's alright." Destiny yells. She and her aunt Donna are speeding down MLK on their way to St Joseph's Hospital. Drena called her phone 5 minutes ago telling her that her dad was in a coma, after damn near being beaten to death at his shop.

10 minutes later, Destiny runs into the emergency room screaming, "I am here for my dad, Deshean Jackson." "3rd floor," the nurse says.
Getting of the hospital elevator destiny sees DJ, Cherelle, and her mom talking to the hospital chaplain. "Noooo!" She yells running up to her mom hugging her. "He's in a coma baby, they won't let us see him yet. They are cleaning him up and checking his brain." "Oh my god! What happened?" Destiny yells. "Some jits out of Ponce De Leon supposedly caught him cheating and pistol whipped him before robbing him and leaving him for dead," DJ answers.

"Did anyone call the police?" "Do they know the jit's names?" "You already know, ain't nobody seen nothing or gonna be willing to testify on them dudes. This is the hood. Have you forgot?" "I can't wait to get my badge," Destiny shouts! "These people are going to start being held accountable for their actions. My father is lying in there almost dead about a petty gambling game and nobody is going to do nothing," Destiny screams.

"I didn't say nobody wasn't gonna do nothing." DJ answers. "Oh no you're not, you are doing too good to get back out there on some Clint Eastwood stuff. Let the police handle it. I am going to file a police report," Destiny says while dialing 911 from her phone.

CASH

"Checkmate," C-Money yells. He and Cash are playing a game of chess while he is waiting on the call to go rescue Tonya. "How did you beat me in 5 moves, Pop?" Cash asks. C-Money Picks up the chess pieces that had lost Cash the game. "You always have to watch out for the queen." The ringing of C-Money's phone breaks the heavy tension in the room. "Hello." "In five minutes, ride in the parking lot of Malibu. Put the money on the bed of the blue Dodge Ram truck and go wait at the 7-Eleven on Skipper Rd. As long as the money is right, she'll be walking up to you. If you play, she'll never walk again." "I am on my way." C-Money says disconnecting the call. "I'll be back," C-Money states while grabbing the duffel bag with half a mil in it. "Pop, you want Fat Dre to tail you?" "No, I'm good. None of y'all do nothing until I return with your mother,"

C-Money says looking at Cash, Cool Al and Fat Dre.

10 minutes later, C-Money is pulling into 7-Eleven's parking lot on Skipper Road and Nebraska Avenue. He drops the money off like he was told and says a silent prayer: "God, I know for years I have lived by the sword. Please don't let my transgressions reflect on my wife. Give her back to me God. I would truly lay down my life for hers right now. Thank you, God. Amen." Soon as C-Money opens his eyes, he sees Tonya walking up Nebraska headed towards his truck. "Thank you, God." He jumps out and rushes up to Tonya giving her a big hug. She is crying. "Baby did they hurt you?" "No, I'm good. Please take me home. I need to take a long hot shower. I feel so violated. They had me in my panties and bra until 20 minutes ago. They did feed me Burger King though," she laughs.

'I'm gonna kill them niggas!" C-Money shouts. Hearing this, she decides not to tell C-Money or Cash one of the dudes slapped her. She doesn't want to see neither one of them killed or in prison trying to get revenge. "I am calling our time shares, we are leaving tomorrow on a 3-week vacation," Tonya says. "Tell Cash I said don't move until we get back. To be sure, I'm calling Carlos to tell him not to deal with Cash until we get back." "Whatever you say baby," C-Money responds. Dirty game.

CHAPTER 14

Money, Cash, Hoes

Mad Max

"If we are gonna make a name for ourselves and get this dope shit poppin, we need to go down there and bust some heads." Mad Max says while looking into the faces of his crew; Tear, Lizanne, Shayla, and Elise. They are all sitting inside the Winnebago they have rented to go to Daytona Beach, Florida for spring break. "I have a nigga I met from Miami in the joint, who has a big brother that's moving major weight. He's gonna hook us up with all the coke, weed and pills we can buy. Our goal need to be $150,000. Is you all with me?"

"You damn right Lizanne says. "Let's get this money," Tear replies. "I am all in!" Says Shayla. Elise says, "what are we waiting on?" "That's what the fuck

I'm talking about. From this point on our crew is called "Dirty Game."

"Let's get it." Mad Max says pulling off heading towards I-4.

Two hours later, Elise is looking stunning in a pair of Ed Hardy boy shorts, tank top to match and some Mark Jacob sandals. She's walking through the lobby of the Adams Mark Hotel. Swinging her hips. "Pssst, Pssst. Hey there pretty." A tall NBA player looking nigga with heavy jewelry on his neck and wrist says. Elise sexily waves but keeps walking.

Jersey is the boss of his crew and can't seem played so he says, "come here sexy. I ain't trying to go back to Jacksonville with all this money." Pulling 2 big stacks of money out of his pockets. He's showing out. It's 3 of his niggas and a big crowd standing around watching. Talking in her lil girl voice, Elise says, "prove it." Putting him on blast. He opens one of the knots of money and gives her $400." "What do you want to smell it for this?" She replies. "Nah ma, that's just a down payment. What are you trying to do?" "Take me to your room and let's see," Elise replies licking her sexy lips. "Hey y'all, I'll be back." He says walking towards the elevator. "Which one of you niggas wanna smell my hand when I get back?" He yells to his crew, trying to stunt. What he ain't see is Tear following them, walking with Shayla like he's on a pussy mission too. A few niggas see Shayla and say, "damn" "My room on the 3rd floor," Jersey says pushing 3. "I hope you don't have a big dick." Says Elise. "Because I have a small pussy." Jersey's dick instantly gets rock hard. "But then if it's small, I can put the whole dick in my mouth and lick your balls at the same time." Jersey is damn near running to his room. As he is opening the door, Tear and Shayla roughly bumps into him. "Damn bruh, y'all need to watch where y'all are going." "My bad, dude." Tear says as Elise steps into the room. She sees that nobody is inside, and she reaches into her purse.

She spins around and ups her .380 at Jersey. "What the fuck is you about to say? Open the door!" Elise shouts. Tear is standing at the door. Shayla is staying outside in case one of Jersey's homeboys come. "You slipped my nigga." Tear says, "run that paper and them jewels and live to see another day." "That's real," Jersey says, giving up all of his money and jewels. "It's a dirty game." Says Elise, grabbing the handcuffs out of her Hermes bag. They handcuff Jersey to a rail in the walk-in closet leaving him broke and blowed.

Ten minutes later.... "Damn black, anybody tell you they will eat all that ass?" A nigga shouts out the passenger's side of a Bentley Coupe. Shayla is walking down the set. At least ten niggas are following her, taking photos and trying to get a feel of her fat ass. "Money makes me cum." She tells the nigga in the Bentley. "I've got more money than I've got places to put it."

Rico says, pulling out a Gucci handbag filled with money. He leans out of the window showing Shayla all of the cash. "Bingo!" She says, knowing it's at least 20 grand in the bag, judging by all the hundreds. "Put my number in your phone," Rico yells. "I'm good," Shayla responds. "I told you money makes me cum, not talking." "Let me out bruh," Rico says to his man Don P. "Fuck that bitch bruh," Don P says. "It's 100,000 hoes out there. We're almost to our room, we'll find some bad shit there." "Fuck that, I want this hoe," Rico says getting out of the car. "I'll be down to the room in a minute." Rico look like he's going to a rap video, he has on so much ice. The Gucci bag is on his shoulder. "Come here ma," Rico says. "My pussy getting wet. You ready to let me ride that big ole dick?" Shayla says, grabbing his dick through the Gucci shorts. "I'll give you a stack ($1,000) to bust this shit," Rico says, grabbing a handful of Shayla's fat ass. "Let's get it," Shayla says, pulling him towards the closest hotel. "Come walk with me. I've got a room at the Adam's Mark Hotel right up the road." "Nah player, you and your man ain't gonna run no train on me and buck me on my money. Get a room right here, I'll let you come back tonight and fuck my face for free, if your dick is good." Rico's dick is bulging out of his pants. "I call that," he says going to the counter at the Holiday Inn & Express to get a room.

"Damn that dick is big," Shayla says gripping Rico's dick as they are getting on the elevator. "Don't go to being nice now," Rico says. Tear and Elise are in the elevator with them. Tear ups his .45. "Nigga if you blink too many times, I'm going to bust your ass. Pat this pussy down," Tear yells. Elise finds a 9mm pistol in Rico's waistline. "Walk nigga," Tear says walking him to the room. "What room is it?" Tear says to Shayla, "422." "Open the door, you already know what it is," Tear says. "Don't make me kill you bout some shit you can get back. Strip this nigga down,"

Tear yells. They take all of his jewelry, the money out of his pockets and put it into the Gucci bag filled with money. "Put the cuffs on this nigga. This weak ass closet ain't gone hold him, we're gonna have to tie him all the way up and lock him the bathroom. I'll put a chair against the door. He'll be alright until housekeeping finds him in the a.m." "It's a dirty game," Shayla says kissing Rico on the cheek.

On the beach...

"Damn slim, pay for it," Don Don says looking at Lizanne's sexy ass legs in her two-piece, Tom Ford bathing suit. "That's what I fuck, straight dimes," Don Don yells to his crew. They are walking down the beach stuntin'. Don Don has money in all four of his pockets and bling galore. He looks like Baby from Cash Money. Seeing how all of his pockets are bulging. Lizanne shows out by dropping in a split and bouncing on one hand. "Can your dick handle this?" She asks, seductively. "I ain't gone lie, I ain't packing like that," Don Don says laughing. "I'll pay to have you ride this dick like that though."

"Where your room at?" Lizanne challenges. "Right down here," he points. "You ready?" She pulls her bikini bottom to the side and puts her finger inside her pussy and pulls it out, showing him the pussy juice all over it. His dick instantly rises. "Oh shit," he yells. "Y'all wait on me, I'll be right back." "I'm coming with you, Boss." Yells his gunman, Tote.

"For show," Don Don yells. "Damn," Lizanne says to herself, walking up to the room. They get on the elevator and head to his room. Mad Max is trailing them. He sees the nigga Tote following behind. Lizanne and Don Don go into the room while Tote stands by a window looking at the beach. "I got him," Mad Max says walking up to him. "My dude, you seen a bitch on this floor with blue hair and a mohawk?" When

Tote turns around, Mad Max has his .45 in his face. "Take your shirt off and I mean slow." Tote lifts up his shirt, revealing a .357 magnum. "Turn around," Mad Max says taking the gun. "Wow you're the real deal," Mad Max says seeing Tote also has a .38 strapped to his back. He puts both guns on him and walks Tote to the room door. Inside of the room....

Don Don slaps Lizanne hard on her ass. "Damn Slim, what's it gone cost for this rodeo?" "$700.00," Lizanne replies taking off her top first. "You call that? All day" Don Don says pulling out his money. "Pay me when we're done big daddy," Lizanne says pushing him onto the bed. She starts to undress him. Knock, knock, knock!

"What the hell does Tote want?" Don Don says. Getting up in his boxers, he peeks through the peep hole and sees Tote before opening the door. Mad Max pushes Tote into Don Don. "The hell you go going on?" Don Don says before seeing Mad Max with the pistol pointed at him. Closing the door behind him, Mad Max says, "y'all niggas strip. I ain't come in here to be playing." After getting all the money and jewelry Tote and Don Don has, Lizanne and Mad Max ties them up and leave the room. After four more successful licks, the Dirty Money crew left Daytona with $110,000 in cash and over $250,000 in jewelry.

"It's some sucker ass niggas in this world," laughs Mad Max. "Nigga we are some bad bitches," laughs Lizanne. "For show, baby it's on now."

"Later in the week we're going to Miami to cop. By Saturday of this coming week, we are opening up shop. We are stealing the game from Miami. We're gonna give niggas ten lays for the hundred. We'll shut down shop. Everybody will start copping their crack from us. I want y'all looking fly everyday Elise and Shayla," Mad Max says.

"Y'all will be selling nigga's work. Lizanne, you will be our accountant and ride with me to cop. Tear you are the enforcer." "Dirty Game baby," yells Lizanne.

DESTINY

"I graduate tomorrow. I'm so excited, I've been waiting to put on a Tampa Police Department uniform since I was six years old." Destiny is on the phone with Chrishonna. "That's great girl. I just finished writing my first play. It's called "Why Do Good Girls Like Bad Guys." "I hope you ain't throwing no stones," Destiny says laughing. "Actually, you and Wugga did inspire me to write this, but you know I'm messed up about them street niggas," Chrishonna laughs. "Alright chic, I'm tired. I'm gonna send you some photos of me in my uniform tomorrow. I love you, chic," Destiny says. "I love you too girl," Chrishonna replies disconnecting the call.

Three months later....

CHAPTER 15

Get Down or Lay Down

CASH

"I'm tired ma," Cash says to Seleena. "You want me to give you a bath and a back massage?" "That would be nice," Cash responds walking towards their bedroom. He's had a rough week. He's had to open up another spot to replace Baby Doll's spot. He had to find another person to pick up the money since Camille is on some New Flame shit. "I'm getting tired," Cash says to himself. "It's too much work to be a kingdom. I could use all this energy opening some legal shit."

"Baby, did I tell you I'm going back to school soon?" Cash says "Yes, I think that is a good idea. My daddy has been trying to get me to go to college like forever," Seleena says. "Why haven't you?" asks Cash. "I have no desire to. I enjoy being a hustler's wife, I'm good. You have been bugging lately, You took out your gold teeth, you haven't driven your Rolls Royce since Baby Doll got arrested, now you're talking about school. What, you're not happy being a King?" Seleena asks. "I'm just trying to take it to the next level," says Cash. "I hear you, for a minute you were starting to scare me," says Seleena. "Fuck you mean?" Cash asks, starting to get upset. "I want to be a Queen and I ain't accepting nothing else," Seleena says; not backing down. "Who do you think you are talking to?" Cash asks. "It ain't but two of us in this house." "Yeah, you're right," Cash says; walking towards the hidden safe behind his Scarface picture. Opening the safe, Cash counts out $60,000.00. He walks over to Seleena and says, "here." "What is this for?" She yells. "It's yours!" Says Cash. "Take it and find you a King. I'm done with you and with being your King. I'm out of here. When I get back, you need to be gone." "This is our house," Seleena yells. "This house belongs to Tonya Jones," Cash says, thankful for listening to his mom when raised. *"Boy,"* she told him, *"when a woman's scorned ain't no telling what they'll do. Don't put that girl on your deed."* "So it's like that huh?" "Straight like that," Cash says headed towards the door. "Please don't make us become enemies," he grills her. She knows Cash could have killed her in the snap of a finger. "Damn," she says to herself, knowing she's blowed. "You can't leave me Cash!" She screams, falling to the floor crying like a newborn baby. Getting into his Ford 150, Cash says, "I need a woman not a 24-year-old girl. I've been tied down with two hoes since I've been a young nigga. Until I get the woman of my dreams, I'm going to hang out.

DESTINY

"I told you I had you," Tiger says to Destiny. They are riding down 22nd in a patrol car. They are the light on Lake Ave. "You did it and I thank you so much." Tiger pulled some strings and got Destiny assigned to his squad. His only backlash was he had to be her partner. He's stuck with a woman-rookie cop. He's cool with it because Destiny is tough, from the hood and really compassionate about doing what's right. "I've got to show you who's who. I know everything that goes on in College Hill, Ponce De Leon, Belmont Heights and all through Jackson Heights. Who sells what, who's who baby's daddy, who steals clothes, etc. I've got a lot of snitches too; these people get caught up and will tell on their mamas." "Wow," Destiny says. She knows how the game goes by being raised in the hood but hearing it from another officer is shocking.

"If you know everything, why are these people not in prison?" "It's not easy," Tiger replies. "I try to focus more on the dangerous criminals. I mean if a guy sells a dime bag of weed in front of me, then he's telling me he has no respect for me and he wants to go to jail. But, if I catch an 18-year-old, lost black male with $60.00 worth of crack, and I know his situation, his mom is a lazy bar fly and his daddy is in prison, I'll take it and give him a one-time chance, along with a long talk." Destiny's respect for Tiger just multiplied tenfold. Her aunt Donna was right, they do have the same mission- To Protect and Serve, but also to uplift and enlighten the blind.

"How about a cuban sandwich?" Tiger asks, turning left onto MLK headed to Buffalo Curtis. "Yes, that will be great," replies Destiny. "I ain't seen Mr. Frank in years."

"Hello, my little princess," Mr. Frank says as Destiny walks into the store. Mr. Frank has owned Buffalo Curtis since Tiger and Destiny can remember.

His cuban sandwiches are legendary. He also has $0.01 candy and cookies. "Heyyyyy Mr. Frank," says Destiny, giving him a big hug. "What is this?" He asks, pointing at her uniform smiling. "I told you I was going to do it." Destiny has been telling Mr. Frank she was going to be a policewoman since she was six years old. "And you?" Frank asks, hugging Tiger. He played baseball at Belmont Heights Little League Park across from Buffalo Curtis and was half raised by Mr. Frank. "I'm so proud of you both," Mr. Frank says. "Thank you," they both reply in unison. "How's your father recovering?" Mr. Frank knows everything that happens in the hood. "He's coming along well. Already back at the car wash doing the same thing," Destiny says sadly.

"You know D," Frank says. "He's been in College Hill forty something years. You see that?" Frank says pointing at a photo of a little league team on the wall.

That's your Pop standing next to Dwight Gooden. Your Pop was a better all-around player than anyone on the team.

Code one, all available units, respond to a robbery in progress at Lake Ave Liquor Store. "Let's go!" Tiger says, grabbing Destiny. "Y'all be safe," Mr. Frank says watching them run to the door.

"You have on your vest?" Tiger asks. "Yes, do you?" Destiny responds. "No." says Tiger. "Well please put it on," Destiny replies. "Okay," Tiger says getting out and grabbing his bullet-proof vest out of the trUnc.

Destiny is so excited; this will be her first action as a cop.

Pulling up to the package store two minutes later, Tiger and Destiny jump out with their guns drawn.

The drUnc robber doesn't know the manager of the liquor store had pushed the silent alarm on him.

He definitely didn't think his luck would be this bad to have two cops outside three minutes after he walked into the store and drew his gun.

"Damn," he says seeing the cop car pull up. He grabs the manager yelling, "is there a back door to this place?" "Yes," the scary manager says. "It's this way," leading him to the back.

Tiger is already on point. "Destiny," he yells! "Stay here and cover the front. I'll watch the back door. Back up should be here in a minute." As soon as the words left Tiger's mouth, two more police cars pulled up. Destiny points to the front and runs to the back to assist Tiger. The door clicks, "freeze, put your hands up and drop the weapon," Tiger says pointing his firearm at the robber. Dropping to a crouch, holding her firearm in both hands, Destiny shouts, "now!" The robber drops his weapon and puts his hands in the air.

"Get down on your knees! Keep your hands up!" Destiny shouts. "I'm gonna secure is weapon," Tiger says grabbing the gun. Destiny puts her handcuffs on the ground. Tiger grabs then and subdues the suspect. "Job well done," Tiger tells her, giving her a hug once they had the suspect in the back of their cruiser. All the other officers cheered her on, congratulating her on her 1st arrest. She was in a zone, wishing she was at the store her uncle Melvin owned, arresting the murderer the night he killed her favorite uncle.

COOL AL

"This is what the fuck I'm talking about," Cool Al says admiring his new car. "What do I owe you, Unc?" "Nothing," Uncle Jaheim says. "I actually have to give you $7,000.00 back. Everything came to $128,000.00; you gave me $135,000.00." "Keep the change Unc. Damn," yells Cool Al looking at the yellow Bentley coupe deluxe. It has all black leather insides, with yellow trimming in the seats, 20-inch chrome Diablo rims with yellow streaks. "Thank you Unc. This is perfect," Cool Al says jumping into the car and speeding off. He turns on the CD player. It's an old school CD in it. Clarence Carter "*Strokin*" comes on. Cool Al is on his way to Tampa Heights to stunt and then head on Main St. It's almost Friday night, he thinks looking at his Jacob watch.

It's 6:15 PM, I've got time to hit the mall.

Cash answers the phone, "Hello."
"Sup bruh, you fucking with me?" Cool Al asks. "What's good, Pretty Boy? I'm trying to hit this mall so I can step out tonight. Club 901 is gonna be swanging. Nothing but executive hoes be in that spot." "Yeah, I'll roll with ya. I'm tied up right now, have Mario pick me out something and I'll come by your house and get ready over there." "That's the business," Cool Al says, hanging up and getting out of the car in Central Court Apartments. Cool Al is smiling from ear to ear as everybody is admiring his whip and pulling his dick. Yeah King status, he says to himself.

One hour later....

Cool Al pulls up to University Mall, trying to decide where to park. Just as he's pulling into an empty parking spot in front of Dillard's, a 740 BMW blocks his path. W.T.F.?

It's Seleena's car. She moves and let him park. Cool Al gets out and Seleena is blowed. She thought she had hit the jackpot seeing the Bentley. Walking to her car, Cool Al leans inside her window. "What's up stranger?" Cool Al asks. He is looking like money. He has on Pelle Pelle jeans set, some Jordans and so much ice on his neck and wrists. Taking her shot, Seleena says, "I can't lie these past four months since Cash and I split, it's been rough. I thought the driver of this Bentley may need a Queen to hold him down and treat his dick right." Licking her lips and opening her Michael Kors pants showing her fat pussy print. Cool Al gets stuck starring at it. "I'm sorry," she says breaking the trance. "What are you doing later on?" Cool Al asks. "I'm gonna go home, take a hot bath, throw on some Frederick's of Hollywood lingerie, turn on some R. Kelly, and play with my lonely pussy. You care to help?"

A damsel in distressed out". Seleena says, rubbing in between her legs. Cool Al's dick is stone. "LOL! Give me your number. I'll be on my way to your crib about 1:00 AM. Where do you live?" "I have a condo in Apollo Beach." "Here," Cool Al says pulling out a fat knot of money. "Grab us something to sip on." He gives her two grand. "I can't wait to taste you," Seleena says while pulling off smiling to herself. "It's more than one King," she says turning her music up. She's listening to Trina's new song, *The Baddest Bitch*.

Cool Al grabs his hard dick and says to himself, "I can't wait to flip this freaky bitch. It's my time to be King!" He shouts, walking into the mall.

CASH

Later that night....

"Damn bro, you fucking up the game with this bitch here," Cash says looking at Cool Al's new Bentley. "I can't lie, I'm on your dick," he laughs. "You should drive this bitch, bruh." "This bitch here is running," Cool Al says. "I'll drive us both to the club," Cash says getting into the driver's seat. "You got me," Cool Al says laughing, while getting into the passenger's seat.

"Listen," Cash says, "it's almost that time. I'm actually pushing it back a couple years. I was gonna retire on my 23rd Birthday in 7 months, but I'm gonna do it at 25. That will give me 2 1/2 years to get my G.E.D. and my AA in Business Management. The good news is, I'm falling back from the day-to-day operations. You're the King my dude," Cash says patting Cool Al on the back. Carlos will only deal with me; so,

I'll grab the work and take care of getting the money to him.

Whatever you feel comfortable with paying me to do that, I'll gladly accept." "Nah bruh, it's C.M.F. till death. I'm gone still bust down with you, the same way you've always did me, you're my brother. The same as Fat Dre, understand me Cool Al? I'm falling back, I start school next month. The next 2 1/2 years I want to stack me another mil and I'm done." "Another mil!" Al shouts. "You got a whole mil put up?" "A little over," Cash says. Cool Al is hot. Because up until recently, the most cash he has ever had was $600,000.00.

"I don't live like you," Cash says already regretting telling Cool Al how much money he has. Carlos told him; information is power. As you hold it to yourself, no one can hold it against you. Silence is golden. "The fuck you mean, you don't live like me?" "Just what I said," Cash says getting upset. "You spend your money on jewelry, hoes, clothes; hell, how many cars does this make you have?"

"You have six so what." Cool Al replies. "Outside of the Rolls Royce, which was a gift, I have a Ford F150, a Mustang, and two duck off cars. You have a 500 Benz, a 740 BMW, a Chevy Silverado, a Range Rover, a Bentley and an Audi. All of them tricked out," Cash states. "Listen bro, we ain't got no business debating. You are the new King, push it to the limit!" Cash yells pulling up to Club 901. "Yeah, you right bro. I apologize." Cool Al says. "I love you bruh." "I love you more," Cash responds.

Later that night....

"I thought you were not gonna make it," Seleena says opening the door to her condo. "Damn, Cool Al says looking at Seleena's sexy body. She has on a see-through yellow sheer gown with some yellow laced thongs underneath.

Closing the door and locking it behind him, Cool Al is in a daze watching pretty ass Seleena walk.

Her body is perfect. She has candles lit everywhere. R. Kelly's, Your Body's Calling, is on her surround sound. *Baby no more stalling*, R. Kelly sings as Seleena brings him a glass of Krug. "I spent your money wisely; it was $1,700.00 a bottle." "Money grows on trees, I'm the King!" He yells. "Let me disrobe King," Seleena says slowly stripping Cool Al of all his clothes. Cool Al's dick is stone (again) LOL! As Bump and Grind comes on, Seleena drops to her knees and grabs Cool Al's dick. She spits on the head and slowly licks all of her saliva off. "Ummmm," she moans. She begins to trace a wet path with her tongue, down Cool Al's 8' dick. She is tickling the head of his dick and shaft as she slowly works his big dick into her hot hungry mouth. "Ooh shit," Cool Al yells.

This is by far the best head he's had in his life. "Relax and enjoy my mouth my King," Seleena says.

"I can't," Cool Al screams as he spasms full of pleasure and cums in her mouth. Seleena continues sucking and swallowing until the last drop is gone. The last thing Cool Al remembered was falling down on her soft bed and 3 minutes later he was sleep.

DESTINY

"Do you want to come inside and have a little night cap before you head home?" Tiger says. As Destiny drops him off home. Tiger has his own home, his parents moved to Valdosta, Georgia 3 years ago and gave him the house off of 22nd he was raised in. "That will be cool. It's only 8:15 PM, I'll stay for 45 minutes." She likes being Tiger's company and he is secretly infatuated with her. She is everything that he has always dreamed of in a woman. Smart, sexy, strong, and has a big heart. "So, did you feel it?" Tiger says pouring Destiny some Zinfandel Wine. "Feel what?" She responds. "The energy every cop feels when they are making an arrest." "Oh yes, here I was thinking it was just me. I was so excited, I had absolutely no fear. Is that weird?" "Yes, it is. This is a dangerous job. A lot of cops get killed every day," Tiger says. "Yeah, I know. It's just the rush I got, gripping my revolver. I guess it took away my fear." "Just don't ever get too comfortable, please." "I've got it," Destiny laughs. "You better," Tiger says grabbing her they began to play wrestle until Tiger ends up on top of her. He gives her a passionate kiss. She responds and they kiss for about 5 full minutes before they break for air. "Wow!" Tiger says. "I've been wanting to do that since I first laid eyes on you." "Get off me," Destiny says laughing. "I've got to get home before aunt Donna put's an A.P.B. out on me." Walking her to the door, Tiger says, "I'll see you at 8:00 AM," before pulling her in for another long kiss. "Call me and let me know you made it home safe." And if I don't?" Destiny says smiling. "I'll arrest you for assault on my heart," Tiger says smiling.

CHAPTER 16

Overnight Celebrity

MAD MAX

"This is what I'm talking about," screams Mad Max. Him and Lizanne is sitting inside a Dodge Intrepid backed in at the Oak Village Apartments in West Tampa. That's where they set up shop. It's been 3 weeks and they have the pack and single stones game in Tampa on lock. People are coming from everywhere to get the 10 big rocks for the hundreds, that's two extra rocks each hundred they spend. The X Pills are going for $10.00, which Blue Dolphins usually go for $20.00, the weed is jumping too. Mad Max is watching Shayla in a pair of short shorts by Prada, a Prada tank top, and some suede Prada tennis shoes making sale after sale.

Elise is matching her in her Nike short set with Nike Air Max shoes and no socks, also going to sale for sale. They have ran through 3 bricks, 200 X pills and 14 pounds of weed the past 2 weeks.

"We have to head to Miami to cop tonight. We only have a kilo and a half left, 100 X pills and 11 more pounds of weed," Lizanne says. "Today is Thursday, this will not last us past Saturday night." "Okay," Mad Max says. "We'll leave early in the morning. I saw the nigga Cool Al come through here in a yellow Bentley while you were inside the trap using the restroom," Lizanne says. "Looks like the nigga Cash and Fat Dre was following behind him in a Yukon, all black. Somebody must have told them it was heavy competition on the rise," Mad Max smiles. "What do you think they are gonna do?"

"I ain't through with them chumps, I'm gonna shoot up two of their traps next week. We need to make their traps hot, so more of their money will come over here." Lizanne laughs, "it's a dirty game." "All day," Mad Max says rubbing her sexy slim thigh.

DESTINY

"Surprise!" Destiny shouts. Everybody goes to yelling and shouting. They are at her parent's apartment in College Hill Projects. Fee got out of prison today and Destiny tricked her into coming to her surprise party. "Oh my GOD," Fee screams. She's so happy to finally be free after 6 years and 3 months in prison. "Come here sis," D says giving her a big hug. "I'm glad you're home baby girl," D says. "You're welcome to stay with us. Ain't nobody but me and your ugly sister in-law." "Fuck you," Drena yells, hugging Fee. "Damn girl, I miss you. Look at my hair," she laughs. "Yeah Chic, you need to get right," Fee laughs. "Thanks bro. I'm gonna stay with Donna and Destiny for a couple of months until I can get on my feet." "Here," D says handing Fee a knot of money. "Welcome home." "You ballin' like that?" Fee says taking the money.

"I had a good night last night at the dice game." "You ain't gone stop," she laughs. "Where is the food?" Fee yells heading towards the kitchen. She's dying to taste some real food, collard greens, potato salad, baked beans, ham hocks, and some real dessert. Red velvet cake, sweet potato pie, pineapple upside down cake, it's all there. The entire family pitched in. Fee piles her plate a foot high and begins to eat like a hungry slave. Destiny is watching her aunt eat and smiles. Ain't nothing like family she thinks to herself. "When she finishes eating, I'm going to introduce y'all," she says, "to Tiger." The past month, him and her have been inseparable making arrest, eating dinner, going on dates, skating, bowling, shooting pool, and dancing. Destiny is having the time of her life, she's about ready to give him a shot of her goodies. She really likes him and she's horny as hell! LOL!

CASH

"We needed this vacation man. I've been so stressed, and I start school next Monday," Cash says. Him and Fat Dre are rolling down I-95 heading to Miami. They're in Cash's Rolls Royce, Cash heard about the new club "King of Diamonds" and wants to go check it out. "Bro what are we going to do about this dirty game situation? I got word that they were the ones that shot up the tram in Robles Park and the one by Central Court," Fat Dre asks. "What do you and Cool AL want to do?" "Cool Al wants to shoot up their spot and kill their leader. Some wild head nigga that's fresh outta prison name Mad Max." "What's up with him?" ask Cash. "The nigga is a robber. He supposedly shot his dad or stepdad up when he was young and did 11 years in prison. He has a lil brother named Tear. He's good and stupid, he shot and robbed a few niggas."
"Who are those bad bitches them niggas got hustling for them?"

"I don't know. I do know they ain't from Tampa because a couple of the niggas I know have tried to fuck em and they say the hoes talk country."

"Is one of them the one who robbed Cool Al? Because I don't like coincidences." "Nah, Cool Al said he'd never forget the bitch's face who set him up." "What about Tear? He's not sure, the nigga who shot him had on a mask and it was late night. I want some more homework done on these dirty game cats before we move on them. Like who is their connect, where do they stay. I want to know where those hoes are from. They could be the power behind the niggas, because from what you are telling me, Mad Max and Tear are dumb goons, but that's not what I'm seeing about their operation. I actually respect their hustle outside of the hatin' shit, like shooting up rivals' traps; that was sucker shit.

The ten for a hundred was a genius move, having them hoes looking sexy while selling the work is too.

Niggas are gonna cop just to see them bad bitches and try to get their mack on." "I'm on it," Fat Dre says. "Why didn't Cool Al want to come and fuck some of these exotic bitches I hear KOD has," ask Cash. Cool Al told him he met a bad bitch during spring break from North Carolina. He was going to visit her and beat her back out all weekend. "Some bitch he met during spring break shit in Daytona," Fat Dre says. Cash was just making sure Cool Al told Fat Dre the same thing. Ever since he told Cool Al about his net worth last month, he's been acting kind of funny. "Let's get our trick on my nigga and worry about Tampa and all the drama later," Cash shouts turning up his sound system; Twister, Overnight Celebrity, is on.

COOL AL

"Damn baby, this is so nice," Seleena says. Her and Cool Al are in 1st class on Delta Airlines flight headed to Hawaii. "It's the only way a King does it baby," Cool Al shouts. "Damn you got my panties wet," Seleena says grabbing Cool Al's hand and putting it under her Dolce & Gabbana skirt. "Oooh shit!" Cool Al says feeling her moisture through the soiled, satin Ed Hardy panties. "Come on," she yells getting up, leading Cool Al to the restroom. They are about to join the-mile-high club. Entering the restroom in a blur, Cool Al is pushed on the toilet seat. Seleena drops between his legs and pulls out his hard dick. "Ummm," she moans covering 5' in her mouth off the top. "Damnnnn," moans Cool Al. She's looking him straight into his eyes as she's devouring his dick. "Slurp, slurp, slurp" "Damn my King this dick tastes so good."

"Gimme some of that good pussy," moans Cool Al. "Your wish is my command daddy," Seleena says lifting up her skirt while pulling her panties to the side. She grabs his pole and puts his dick inside of her as she straddles him on the toilet seat. "Ooooh fuck daddy," yells Seleena as she begins to ride him slowly. Feeling Seleena's tight, wet pussy grip his dick has Cool Al's eyes rolling into the back of his head. "Damn this pussy is good," he moans. Seleena grabs him around the neck and goes to throwing her pussy wildly on him. "Get this pussy," she screams. "Ooooh shiiiit, baby I'm cummin," Seleena yells. "Meeeee too," Cool Al screams shooting his seed into Seleena.

DESTINY

"I want to thank you. You have made my life so meaningful. I feel so powerful around you. You keep me smiling and happy," Destiny says. Her and Tiger are walking down Clearwater Beach while holding hands. "You're so welcome. If you only knew how much I have enjoyed every second I've been around you, you would understand why I'm returning the thank you. You have made me whole, you have been the answer to my prayers, you make my days so much brighter. You have brought nothing but joy to my world," Tiger says. "Ooh Tiger you are about to make me cry," Destiny says with a smile. "I sure am," Tiger replies grabbing her hand and leading her towards the Hilton Hotel that sits on the beach. Tiger gets a room and leads Destiny to the suite.

"OMG this is beautiful." Destiny has never been inside a suite.

"Look at this," she yells looking at the garden tub, his and her gold sinks, the standing room crystal showers. "This has to be the biggest and most beautiful beds I've ever seen," Destiny says pointing at the huge King size canopy bed. "Come here," Tiger says grabbing Destiny passionately, kissing her softly on her lips. She kisses him back and whispers, "I'm a little nervous to be honest with you. I've only been intimate with one guy and the last time was 18 months ago, but I'm ready." Tiger lays Destiny back on the bed and just look at her sexy body. "What's wrong?" Destiny ask. "Absolutely nothing, you are just so damn beautiful. I wanted to look at you. I'm a lucky man!" Destiny's panties get wet instantly, they both disrobe immediately.

Tiger grabs Destiny, places her in the center of the bed and lifts her leg and begins to sprinkle kisses from the back of her ankle down to the back of her thigh, sniffing her sweet-smelling scent. Tiger opens Destiny's thighs and begins to lick her clit and tongue fucks her pussy. "Oooh GOD," Destiny yells. "Tiger that feels so good." Tiger continues his oral assault until Destiny's body couldn't take it anymore. In seconds he has made her cum, leaving her entire body in shock. Tiger's dick is brick hard, he pulls Destiny's body down towards him and slides his dick into her dripping wet pussy, causing her to arch her back as he fills up her insides. "Damn Destiny," Tiger says. "Your pussy feels so good baby." "Hmmmm," Destiny moans as the initial pain of Tiger's 8' fat dick entering her turns into intense pleasure.

"Fuuuuck," she yells as Tiger is gently sliding in and out of her wet pussy, while licking her hard nipples. "Oooh God, Tiger I'm cummin' again," Destiny shouts. Tiger getting lost in her sweet juices, screams, "oh shit, me too," while shaking and twisting from the intense pleasure.

CASH

My Goodies by Ciara is playing. Cash and Fat Dre are in the VIP at King of Diamonds. Hoes are everywhere and its so much money flying around. Money is literally all over the floor. Cash is stuck watching a tall Asian chic with long black hair down to her ass, work the pole. "Damn ma is beautiful," Cash says to Fat Dre. "I see," Fat Dre says laughing. "Nigga you have thrown over two grand at that bitch," Fat Dre says laughing again. "Fuck you," says Cash. "Nigga you have had over 10 lap dances, you got any pussy yet?" Asks Cash. "I have one leaving with me," Fat Dre boasts. "Yeah, well this beauty here is leaving with me," says Cash pointing at the Asian chic. Cash motions with his finger for her to come to him.
"Yes," she says in a beautiful accent. Cash replies, "I want you to come have a drink with me. I know time is money, I got you."

Asia is actually her stage name. She grabs up all her money that Cash and a host of other ballers have thrown her and walks off of the stage. "Listen baby," Cash says. "I'm only gonna be in town a day or two, I'm from California and I would like for you to keep me company. I'll pay you $6,000.00," Cash says. He ain't got time to play the wine and dine routine. He sees something he wants; he buys it. You only live once, C-Money taught him. "Let me go get my things," Asia says. "You ready bro?" Cash asks Fat Dre while smiling. "Nah, I'm never going to be ready to leave with all these beautiful hoes. I wonder how much the owner will charge to let me live in this bitch. I'll meet you at the door."

Ten minutes later, they are waiting for valet to bring Cash's Rolls Royce to them. Both of the hoes yell, "Damn!" while seeing the Rolls Royce pull up.

Fat Dre has a thick white chic that resembles Ice T's wife, Coco. "Here, you drive," Cash says to Fat Dre while getting in the back seat with Asia. "Y'all hungry? Because I am. Let's go to the restaurant inside our hotel," Cash says to Fat Dre. "That's what it is," Fat Dre says while driving off. Cash fucks Asia eight different ways and get's her to give him a full body massage before he passes out at about 3:00 AM. Fat Dre is still up fucking Becky like she stole something. LOL! The good life!

MAD MAX

"Yeah, I smell you big homie. That makes a lot of sense," Mad Max says to Rondo; his Miami connect. Rondo just told him to slow down all the trips back and forth that whatever he buys from now on he will front him the same on consignment. "My lil brother says you were his main man up the road (prison) and you are loyal, so I'm gone trust you like that. Please don't make me regret this choice," Rondo says looking at Mad Max in the eyes. Going at him with the same intensity, Mad Max says, "it's death by dishonor with me main man." "I'm glad you know," Rondo says shaking his hand. Getting back inside the Ford Expedition rental, Mad Max is so excited he reveals to Lizanne the convo him and Rondo just had. "Damn baby, we're leaving this bitch with 10 keys, 300 X pills and 50 pounds of pressure weed," Lizanne shouts.

"All day," Mad Max says. "He told me to be ready in the A.M. Let's get a room."

...later that night

"So, you playing like that?" Asks Mad Max. Lizanne just walked out of the restroom smelling so good in Apple Crush Victoria's Secret body wash and lotion, with only a pair of light blue Victoria's Secret t-backs on. Mad Max has fucked a few hood rats and one older bitch since he's been home. But nothing nowhere close to a dime piece like Lizanne. She knows he's crazy about her, she likes him too, but her motives are strictly about money and security. She sees he's about to be King and she plans to be the Queen right by his side. "What are you talking about?" She asks while bending over to put her things into her Coach Tote bag. Seeing her sexy slim, long legs and her firm ass eat the panties; Mad Max's dick gets harder than it ever has in his life.

Looking back at him, Lizanne says, "come and get it daddy."

Mad Max wastes no time, he goes to kissing both of her ass cheeks. "Damn ma. Your body is beautiful," he says between kisses. "Open your legs," Mad Max says. He pulls the t-backs to the side and goes to eating her pussy from the back. "Oooh shit," moans Lizanne. She has to hold on to the wall, the sensation is feeling so good. Mad Max licks up to her asshole and puts his tongue inside of it. Lizanne damn nears falls down from the intense pleasure. "Oooh," she yells. Mad Max has two fingers inside of her wet, tight pussy. "I'm cummmmmmmmming," yells Lizanne. Mad Max continues his oral assault. He's never eaten pussy, doing what he's heard so many niggas brag about, telling whore stories in prison. "Fuck me," yells Lizanne. "Give me my big black dick." She spins around and grabs Mad Max nice size 9' dick.

"Ummmm, slurp, slurp, ummmm," she's giving him a master blow job. "Uggggh, hold on," Mad Max tries to run. "Ooh shit baby, this mouth feels good."

Stepping out of her panties, Lizanne bends over the bed and says, "give me that big ole dick." Mad Max plunges his dick inside of Lizanne's tight, wet pussy. Lizanne's moan is with delight, "yes, yes, yes." It's so good, but so big. "Please, oh God," she whimpers as each of Mad Max's powerful thrusts stretched her tight walls to the limit. "Whose pussy is this?" Mad Max yells. "Yours my King, it's all yours," Lizanne yells. "That's all I needed to hear," Mad Max screams pumping in and out of her pussy like a man possessed. "Damn this is the best pussy in the world," Mad Max shouts as he begins to pump his load into her. Lizanne violently shakes, having another orgasm.

CHAPTER 17

Love at 1st Sight

"Meme," I am so proud of you, Destiny says. They are riding in Destiny's new car, a 2000 Nissan Altima, heading to Gary Adult. Meme is about to sign up to get her GED. "Yes, girl, it seems like since I met Rick, my whole life has changed for the better. I met his mom last week. She was so nice and motivating. She told me how she struggled to raise Rick as a single parent. How she had dropped out of school, and once had to sell her body to make sure Rick and her had a place to stay. She offered to help me out with the kids while I go to school. Rick stays with me now, so on the days I have to go to school, he's gonna take the kids with him to his mom's house before he goes to work and go get them and bring them home when he gets off.

"That's great. I knew you were gonna find somebody to treat you and the kids right. What do you want to do once you finish school?" Destiny asks. "My mother-in-law is a manager at Verizon. She says she can get me on at the store she's at." "Yaaahh girl. They pay better than what I make now, and I had to go to college." "No, you didn't," replied Meme. "Yes, I did. This ain't it for me. I told you I want to be a detective. Then, maybe a Prosecutor when I get into my 30's." "Alrighty then!" Yells Meme, laughing. "I know you're going in with me," Meme says, noticing they had pulled up to Gary Adult. "For sure chic. I got you," Destiny says, getting out.

CASH

"Pop, ya'll made it back just in time." Cash says. C-Money and Tonya have been gone 6 weeks. "Yeah barely," C-Money says. "We were supposed to come back 3 weeks ago, but your mom fell in love with California. We ended up hooking up with a realtor, house shopping, and eventually buying a house in the Hamptons. You know how your mom is. So, another week was spent decorating and getting it how she wanted it." "California?" Cash yells. "Ya'll moving?" "We are," C-Money says. "We are gonna keep this house in Lutz. Everything else is gone. You can have the house in Tampa Heights. We are giving the beauty salon to Camille. All our other properties, we are putting on the market. Son, I was in the game for 25 years. I had rivals. I had to bust a few heads. I've been robbed. Even shot at. I have never been scared.

Son, when those guys had your momma, I was scared. That woman has been with me through thick and thin. I fell in love with her the day I laid my eyes on her. If something tragic had happened to her, they might as well as killed me too. Because my soul would have died with her. This new way they play the game, is scary. Ain't no respect anymore. When I had beef with a cat, I played it like Scarface. Man to man. All the things you have told me about your dreams to become a successful legit entrepreneur, you have my full support and blessing. I love you son," C-Money says, hugging his son. "Good, because I need you to go with me to sign up for school." "School?" "Yes, pop. I was so busy running an empire, I never graduated. I want to get my G.E.D. and then my A.A. degree in Business Management.

If I'm gonna go legit and open businesses, I want the skills to be successful." "That's the only way to win, son. What were you doing at our house?" C-Money questions. "I'm selling my house. I need to use ya'lls garage to put my R.R. in."

"You don't want to drive it to enroll in school? You might catch you a good lil chic, or are you still heartbroken about Seleena?" His pop teases. "I ain't lost nothing losing her. I gained. And no, I'm not driving this fancy car to go sign up to get a G.E.D. If I meet a chic, it will be like in the movie Coming to America. I want her to want me for me, not what I have in materialistic possessions."

"True. When I met your mom, I was outside Princess Grocery selling nickel bags of weed. Before we pull off, have you heard anything about who them chumps were who grabbed my Queen?" C-Money asks.

"They would be dead by now, pop. I'm on it though.

I put $100,000 out there for some info that's gonna lead to the guys responsible. Some new crew of robbers have popped up with a lot of work, out of the blue. I've got Fat Dre checking them out now." "Okay. You know it is not about the money we paid to get her back." "I already know, pop." Cash says, cutting him off. "It's the principle." "You better believe it. You're the only other man that has seen my wife in panties, before these creeps violated my Queen." "We'll get them, Pop." Cash says, pulling up to Gary Adult. "Damn," C-Money says, looking at all the cars in front of the school. "The new semester starts today?" "No, Pop. We sign up today. We'll start classes in a couple of days. Come on, old man."

Cash says, getting out of his Dodge Intrepid.

He's fresh in a pair of Roca Wear shorts, with the shirt to match. A pair of all white high-top Air Force One's, with a red G-Shock watch. He has on no other jewelry. His fade is cut to perfection. As they head up the steps to the registration office, Cash sees it's a long line. C-Money says, "I need to call your mom. It looks like we're gonna be here a while. I dropped her off at the salon earlier. She has to tie up a few loose ends." "I'm sending Black Isaac over there to watch her." Cash says, pulling out his phone.

DESTINY

"Yes Ma'am. She will take the class that starts in two days," Destiny says. Her and Meme are inside the office finishing the paperwork and talking to a counselor to get Meme enrolled in adult school to obtain her G.E.D. "I need your signature right here, Jomesha." The counselor says, pointing at a piece of paper. "Okay, you start Thursday. Good luck. The class is 16 weeks." "Thank you." Destiny and Meme say to the counselor as they are exiting the office. "Okay girl let's go see my nephew and niece," Destiny says, walking towards her car. Not looking up, she bumps into Cash, who is also not looking up because he's busy on his phone. "Oops! Excuse me," Destiny says, locking eyes with Cash. For a slight moment she's stuck looking at him.

"No, I'm the one who owes you an apology," Cash says, apologizing. "I was so busy with this phone; I didn't notice you walking by me." "It's no problem. You have a nice day," Destiny says, walking toward her car. Pulling off, Meme says, "damn chic, why was you looking at dude like that? Don't make me tell Tiger," she teases. "Ain't nothing to tell. Dude was cute though." Destiny laughs, pulling off.

CASH

"Damn son close your mouth," C-Money says to Cash. He's stuck looking at Destiny walk off. Destiny is looking to fly in a pair of white skinny jeans. Hugging her sexy slim frame; a white Forever 21 t-shirt with the words PROUD in black letters; a black belt and some laced up black heels. Her hair is on point because Fee just did her a lace front last night; toes and nails were painted with white tips.

"Man, Pop, lil momma there is bad," Cash says. "You talking about Shorty with all that ass?" C-Money replies. He's speaking of Meme. "Naw, Pop. The one I bumped into. When she looked at me, I felt a strange feeling."

"I told you earlier today, when I saw your mother, I knew she was the one." "I don't know what it was Pop, but it was something," Cash says, watching Destiny pull off in her Altima.

COOL AL

"Sup, Cuzzo," Cool Al says. "This is Rolo. What it is?" "Nigga miss me with all that fly shit. What's going on over there in the burg?" "Just doing me. Got a lil young bitch I met in Tampa last week at the new lounge over there, eating me up," laughs Rolo. "The trap is booming. I really appreciate you putting me on, Cuzzo. Me and my nigga Ike was starving. Them $150,000 set a nigga right, and the stash whip you shot me; good looking out." Rolo is Cool Al's cousin on his mom's side of the family. He lives in St. Pete. He's 4 years younger than Cool Al. His BFF Ike is his main man. They were robbing and breaking in houses a couple months ago, before Cool Al gave them life. "I may have a job for ya'll. Be on point next week." "For show Cuzzo," Rolo replies, hanging up.

"You hungry babe?" Seleena asks. She's laying on Cool Al's chest. They are in his king size bed, looking at his favorite movie, New Jack City. "Naw, baby. Not for no food. My hunger is for power and money. These pussy-boys and creep hoes, Dirty Game, think C.M.F. is something to play with. Cash been playing with these pussies. Now they feel like it ain't no repercussion behind playing with our money." "You know we can't have that babe," Seleena says, yeasting him on. "You're the King, daddy. Make your presence felt." "You already know" Cool Al says, guiding her mouth towards his semi-erect dick. "Uuum,"
she says, swallowing a mouthful. "Daamnn baby," moans Cool Al. Seleena sucks the life outta him, then blows bubbles with his cum. "Fuck, I'm a lucky dude," Cool Al says, watching her lil freak show.

Two days later....

CASH

"What? Are you following me?" He says, smiling at Meme. They are headed to the vending machine. They just left their 2nd class, on a break. "I ain't thinking about you boy," Meme says. "It ain't my fault we are in the same classes and happen to be thirsty at the same time. What is your name, anyways?" "Cashmere. And yours?" He says. "Jomesha, but everybody calls me Meme." "How come I ain't never seen you or your home girl around? Where are ya'll from?" "Ooh," Meme says, smiling. "You are feeling my home girl?" "I didn't say that" Cash tries to slyly reply. "You're out of luck," Meme says. "She has a boyfriend." "Who is she?" "Her name is Destiny. She's my best friend. We grew up in College Hill. I'm so proud of her. She graduated from FAMU and is a police officer, waiting to be a detective."

Cash is speechless. "Still kinda ghetto," Meme says. "I'm happy with my dude, so I'm off limits too." "Hold on," Cash smiles. "What type of monster do you think I am? If I can't have your home girl, I'm gonna try you?" He holds his hands up in defense. "I'm not that type of dude. I think that your home girl is cute, and I felt a vibe when we bumped into each other." "Un huh," Meme responds. "Well, you can fall back
because she is definitely not the cheating or creeping type." Good, Cash thinks to himself. "Anyways, if I need some help, I'm gonna cheat off of you," Cash says. "Whatever. I haven't been in school in 10 years. I quit when I had my baby and never came back until now." "That's okay. I guess we will be learning together, because it's been a while for me too. Partners?" Cash says, offering his hand. "Deal me in," Meme says, shaking it.

CHAPTER 18

Never Die Alone

DESTINY

"What's wrong, Auntie? Why are you sitting in this dark room, crying?"

"I'm okay, Destiny," Auntie Donna replies. "No you are not. You are one of the strongest women I've ever met. If you are crying, something is wrong," Destiny says, grabbing her Auntie's hand. "I have cancer, Destiny. I went to the doctor today. They have to run some more tests to see how severe it is. And what will be the treatment process." "Ooh God, Auntie," destiny says, hugging her. She also has begun to cry. "I'm gonna be there every step of the way. Let's say a prayer. God is not gonna let us down."

After saying their prayers, Destiny asks, "are you hungry, Auntie?"

"Yes!" "Come on. Let's go to Red Lobster, Destiny says."

"It's on me. Hearing this terrible news has me feeling like I'm missing something. I mean, I have a good guy that I'm falling in love with. I love my job. It's to the point where we are averaging at least two arrests per day. Tiger says I should get rookie of the year. I just bought my first real car. It's like I have so much to be happy and grateful for, but I'm missing something." "I feel you, Destiny. I've been feeling like that the past 10 years. I've had one decent relationship, and that guy lied to me because he was married the whole time. I have a career I love. A nice house. Good friends.

But, I'm still single and haven't been nowhere." Now you got me, Auntie. I want to travel. I like adventure. I feel like my purpose has only scratched the surface." "Well, please don't let your good years get away like I did. I'm 41 and live like an old lady," Auntie Donna says.

CASH

"Meet me and your mom at Tampa General," C-Money says into the phone. "Okay, Pop. What is going on?" "Your Auntie Roxy just got rushed there. She's been sick the past two days with pneumonia." "I'm on my way," Cash says, disconnecting the phone. "Damn!" He says aloud.

"What's up, main man?" Fat Dre says. Him and Cash are at Baker's Pool Hall on Tampa Street, shooting pool and drinking beers. "I have to go to the hospital. My Auntie Roxy is not feeling well." "That's like my Aunt too...I'm rolling with you bro," Fat Dre replies.

Ten minutes later....

"How is she?" Cash says to his mom, while giving her a hug. "I'm not sure. We're waiting on the doctor now. I just did her hair a couple of days ago.

I was telling her she needs to find another beautician because I was moving to California," Tonya says. We paid off Veronica's condo and was gonna let her hold it down for her. She was all excited, telling me how much she's changed. Saying she's even found a man she likes." Tonya starts to cry.

"Hello. Is this the family for Ms. Williams?" "Yes, I'm her Sister," Ms. Tonya says to the tall, attractive black doctor. "Hello. I'm Doctor Willis. Did you know that Roxy has full-blown AIDS?" C-Money and Tonya were the only ones Roxy trusted with this info. "Yes sir, I did," Tonya replies. "I'm sorry. She's not gonna make it. She has, at the most, 3 days to live." "Ooooh God," Tonya screams, grabbing C-Money. Boohoo crying, Cash is torn. His Auntie Roxy is like a second mother to him.

He never judged her or disrespected her because of her addiction to drugs.

He's upset because somebody should have been put an end to her tricking for drugs. He has no idea that C-Money and Tonya has spent over a $100,000 on drug treatment centers, trying to get her to stop doing drugs. "I'm sorry," Mr. Willis says. "The pneumonia was too strong. Her T-cells can't fight it. It's nothing that can be done. Ya'll can go see her. She's responsive." "Thank you," C-Money says, shaking his hand. "Oh my God," yells Tonya. Roxy is all the family she has left. Her mother and father passed away when she was young. "Come on ma. Let's go see her," Cash says, walking into Roxy's room. "I want to see my baby. Cash, please make it happen.

I already know I'm not gonna make it. I have to talk to her. Please," Roxy says. Tears are running down her face. Cash starts crying and walks out of the room. "Fuuuuck," he yells. He pulls out his cellphone and calls Eric Kuske. "Hello," Kuske says, answering his personal cellphone.

"This is Cashmere. I don't care how much it costs. I need my cousin Veronica Williams here in Tampa in the next 24 hours." "Hold it. What's going on?" Kuske replies. He's a money-hungry lawyer. If it's a will, he will make a way for the right amount of cash. "I'm at Tampa General Hospital. Her mom, Roxy Williams is in hospice. She only has 3 days to live and needs to see her." "I'm on it," Kuske says. "She's at Coleman, right?" Kuske asks. "Yes!" "Okay. You may have to pay for federal escort. Let me make a few phone calls and hit you back." "Ain't no limit," Cash says before disconnecting the call.

DESTINY

"Come here baby," Tiger says, reaching for Destiny. They are in his house watching the movie, Final Destination. Grabbing her in a hug, Tiger says, "you know I love you, right?" "I know," Destiny replies. "Baby, you have not been yourself since your Aunt Donna was diagnosed with cancer, and I don't expect you to. But I do expect you to be strong. Your Aunt is really gonna need you. You here watching a scary movie and you're crying. I'm with you all the way baby. I love your auntie Donna too. I'm sorry baby, Destiny says. It's just my life has been a constant black hole. I lost Ms. Tracy, my uncle Melvin, my auntie Fee goes to prison, my dad almost lost his life. I'm only 23 years old. Is God punishing me? Am I cursed? Looking at her phone ringing, Destiny sees it's Aunt Donna and answers.

"Hello?" "Hey baby," shouts Aunt Donna. "I'm leaving the doctor's office. I have great news. The cancer is right above my left breast. He said, with immediate surgery, he should be able to cut it out and I should be good. I won't have to do chemo or nothing." "Ooh God, Auntie," Destiny shouts. "God is so good, baby." Aunt Donna says. "We have to stay in prayer. It's not over, but it's a sign that he heard our prayers. Come and get me. I'm at Tiger's house. Let's go to Dairy Queen and eat some Banana Splits." "I'm on my way," Aunt Donna says, disconnecting the call. "I'm so excited," Destiny yells. She tells Tiger the good news. "Thank God," he replies. Getting down on one knee, Tiger pulls out a 2-karat white-gold diamond ring and says, "Destiny, will you marry me?" Destiny is stunned.

"Yes! Tiger, I'll be your wife," she happily says, hugging him.

"So tomorrow, I'll be helping you pack your things, so you can live with your fiance?" "Yesss. I'll be back. I'm going with Auntie for a minute," Destiny says, walking outside to get with Auntie. She calls Meme and tells her and then tries to call Chrishonna. She doesn't answer, so she leaves her a text to hit her back when she's not busy. Destiny is so happy.

CASH

"Thank you for working your magic," Cash says, handing $12,000 to Kuske. They are standing outside Tampa General waiting for Baby Doll to be brought to the hospital by two federal marshals. "22 hours," Kuske says, looking at his Rolex watch. "You're the man," Cash says, stroking his ego while shaking his hand. "I have to go as soon as they get here. I have a client I have to meet at my office. Here they go now," Kuske says, seeing a black federal escort van pull up. Baby Doll is escorted out of the van. She has on street clothes Kuske dropped off for her. "We're gonna take the cuffs off, please don't make us regret it," one of the agents say. "I have 2 years before I go to the halfway house. I just want to see my mom," Baby Doll says.

"Sup, Cuzzo?" Baby Doll says, giving Cash a hug. "I ain't slept since yesterday, but I'm good," Cash replies. "Gone on up to see Auntie. She's on the 3rd floor, room 317. I'm gone step inside this McDonald's and grab me a bite to eat."

BABY DOLL

"Hello momma," she says, kissing Roxy on her cheek. "Hey Baby," Roxy says excited, he did it, she says. Oh, God. He got my baby here. Hey Auntie. Tonya! Baby Doll says to her Auntie. Tonya hasn't left the hospital. Hey Baby, Tonya says, giving Baby Doll a hug. Where is Cash? He went to McDonald's downstairs, to get something to eat. Looking at the two marshals, Tonya says, let me go. Get me something to eat, so ya'll can have a lil privacy. I'll be back, Roxy, she yells, walking outta the door. The agents say, we will be outside. You have 4 more hours before we have to head back. Thank you, Baby Doll says. I'm so sorry, Roxy says, tears rolling down her face. You're my only child, and because of my addiction, I deprived you of so much. Momma, I..... Hold on, let me finish, Roxy says, cutting her off. Veronica, no matter how bad this drug had me, there is nothing in this world I love more than you. I wouldn't trade you for no other mother in this world. Crying, Baby Doll holds her mom's hand and says, momma, I'm gonna make you proud. I'm taking a business management course at my camp, and when I get out, I'm gonna invest my money with Cash, and open some legit businesses. I'm even gonna settle down and have you some grandchildren. My daughter, God's will I have one, I'm gonna name after you. Thank you, baby. Baby Doll, please cremate me and keep me in an urn. I want to see you be successful and watch over you and my grandkids. Let's stop all this crying. We are boss bitches till the end, Roxy says.

I love you, baby girl. I love you too momma. Cash, Ms. Tonya, and Roxy reminisce a couple of hours telling old stories, until the marshal peeps inside and tells Baby Doll she has 15 minutes before they have to leave. Roxy grabs her hand and squeezes it with all her might. Baby Doll can't help it, she starts crying again. I'll always love you momma, she says, giving her *--*- mother one last hug. The pain is tremendous, knowing this will be the last time she will ever see her mom alive. Baby Doll breaks · the embrace and says, Cash, let me have a word with you. Sup, Cuzzo? He says, going into the rest room.

Inside the room with Baby Doll...

I want this fuck nigga Pancho dead before the funeral, Baby Doll whispers. Say no more, Cuzzo. I'll put Fat Dre on it ASAP.

DESTINY

Don't be so tuff. It's okay to cry sometimes, Destiny says to her aunt Donna. They are in Destiny's car on the way to St. Joseph's Hospital. Aunt Donna's surgery is today. I have prayed about it and I have faith in the Lord. Crying would only mean I don't trust my God, which I do. Am I scared? Yes. Am I worried? No. I am one of his children, aunt Donna says. I'm still a work in progress. Destiny responds. Because I am gonna be crying and praying until the doctor comes out and tells me that your operation was a success. Laughing, Aunt Donna says if the shoe was on the other foot, I would be doing the same thing.

FAT DRE

"Here you go, main man." Fat Dre says, handing a petty hustler by the name of Tone 10 grand. Tone cops dope from police-ass Pancho, when he heard through the hood gossip vine, money was on Pancho's head. He got in touch with Fat Dre ASAP. For the past 5 months Tone has been copping packs from Pancho. Pancho has a spot in Port Tampa, where he's been hiding out and making money like nothing ever happened. Tonight, Tone talked him into going to a strip club on Dale Mabry across from Raymond James football stadium with him. Its called The Pink Pussy. Taking the 10 stacks, Tone says, "his bitch ass is in there tricking off with some strippers. You need me to lure him outside?" "Naw, just tell the nigga you had to go make a sale, one of your crackers is coming to get you."

"Okay, I got it."

"Thanks, main man." Fat Dre says. 30 minutes later Pancho stumbles out the front door of the club, he's drUnc and high as hell. As he approaches his Chrysler 300, Fat Dre hits him on the top of his head with his .45 caliber, knocking him out instantly. Fat Dre puts him inside the trUnc of the Chrysler 300 and gets inside and motions for Black Isaac to follow him. Fat Dre drives to the graveyard out on 43rd and Hanna. He gets out and pours gasoline all inside the car and around it. He opens the trUnc, shoots Pancho 6 times… boom, boom, boom, boom, boom, boom. He lights a match, throws it at the car, and walks off. Black Isaac picks him up along 46th and Hillsborough by the Jet gas station. "Snitches get more than stitches."

DESTINY

"You can go inside the room. She's up," says Doctor Chinson. "I'll be back in a minute. I have to go review the x-rays and check on a few things." "Hey, lady!" Destiny says, walking into the post-op room. "Drowsy," is all Donna responds. "I still think you should have allowed the whole family to be here to support you," Destiny says. Donna made her promise she wouldn't tell nobody her surgery date. She only wanted her there. Her reason was, she didn't want nobody stressing her or the doctor before the surgery. "How do you feel?" Ask Destiny. "I feel like we're about to hear a blessing." "Me too,' Destiny says, holding her hand. 5 minutes later Doctor Chinson comes in the room with a big smile on his face.

"I got 99.7 percent of it out. The surgery was a success. You are gonna have to come in every 6 months to do an x-ray to stay safe. As of today, you are cancer-free." "Thank you so much," Donna screams. "God is so good!" "Ya'll ladies have a great day," Dr. Chinson says walking out of the room. "Thank you, Lord," Destiny screams. "You know I need my favorite Auntie," she laughs. "I have to plan this wedding," Aunt Donna says, smiling.

CASH

3 days later....

"She's gone!" Tonya screams into the phone. "Oh God she's gone, Cash!" "I'm sorry momma," Cash says into the phone. It's killing him to hear his mother in so much pain. "Ma, I love you. I'll see you soon." "Bye baby," Tonya says, disconnecting the call. Calling Kuske a few minutes later, he says call the prison and have them have Veronica call me. "Her mother just passed away." "Damn," Kuske says. "I'll handle that right away."

30 minutes later...

"Sup Cuzzo." Baby Doll says, as Cash answers the phone. She's calling from the Chaplain's office at Coleman Federal Institution. "She's gone Cuzzo." Cash says. "Fuuuck," screams Baby Doll.

"It's weird, this guy Pancho was found in a burning car, shot 6 times in a graveyard, the other day. Life is short," Cash says. Telling Baby Doll in code that Pancho was handled. "All day," Baby Doll responds. "I'm not trying to see my mother in no casket," Cuzzo. "Please send her out in the best and put up her ashes for me. I'll call you back in a couple days. Be strong for Auntie Tonya. I love you, cuzzo."   "I love you more," Cash replies.

CHAPTER 19

Gangsta Lean

DESTINY

"What time are you heading home?" Tiger says. He is talking to Destiny on the cellphone. "I'm leaving Auntie's house now. I should be there in 20 minutes." "There? This is home," he shouts, hanging up the phone.

30 minutes later....

"You finally made it?" Tiger snaps. He is sitting on the couch watching Monday Night Football. "Well, I figured since you watch Monday Night Football, I would hang out with my Aunts and get a few laughs in," Destiny says.

"I feel you, baby. I just wanted a lil QT with my fiance," Tiger coos. "Oh, baby I'm sorry. Let me give you a back massage and make you feel a little better." "You thought about what I asked you the other day?" Tiger says.

A couple of days ago Tiger asked her for some head. He told her that he was really turned on by giving and receiving oral sex. "Yes! And when I feel comfortable, I will do it," Destiny replies. "What happened to hello baby, how was your day?" The past two weeks, Destiny has been training with the Vice Squad. She's having fun being a cop, but she's fully committed to being a narcotics detective. She believes drugs are the centerpiece to criminal activity. "Why didn't you ask me how my day was?" Tiger says. "Every day I ask you how your day was."

"I'm not trying to argue. Have you eaten yet?" "Well, yeah. It's 9:30 p.m. Normal people eat dinner around 7:30 or 8:00 p.m." Destiny is getting frustrated. Ever since she moved into Tiger's home, he's been a different man.

CASH

"That was a helluva test, Shorty," Cash says to Meme. They are walking out of their math class. They took the Pre-GED test today. "I know right." Meme responds. "How is your homegirl doing?" Cash asks. "She's doing great. She's started detective training and got engaged a couple of months ago." "That's a lucky dude," Cash replies. "Yeah, he's a cop. I like him. I think he's nice. You still thinking about my homegirl huh?" Meme asks. "I have not had a feeling like I felt when I saw her, so yes, I am," cash admits. "You don't have a girlfriend?" "No. The past two were not on the same page as me." Who are you, anyways?" Meme asks. "I grew up in Tampa Heights, my dad is a contractor, and my mom owns Super T's. beauty salon." "What? Mrs. Tonya is your mom?

I've seen her work. I just never had the money to afford to go to her," Meme laughs.

"I work part time at my uncle's car lot on 40th off of Hillsborough Avenue. I'm getting my A.A. in business management once we graduate from here," Cash says. Then I'm going to open business as business. Restaurants, real estate, promoting. I'm going to open a lot of doors for people of color." "That's what's up," says Meme. "Come on, lunch is on me," Cash says. "Let's walk to Abellas." "Now you're talking," Meme says, smiling.

5 days later....

DESTINY

"Bae are you going with me to take my nieces and nephews to Lowry Park or do you want me to call you after we leave?" "I need to cut this yard and wash my car. You go ahead. We'll go out to eat later on tonight." "Okay. I love you," Destiny shouts, pulling off. "Yaaaah, Auntie Destiny is taking us to Lowry Park," yells Deshean III, her oldest nephew. She has him and 3 of Cherell's kids. 1 nephew, Donte and 2 nieces, Jayla and Janine. She promised them 2 weeks ago she was gonna take them to see the animals and ride the rides. "Alright, Yall buckle up. We are headed to have some fun!" Destiny shouts. "You're going by yourself?" Cherell asks. "You want me to go with you?" "No. I'm good. Tiger had some things to do.

I'll be alright. I like being auntie. You know, we never got to get much of this, outside of Auntie Donna and Uncle Melvin, we had no family trips." "Yeah Sis. I feel you. That's why I'm working now. So, me and Coop have more income coming into our house. We are supposed to take the kids to Disney World in Orlando next month." "That's good." "It's sad, I'm 24, and have never been there," Destiny says. "Me either," Cherell says. "Alright. I'll call you to get them as soon as I'm pulling out of Lowry Park". Laughing, Cherell says, "okay. I love y'all she shouts."

CASH

"Sup, big sis?" Cash answers his phone. "I need a big favor lil bruh! I need you to watch your nephew and niece for a couple of hours. Me and Pale need to take his parents to the airport. They are..." "Hold up," Cash says. "I'll be at the salon in 15 minutes. Are you close by?" "I'll be there in 20," Cash says, disconnecting the call.

20 minutes later...

"Hey Uncle Cash!" Supreme yells, running up to his car. "Sup, nephew," Cash says, hugging him. Brooklyn says, "hug me too, Uncle Cash." Looking super-cute in a pink Baby Fat kid's short set. "Where do ya'll want to go? Chuck E Cheese? Or to see the animals at Lowry Park?" "We want to see the animals," they shout in unison.

"Can I ride the horses?" Brooklyn asks. "I got ya'll. You can ride all the rides and the horses, baby girl." "Thank you, bro., I'll call you when we get done." "Fa sho." Cash says, putting the kids in their seat belts. "Ya'll be good. I love ya'll." Camille says. "We love you too."

20 minutes later....

"What do ya'll want to do first? Play the games? See the animals? Or ride the rides?" "Let's see the animals first," they yell. "Oooh, look at that big Elephant," Brooklyn shouts. "Can we feed him, Uncle Cash?" "Come on, let's go get some peanuts and come right back.' Standing in line to buy the peanuts, Cash thinks he's seeing things. He sees Destiny at the front of the line waiting to buy peanuts. She has 4 kids with her. His heart is racing.

For some reason, he gets excited, and butterflies in his stomach, almost to the point he wants to hide or run. Turning around after making her purchase, she sees him.

DESTINY

"Thank you, maam." Destiny says, getting her change from the girl selling her the peanuts. As she turns around to hand the kids the peanuts, she gets stuck, she sees Cash looking directly at her. She feels like a deer caught in the headlights. "Oh God, how do I look?" She thinks to herself. Destiny is looking good in a pair of all white Nike Air shocks, some white and green Nike shorts, and a white Nike tank top. Her hair is done in a bob. "Why am I feeling like this, with this guy? And I'm engaged?" She thinks, feeling nervous. "Damn, he looking good," she observes. Cash has on a navy blue and white Polo shirt, navy blue baggy cargo Polo shorts, and some all-white Air Force one's and a white G-Shock watch, with a Polo visor on his head. Heading his way, she says, "so we meet again?' Putting her hand out to shake his, she feels the current again.

CASH

"Damn. This woman is beautiful," Cash says to himself, watching Destiny walk towards him; her walk is so sexy. "It's a small world," Cash replying to Destiny, saying, "so we meet again."

"I was getting in some quality time with my niece and nephew. This is Brooklyn and my main man, Supreme." "Hello," they yell. "I'm on the same mission," Destiny says, introducing her nephews and nieces. They are both secretly happy that neither had kids of their own. Cash knows Destiny doesn't have any, but Destiny was not sure. "Are ya'll just getting here?" Cash asks. "Yes, I was buying some peanuts so they can feed the animals." "That's where I'm headed. Maybe we can all have a lil fun together," Cash says. He wants to get some time in with Destiny and

he could use a woman's help with the kids. "Sounds like a plan. I'll wait here with the kids while you go get more peanuts." "Thank you," Cash says, walking off.

They had a great day, the kids rode, ate good, and they all played games. Destiny and Cash are both very competitive, so they had a great time and a lot of laughs. Cash didn't want the day to end. Truth be told, Destiny neither. Leaving the park, Cash says, "thank you. You and the kids really made my day." "The feeling is mutual," Destiny says. "Bye ya'll," Destiny says to Supreme and Brooklyn. "And by to you," Destiny says, shaking his hand. Cash wanted to grab her and give her a hug.

DESTINY

"Meme, guess what?" Destiny says. "I'm getting my hair done by Tracy in the projects. What do you want?" Meme replies. "I just left Lowry Park taking my nephew's and niece's there. I ran into the dude Cashmere. That guy I bumped into when we were signing you up for school." "And?" Meme says. "He had his nephew and niece with him. We all hung out and had a good time." "Let me finish with my hair. I will call you back soon as I'm done. Better yet, where are you dropping the kids off to?" "My mom's house." "Okay. Tracy is almost done. I'll be over there in less than an hour." "Okay, chic." Destiny says, hanging up.

TIGER

"Oooh shit, eat that dick, ma!" Tiger eyes are closed. He's getting a massive blowjob.

Trina has the best head in College Hill, maybe the world. She also steals clothes, tricks, and snorts powder. "Slurp, slurp, slurp." Trina takes Tiger's whole dick in her throat and holds it. "Ooh shit," Tiger moans, seeing his dick disappear down Trina's throat, Trina squeezes his balls. "Uuum, let me taste these," she says, sucking each ball. "Oooh shit ma, ooh shit," Tiger moans. Trina puts his dick back in her mouth and begins to suck with all her might. "Damn, I'm cumin!" shouts Tiger, as his knees buckle. Reaching for his pants while panting, he says, "here," handing her a $100.

"I can't do this anymore," he says. Trina replies, "that's what you say every time we get finished. Gimme my clothes back before you leave Mr. Officer." Tiger had caught her two days ago with a couple grams of powder and two big bags of stolen clothes. He let her keep the powder but took the clothes. When he called her and told her he was on his way, he promised her he was gonna bring them and give them back. Tiger has about 5 girls in the projects he gets head from, but Trina is the best. Since he got engaged to Destiny, he had cut them all off. His freak light came on today and it's about to cost him dearly. It's a small world.

Especially in the hood.

MEME

"Thank you, Tracey. Bitch, once again you did your thang," Meme says, admiring her lace front Tracey just put on for her. She's standing in Tracey's living room, looking at a big wall mirror. Tracey has one of the nicest apartments in College Hill. "Just pay me hoe," Tracey replies, smiling. She loves doing hair, fucking, thug niggas and clubbing. "Who is it?" Tracey says, hearing somebody knocking at her door. "Bitch, it's me!" Trina says, walking in without acceptance. "I have some clothes. BeBe, Kate Spade, and a few Baby Phat body suits." "Ooh let me see," Tracey says opening the bag. Meme comes over and goes to puling stuff out too. "When did you get this, bitch?" Tracey says. She likes to be the first one Trina sells clothing to, because if not, everybody will have on the same shit, and Tracy doesn't like to be dressed like the other girls in the hood. "Bitch, how about I hit Macy's last week and soon as I was getting out of the rental car with Starla, Tiger sees me, and grabs me. He took my shit because I didn't have a receipt for them, but 30 minutes ago, he calls me with his freak light on." Tracey is trying to stop Trina from running her mouth - saying "ummm." She knows everything by being the hood stylist. She's even tricked with Tiger in the past. But the hood has a code – don't ask, don't tell, so she wasn't trying to get involved in what was about to go down. She grew up with Destiny and Meme. She knew Destiny and Tiger were engaged. Trina continued, saying he needed some of her pressure head. He said he was going to give me a $100 and my clothes back; "so bitch, you already know I knocked his ass down. That nigga is crazy.

Every time I get off his dick, he says this is the last time he's doing this! Bitch, I'm the real super head. Nigga's can't stay away, police officers and all," she brags. Meme can't believe her ears. She is so upset. She knows Destiny is gonna be hurt, but she has to tell her because that's her best friend and she deserves better than a nigga cheating and lying to her.

20 minutes later....

DESTINY

"Damn, chic," says Destiny as Meme comes into her mom's apartment. "Beauty takes time," Meme replies. She's so nervous. She doesn't know how to tell Destiny what she just heard. "Have you ate yet chic?" Meme says. No. I'm going out to eat with my fiance in a little while. I had a li1 kiddie plate at Lowry Park." "Take me to Burger King right quick," Meme says. "Come on chic. What's on your mind? I'm a cop. I can tell when somebody has something to say." Turning off the music, Meme says, "this is what just happened at Tracey's house." She tells Destiny in detail the story. "Wow," Destiny says. I leave my part time love because he was a hustler and I fall for a cop that's a lying, cheating scumbag. I'm beyond hurt. This is so reckless.

I guess it's my fault because I wouldn't suck his dick." "Naw girl. He's a dirty disrespectful dog. He knows you grew up around here. Hell, ya'll patrol this area. He showed no respect for you." Meme says. They both start to cry. "I'm done with him. I'm gonna need you to do me a big favor," Destiny says, taking Tiger's house keys off of her key ring. "Whatever chic. You know I'm down for whatever bout my homegirl." "Listen, I want you to take my keys. As a matter of fact, here, take all of them." Destiny says, handing her keys to Meme. "I'm gonna go with Tiger to the restaurant. You are gonna leave after he picks me up; and go to his house. Pack up all of my things and put them in my backseat and in the trUnc if you need more room. When you are done, text me and I'll tell you where we are going to eat. I want you to come and get me from there."

"Ain't that's a burglary?" Meme says. "No. I'm a resident. I'm giving you the keys and permission, Duh. Let's get him, girl." They dap up.

2 hours later...

"How did the yard fixing go?" Destiny asks. Her and Tiger are at the Olive Garden on 30th and Bush. "I would have had a better time with you and the kids. Next weekend let's get Meme's kids too and take them all to Chuck E Cheese," Tiger says. Destiny grabs Tiger's hands inside hers and says, "are you in love with me?" "Of course, baby. I've never felt the way I feel about you with any other woman in my life, and I want to prove it by making you a very happy wife." A tear falls down Destiny's cheek. "What's wrong, baby?" Tiger asks, seeing Destiny's tear escape her eyes.

I don't know if it's me, or is it you, or men in general. Hold on," Destiny says, picking up her phone. It's the okay from Meme. She responds with the location she's at and says, I'm ready. "Who was that?" Tiger says. "Meme." Destiny replies. "Tiger, why did you break my heart?" "What?" Tiger says, getting nervous. "Why have you hurt me?" I asked, "you couldn't wait until I felt comfortable giving you oral sex? You had to go get it from somewhere else?" Stuck, blowed and tongue-tied, Tiger says, "baby, I baby." "I what?" Destiny stops him. "You're sorry? Or I won't do it again? Or I wasn't thinking? Ain't no excuse you can give me. You don't love me. You only love yourself. You were that impatient, you had to have some sexual satisfaction that bad? You totally disregarded all your loyalty and respect for me too?"

"I'm sorry," Tiger says. "Yes, you are," Destiny says, getting up. "You're very sorry and you need help. I'll always be your friend, but there is no way I can accept a man that has no respect for me or himself." "Where are you going?" Tiger says, getting up. "I'm going home." "We'll go home together and talk about this." "Why bother? What's understood doesn't need to be explained." Destiny says, walking out of the door. As her car pulls up, she gets inside and says goodbye.

CHAPTER 20

Teflon Don

FAT DRE

"I'm on 50th and Sligh by King High School. What's the bizz-ness?" Fat Dre says into his cellphone. "I need to get at you fat boy," Cool Al says. "Where you want me to come to?" "I'll come to you," Cool Al replies. "Just gone on to your spot. I'll be there in 20 minutes." "One," Fat Dre says, disconnecting the call. Fat Dre has a nice condo across from Long John Silver's on 50th Street.

He has plenty of hoes, but he lives solo in his laid-out spot. He turns into his carport and says to himself, "damn a nigga is actually living." Fat Dre has $400,000 put up, he's got 3 nice whips; an all-black Denali truck, a black GS300 Lexus, and his baby, a Dodge Viper which is also all black. He's $18,000 from owning his $93,000 condo; he could easily have bought it cash, but

Cash taught him how to build his credit; slowly paying things off. That' how you show a pattern being responsible. His wardrobe is exclusive, he has over $80,000 in jewelry, even though he rarely wears it. At 25, he can actually say he's successful. I wonder what Cool Al wants; Fat Dre says to himself while entering his condo. He turns off his alarm, goes into his kitchen, and grabs a pink grapefruit juice.

Ten minutes later …

Cool Al is knocking at his door. "What's good pretty boy?" Fat Dre says giving him some dap while entering the condo. "I'm not gonna be long, because I got this lil freak that says she wants me to

Make her holler for a couple dollars. She even said she was gonna suck my dick from the back.

I ain't never had that there," Cool Al laughs, mimicking Day Day off of the Last Friday. "She ain't got no partner?" Fat Dre yells. "Naw, fat boy. You're dead. Listen, Cash is on some get out of the game shit, what direction are you going in?" Cool Al says seriously. "I've got me a lil paper put up. The idea of going legit sounds good to me. I love this life, but I know ain't but two outcomes: jail or death. I'm ready either way, but if I have the opportunity to stay free and alive, and come up even more, then I'm rolling with Cash." "My dude. Fat Dre says, "if you ever need me to put in some work, I'm all in. I love you my nigga." "I feel you and I respect your mind.

I ain't giving up the throne like that. I'm married to the game. I'm about to tum up the heat. I'll call you later, main man. I do have another lil freak I met out of St. Pete last week that had a lil cutie with her." "All day," Fat Dre says, walking him to the door.

DESTINY

"Hey baby. How about we meet up this Friday. I have to pick my brother up from the airport. He goes to school in Atlanta, which is really a front. He's eating good down there in the A. They are taxing him so hard for the work down there. I told him that I could maybe get him a better price here in Tampa," Destiny says, "what is he pushing?" Ask Ant Ant. "Weed and crack." "Yeah, see what's good and holler back at me. You see I keep that good." Ant Ant just sold Destiny an ounce of crack cocaine. She is working undercover. He thinks she's a female hustler trying to get her weight up. He met her through a C.I. a week ago, trying to work his own case off. Destiny being so sexy Ant Ant is trying to fuck and get some money.

COOL AL

"Sup Cuzzo?" Cool Al says, giving Rolo and Ike some dap. "Getting pussy and money," Rolo replies. He just copped a Dodge Magnum and put it on 24's. Ike grabbed a Chrysler 300 and put 24's on it too. They are fucking mad hoes and having the time of their lives. "Is this all you want?" Cool Al says, pointing to their whips. "Hell naw," Rolo says. "This is just a lil toy to get the lil hood hoes pussies wet. Nigga, we are trying to eat, what's up? You ready to take us outta this trap?" "I'm giving out positions by performance. Ya'll wanna make 50 g's a piece?" "You damn right," they scream in union. "Okay, check this out. This is what I want ya'll to do....

CASH

"I am so glad we are finished with all these tests. I never thought going back to school would be this aggravating. I mean, the work is easy, it's just the constant testing." "I'm with you, big bro," Meme responds. Her and Cash just took the last part of the GED. If they pass, they graduate next week and get their diploma's. "It is worth it though. I know my momma is looking down from heaven with a smile on her face." "I'm sorry to hear that," Cash replies. "It's okay. I lost my momma when I was 17. She had a drug overdose." "Damn!" Wanting to change the subject, Cash says, "if you walk to Abella's with me, the food is on me." "By now, you already know I am not turning down no free food." "Got her," Cash says to himself. He wants to talk about Destiny.

He has not been able to stop thinking about her since they left Lowery Park a couple weeks ago.

"How is your bestie?" Cash says while they are walking down 8th Avenue. "Better now. That prick of a fiancé she had was caught cheating on her and Cashmere, he did it with a dirty cokehead girl that steals clothes and sucks all the dicks she can get down her throat." "What?" Cash says, getting excited. "Dude played like that?" "My Chic didn't play. She left him the same day and has been going hard, focusing on her career ever since. I bet she's made 100 arrests in the past 3 weeks." "I have to head to work," Cash says giving her a $20 bill. "Thanks for the walk." He heads back towards school to get his truck.

30 minutes later...

"I need a job," Cash says. "What?" "I need a job." "I'm not hiring," his uncle Jahiem says smiling. "Unc I'm for real. I need the job training and I need a good front." "For what?" "I've met this woman that I'm head over heels about. Well, I sorta met her." "Boy tell your uncle the lick."

Cash tells his Uncle Jahiem about both encounters with Destiny and how she makes him feel. Then he says, "she's a cop with the Tampa Police Department." Uncle Jahiem bust out laughing, "my nephew the kingpin is crazy about a cop." "Former kingpin, and yes. I think it's something special between us." "Former?" Uncle Jahiem says. "I still grab the work from Mr. Carlos, but since I started school 4 months ago, I've been playing the backseat." "Your hands are still dirty, and the feds or state will give you just as much time as anybody else in the organization."

"I know Unc. I can't just give up on my team like that. Not just yet. I gave them until I graduate from community college to get right because after I get my degree, I'm done. I'm going all the way legit." "Why wait, Cash? Tomorrow is not guaranteed to us. In a split second, things can go from O to 60. I'm not going to badger you because I am proud of you for seeing the big picture; at least part of it. You say Chic is a cop? I don't think being with a kingpin or even a supplier will pique her interest." "Duh! That's why I work with my favorite uncle selling cars and inherited some money when I turned 18 from my wealthy business owner parents." "If you start out lying, you will have to live out the lies, and your relationship will be based on lies. Do you want her to lie to you?

Do you want a real woman? You're gonna have to do real things."

"I feel you Unc. That's why I'm really gonna take this job and all the life skills you give me, dead serious. I will have a talk with Cool Al about the supply situation. When do I start work?" Cash says, laughing.

MAD MAX

"Baby, I'm tired of hiding. I'm your queen and I barely get to stunt with my king," Lizanne whines.

Her and Mad Max are laying in their king-size bed overlooking the beach. They are in a suite at Ballast Point. They just got finished having a powerful round of wild sex. "Baby girl, you ain't got to hide from no one. Them pussies don't want none of Dirty Game. Next month when I bring our new toy out, you are gonna step out with me straight stuntin'. I'm about to make a power move to show these chumps who's boss. Hand me my phone…. Tear, check this out."

DESTINY

"Girl, I'm so sorry I've been so busy," Chrishonna says. "I feel you. I've been doing a lot of running too," Destiny replies. "So what's on your mind Chic?" "You first." Destiny says. "How is Cali??" "It's great. I love the weather. It's a lot of hunks, and I'm having fun. I did a lot of production for The Color Purple play. I've been busy trying to finish my own, get financing for it, people to play in it; it's a lot of work that people don't see behind the scenes. I got me a lil piece last night." "Please tell," Destiny laughs. "Well, he's a NBA player, who plays for the Lakers. He has taken me on two dates and last night I rocked his world. I'm not playing myself, it was fun, and I may even get seconds," she laughs, "but a relationship? Neither of us are on that level.

Anyways, what's up with you? And when do I need to come try on my bridal dress?" Destiny busts out crying. "Chrishonna, he cheated on me." "What?" "Yes, he asked me to give him some head. I told him to give me some time, and low and behold, he went and got him some, somewhere else." "Wow!" Chrishonna shouts. "He was also starting to get argumentative, possessive and abusive." "He hit you, Chic?" "No, not physically, but mentally and emotionally. His behavior wouldn't surprise me if in the future he would have put his hands on me." "I know you're hurt, but I'm glad that is over, because I would have had to come down and get him." "I did have a weird experience though." Destiny went on telling her about her two meetings with Cashmere. "Do you like him? What does he do?" Chrishonna asks.

"I don't know. I told you what happened. But yes he's nice and definitely something good to look at." "Chic, get off my phone," Chrishonna says, laughing. "Later," Destiny says, hanging up.

FAT DRE

"Let me get two pair of the low top all white Air Force Ones, a pair of the new Jordan's and a pair of Kobe Bryant's new shoes," Fat Dre says to the sexy, slim assistant manager, Tisa, who works at Finish Line in University Mall. Fat Dre buys all his tennis shoes from her because he wants to fuck her, and because she's a single mom of two young boys. He likes helping her out by giving her big tips and letting her get a nice commission off of him. "Will that be all?" Tisa sexily says. "Besides if I could get you, Yes, I'm good. I'm going next door to Lids to get some hats and jerseys to match." "Size 12, right?" "You already know my shoe size," he smiles. "That's probably why you're so scared to give me a shot," he says, winking at her while pulling out a fat wad of money. "Whatever.

You keep on playing. I'm gone see what you're always talking slick about," Tisa challenges. Put my number in your phone and let me change you and your boy's lives." "Give it here," she say's pulling out her phone. "Your bill comes to $622." Peeling 7 $100 dollar bills off of his knot, he says his phone number while handing her the money. "You already know better than to insult me." Talking about the change se tried t give him back. "I'm gone call you soon," she says, handing him his bags. "For sure," Fat Dre says, walking out of the store. A bad bitch bump into him. "Excuse me, big man," she sexily says. Fat Dre looks her up and down. She's a full all-out dime piece. 5'9, maybe 125 lbs., light skin complexion, hazel eyes, nice hips, and the Prada pantsuit she has on is hugging her body.

Her pussy print looking like she has elephant teeth in her panties. "Assault!" Fat Dre says, laughing.

"I'm gonna call mall security if you don't let me get your number and take you somewhere nice tonight."

"I don't have anything to wear." Playing her game, Fat Dre says, "lets head to your favorite store to fix that problem. What's your name, pretty?" "Kadija, and you are?" "Fat Dre but you can call me Big Daddy," he teases her. "I like Big Daddy better," Kadija coos, licking her sexy lips. Wait until Cash and Cool Al see's this bitch, Fat Dre thinks to himself. He's had his share of bad hoes, but this Kadija is straight model material.

After they hit a few high-end stores, Fat Dre spends about $1,600 on her. He says, "so what time are we hooking up?" "How about 9:00 p.m?

That will give me time to get me a hot bath in, lotion my body down, and play in my pussy.

I haven't had a man enter me in 7 months. I don't want it too tight when I do finally get me some dick." "Stop playing," Fat Dre says, grabbing his rock-hard dick through his Roca Wear shorts. "Really, I'm Bi-Sexual, but I do love a big man inside me every 6 months or so." "Dammit man," Fat Dre says to himself, imagining how good Kadija's pussy must be. "Should I bring my overnight bag? Or is this just gonna be a movie and a walk down the beach?" Kadija asks. "I ain't planning on never letting you go back to your spot. Hell, I'll send some movers around there now," Fat Dre says, smiling. "We'll see. I'm bringing over my overnight bag." "Call me when you get ready. My number is 813-691-4773. I have one rule though.

I drive on all first dates, so I'm coming to get you. Don't go to looking crazy, I can drive," she laughs, walking off.

Later that night......

"Hello," Kadija sexily answers her phone. "Sup, sexy. This is Big Daddy; what's the deal?" "I've been sitting here in my t-back and bra, waiting on your call. I wasn't putting on my clothes until I was sure you weren't going to air me." "Imagine that," Fat Dre says, getting an erection thinking of her in a t-back. "What color t-backs do you have on?" "Light pink. I feel real girly tonight." Going against the rule of the game; never allow a stranger to know where you rest your head. Fat Dre says, "I live on 50th in the condo's across from Long John Silver. You know how to get here?" "Yes, I am from Tampa," she lies. "I'll be there in 30 minutes, Big Daddy. I'll call you when I'm pulling in." "All day." Fat Dre says, disconnecting the call.

30 minutes later....

"I live in the back." Showing out, he says, you will see my black Dodge Viper parked down there. I'm walking out the door." Looking in the mirror, Fat Dre says to himself, "yeah, I see what Cool Al says about being king. It does have its advantages." He's so fresh in an all-black Havana Joe boots, black Aqua Master diamond watch, a big Cuban link chain and bracelet with diamonds all through them, smelling like 360°. "I'll be back," he says, grabbing his .40 cal. Off the couch. "Damn, you looking good," Kadija says, getting out of her silver Audi A4 to give him a hug. She's absolutely stunning in a white Azzedine Alaia tight fitting short dress. A pair of pink Christian Louboutin heels, Jennifer Meyer jewelry. She smells of Rose Rush by Paris Hilton. Hugging her, Fat Dre says, "damn, you smell good." "Wait until you get a taste, Big Daddy," she smiles. "I'm ready," Fat Dre says. "Let's go to the sponge docks in Tarpon Springs.

It's a 5-star restaurant called Pappas. I've been begging to try," Fat Dre says. He heard Cash talking about him and

Seleena went their once, and the food was all that. Kadija put it in her Google Map and takes off. After dinner they walked down the dock holding hands and talking. Kadija made up a story that she was a 5th year senior at USF in the medical program. Fat Dre told her he was an entrepreneur and did a lot of real estate; house flipping, he called it. "Well, it's 1:15 a.m. What do you want to do?" "Get a suite and put my tongue all over your body," Fat Dre replies. "No offense, but I don't do hotels on the first night. I'm horny and I want to get my freak on, but I do have morals. If you can't take me back to your place, we'll try out a few more dates and see where we go from there." Thinking with his dick, Fat Dre says, "I feel you, and I apologize for acting like you're some trick. Let's go back to my place." "Thank you. Let me see what you're working with. I might change my mind," Kadija says, rubbing Fat Dre's semi-erect dick through his pants. "Oooooo, nice and fat she moans."

One hour later....

"Oohh, fuck Big Daddy beat this pussy," yells Kadija. "You like that ma?" Fat Dre says smacking her hard on the ass. "Ooh yes, ooh fuck this dick feels sooo good. Let me taste it baby," Kadija yells. She pulls Fat Dre's dick out of her wet pussy and goes to licking all of her pussy juice off of it. "Uuuum, slurp, slurp, slurp, oooh," she moans. "Damn, it's so fat, and tastes so good. Lay back," she says, pushing him flat on his back, she climbs on to him and goes to riding his dick backwards. "Damn," Fat Dre screams, watching his dick disappear in and out of Kadija's tight pussy. It's by far the best pussy he's ever had. "Oooh God, Big Daddy, I'm cummin." "Oooh shit, me too!" Fat Dre yells as they shake and twist together, having a maximum orgasm.

5 minutes later....

"Lay back Daddy. Let me treat you like the king you are," Kadija says, getting up to go get a hot soapy rag. She's cleaning off Fat Dre's dick as she notices him sending a text. Damn, she gets nervous but thinks, this is the perfect distraction. She pulls her .380 out of her purse and yells, "if you act like you're moving, I'm gonna shoot you in the face!" "WTF?" Fat Dre says, trying to think of a way to grab his .40 Cal. from underneath the pillow. "I saw where you put your gun don't try to play me nigga. Stand up. Put your hands up while you do."

"What do you want? Some money?" Fat Dre says. "Shut up and walk towards the door. Open it," Kadija says. As he does, two guys come in the condo with all black on with black ski masks. One hits Fat Dre in the face with his .357 off top. "Nigga, you got you some pussy, ate good, now pay your tab. Where is the money?" "Look in my drawer and in my pants pockets." Rushing off, Kadija comes back and shows the gunmen all the money. "I grabbed the jewelry too," she says, looking at the money. The robber that hit Fat Dre with the pistol says, "put the handcuffs on this nigga." "Man, I gave ya'll the money. Why I...." That was all he got out before he felt the power of the .357 hitting him in the mouth, the blow was so forceful it knocked Fat Dre down. "All you do is listen, Fat Boy and you may live. I know you're C.M.F. Give me the safe and I'll leave. If you don't, I'm gonna get mad, find it anyways, then I'm gonna kill you."

Slapping Fat Dre with the pistol, he says, "what's it gonna be?" "It's in the closet. Look behind the wall where the shoe boxes are stacked. The combination is 38-38-32." Fat Dre has $250,000 in the safe, along with the rest of his jewelry. He figures the $150,000 he has stashed in his room at his mom's house and the fact that he's gonna hunt down and kill whoever this is violating him is good. At least he can live to see another day.

After the robbers open the safe, they put all of Fat Dre's money and other jewelry inside, along with his pistol. One of the robbers tell the girl and the other robber to go and get the car. On his way out of the door, he puts the muzzle to the back of Fat Dre's head and fires, Boom!! Blowing half of his skull off.

CHAPTER 21

One Day Plies

DESTINY

"What's up sexy?" Destiny coos into the phone. "You baby girl. You. Trying to see me?" Ant Ant says. "For sure. My brother is acting all paranoid and shit, so I'm just gonna bring his money with me and spend it all with you. I know you gone look out, right?" "You know I got you ma. I'm at my spot. Come on through." Destiny had to learn how to talk ghetto, and like a hustler, because even though she was born and raised in the hood, she never let it define her. She didn't mess with drug dealers and she kept her focus on her education. The environment did help her pick up fast though. She's on her way to make her biggest bust.

"Everybody ready?" The Quad Squad leader, Sgt. Graham shouts. "Once you walk to your car, we're going in.

Let's go." Tiger is on the squad. He says, "be careful and good luck." "Thank you," Destiny replies. They have remained good friends. Destiny even forgave him but going backwards was not the plan.

10 minutes later....

"Come on in," Ant Ant says. They are at his trap off of 34th and Chelsea. "What are you trying to do?" "I have $850 of my own money and my brother gave me $6,500. He wants some crack and a few pounds of weed." "How about I'm about to bless you like this... I'm gonna sell you a quarter (9 oz) for $6,000. I usually sell my pounds for $800 apiece. I'm gonna give you two pounds of mid too." "I call that," Destiny says, pulling out the money. Thanks for looking out. "You need to look out," Ant Ant says, looking at Destiny's sexy shape. "Whatever, boy. I know you have 1000 hoes," she says, smiling while handing him a foot action bag.

"I'll call you in a couple days," Destiny says, exiting the house. By the time her key is in the ignition, she sees Quad Squad officers rushing in from everywhere.

At the substation 30 minutes later....

Everybody is high fiving and celebrating. They found a half a kilo (500 grams) 22 pounds of weed, $16,000 in cash and two firearms. Ant Ant is charged with armed trafficking of cocaine, possession with intent to sell marijuana, and felon in possession of a firearm. "You made it happen," Tiger says. Congratulating her. Sgt. Graham and all of the crew are trying to get her to come out with them later to celebrate. "I'm good, ya'll. I will celebrate once I make detective.

CASH

"What the hell big boy got going on?" Cash says, seeing the text from Fat Dre. It's 2:35 a.m. Cash had fell asleep on his couch watching the Orlando Magic and Dwight Howard beat up on the NY Nicks. He opens the text...

Big bro, I've died and went to heaven. I'm lying in my bed, getting wiped off by a full fledge dime piece I met at the mall earlier. Man, she's all that. I can't wait to let you meet her. She rode and sucked my dick like a porn star. I'll hit you in the a.m. I love ya bro. Fat Dre- at 2:12 a.m. it was sent.

Cash calls Fat Dre's phone about to question him on why he has a new chic at his spot, and to see who this mystery woman is. He's not getting no answer. He tries 3 more times before he gets an eerie feeling in the pit of his stomach.

He dials Cool Al's number. After 5 rings he groggily answers, "what's up, dude?" "You heard from Fat Dre?" Cash asks. "Earlier he was headed to the mall. He asked me if I wanted to ride with him." "Yeah, he called and asked me too," Cash replies. "Why, what's up? It's almost 3:00 in the morning." "I don't know. He sent me a text about 40 minutes ago about some bitch he had just fucked. Now he ain't answering his phone. Get Black Isaac and a couple of shooters together, and ya'll meet me at the McDonalds on 50th in 30 minutes. We are going to check on fat boy," Cash says. "I'm walking out of the door now."

DESTINY

"I did it, Destiny. Oh, my God. I'm so excited. I passed the GED," Meme shouts. "Yes," Destiny shouts. "Girl I knew you could do it. When do you graduate?" "Next week is the actual graduation. I know you are coming, right?" "I wouldn't miss it for the world, Chic". I'm so proud of you. I know Ms. Tracy is smiling down from heaven." "I love you, chic," Destiny says, "I love you too." "I'm about to head to Red Lobster to celebrate. Rick, the kids and his mom are coming. I would love for you to be there, Chic." "You know I love me some seafood. Which one are ya'll going to? And how long before ya'll leave?" "The one on Dale Mabry, and we are leaving now. We will be waiting in the parking lot for you." "I'm on my way Chic," Destiny says, disconnecting the call.

CASH

Getting out of his truck, Cash feels that everything is okay because he sees all of Fat Dre's cars in place. Him, Cool Al, Black Isaac, and Trigger are walking up to Fat Dre's condo. Black Isaac pulls out his gun and says, "I've got a funny feeling." "Let me knock on the door. Fuck that," Cash says, pulling out a Glock .40. Cool Al and Trigger whip out too, after knocking 5 times, Cash turns the doorknob and it opens. As soon as he steps inside the house, he sees Fat Dre in a puddle of blood. Rushing up to him, he says, "check the place out and call 911." "Ain't nobody else in here." "Quick, all ya'll give me ya'lls gun," Trigger says. "The police will be here asap. This is Temple Terrace." "Oh, shit, he's right," Cash says, handing him the gun.

"Ooh my God," he yells seeing half of Fat Dre's head torn off, his brains and blood is all over the floor. "Fuuuck!!" He yells at the top of his lungs. Cool Al falls next to him on the floor. They are both crying. "I swear to God, I'm about to bring the pain to these niggas. It sounds like that same crew who robbed you," Cash says. "Sure do," Cool Al replies. "What are we gonna do?? "Let's check this apartment real quick to make sure ain't nothing incriminating in here." "I've already did that," Isaac says. "Damn, my nigga is gone," Cash shouts. He is in so much pain, Fat Dre is his main man. Fat Dre would have taken a bullet for him. "I love you, my nigga," Cash says, kissing Fat Dre's hand. "Here come the cops. I hear sirens," Cool Al says. "Ya'll go ahead. I got this," Cash yells.

He is not leaving his man laying here alone like this. "Okay bruh. Call us as soon as you can," Cool Al says, walking outta the door. Cash feels something ain't right. Why kill if he's in handcuffs? This was a hit. Hits are personal. Cash thinks, either that or to send a message.

DESTINY

"I feel so giddy," Destiny says. She's at Gary Adult with their family. Her and Aunt donna are sitting next to each other. "I'm so proud of her. She has gone from dancing and tricking off with sorry dope-boys, to having a real man in Rick who's an engineer and a great step-dad. His mother is like a mother to her. They just moved into a HUD house, and she starts next week at Verizon. "That's great," Aunt Donna says, smiling. Meme is her niece too in her mind, because she helped raise her and loves her too. "Here they come," Destiny yells, seeing all the grads lining up, she spots Cash standing next to Meme and her heart flutters. "That's him, Auntie!" She says, nudging Aunt Donna.

She has talked Aunt Donna & Fee's ears off about Cashmere. "Where, child?" The handsome fellow next to Meme." "Oooh, he's cute," Aunt Donna says. "Alright," Destiny says, laughing.

CASH

"I'm okay. I just have a lot on my mind," Cash says. "Okay, I was just checking, because you're not acting like your usual self," Meme says. "I lost my best friend 3 days ago," Cash says sadly. "Ooh, Cashmere. I'm so sorry to hear that," Meme responds.

For the past 72 hours cash has been like a mummy. He has barely even slept or eaten. If it wasn't for his parents and uncle Jahiem, he wasn't even gonna attend his graduation. Looking into the crowd, he locks eyes with Destiny. Seeing her gives him a jolt of joy. She's smiling and waving at him. He gives her a wink and continues to stare at her. She is everything he's dreamed of in a woman. If only they were not on opposite sides of the law, because he is gonna get revenge on who killed his main man, even if he dies in the process. He goes to feeling sad again, knowing Fat Dre would have been right there right now, proud of him, cheering him on just as loud as C-Money and Tonya are. Bad as he wants Destiny, he's gonna put his heart on hold until he can fully give her the realness and love a woman like she deserves.

DESTINY

"Why don't you stop all that smiling and go congratulate the man," Aunt Donna says. "I ain't going over there with all of his family around him." "Why not?" Aunt Fee says. "If you feel it in your heart, don't let nothing stop you." Building her courage, Destiny walks over to Cash, and says, "excuse me." He turns around and says, "hello." "I wanted to congratulate you and tell you I haven't stopped thinking about you since we left Lowry Park." Cash is speechless. He's looking so blowed. Destiny says, "I'm sorry!" .... cutting her off, he says, "no, I'm sorry. I'm so speechless because I have not allowed an hour to go without thinking about you, since I bumped into you when I was signing up for class." "Oooh, "Where are ya'll going to celebrate?" Destiny says.

"We're gonna have a big family get-together at my mom and dad's house. They are leaving Saturday to move to California." "Wow! That must be nice." "Yeah, I'm gonna miss them, but I'm glad they're happy. How about you? Where are ya'll taking Meme?" "I rented the Orange Blossom Hall on 34th. We're gonna have a nice party. You and your family are welcome to come." "Actually, I would love to, but I have to go to a funeral this weekend and I'm not really in a partying mood. I lost my best friend." Tampa is so big. Temple Terrace Police caught the homicide case of Fat Dre. Destiny didn't even hear about it. "I'm so sorry," Destiny says, giving him a hug. Cash is blowed, but her warmth and comfort give him some much-needed relief. "Thank you," he says, hugging her back tightly. He doesn't want to ever let her go.

Breaking the embrace, Destiny says, "put my number in your phone. I'm gonna take you somewhere after the funeral, if you'll let me." They exchange numbers. "I'll call you later tonight to check on you," Cash says. "Tell Meme I said we did it!" Cash yells, walking off.

Two days later....

CASH

Fat Dre's wake is like a block party. So many niggas and hoes have shown up to send a street legend out in style. Cool Al is the star of the show. He has his Bentley parked in the front. C.M.F. signs are everywhere. They are even engraved in gold on Fat Dre's casket. Cool Al and Cash sent their main man out in style. They bought him a fat Cuban chain with a big C.M.F. medallion in diamonds. They paid an extra 2 grand to have it custom made in 3 days. His casket is his favorite color (Black) with 14 karat gold trimming. Fat Dre has on an all-black Armani suit. The funeral home did a great job. You can see his face, neatly trimmed goatee, and the way they have him in the casket, you can't tell the whole back of his head is missing.

His mom and dad, along with C-Money, Tonya and Cool Al's parents are in the front.

Cool Al and Cash are behind them. Camille, Black Isaac, and the rest of the C.M.F. crew are all in Black and heavy jewelry. Cash says, "I have to go" and kisses all the parents on the cheek. "I'll see ya'll tomorrow," he says to the C.M.F. crew. He heads out to his Intrepid and leaves.

He drives over to Oak Village and rides through. It's a Friday, so it's jumping. He sees major money being made. He spots Shayla making a sell. Turning out the backside, he sees Tear talking on his cellphone with his head down. This shit won't be like this next week, he says to himself, pulling off.

The next day....

Cash has only been to two funerals his whole life; his Aunt Roxy, and now his main man, Fat Dre.

As he looks around the crowded church, he gets angry, thinking, in a few days most of the people in here will have moved on and won't even be thinking about Fat Dre. C.M.F. is on deck stunting once again. Cash says the eulogy, going back to when they were kids sneaking weed from their dad to sell in school, to Fat Dre beating up all the school bullies. Him, Cool Al and Fat Dre going to East Lake Mall, going to Chic Fil A, the game room, and to get girls phone numbers. When he is done, the whole chapel is in tears. He sees Seleena in all Black sitting in the back. She's looking stunning. He nods his head at her.

After the funeral, Cash calls a C.M.F. only meeting. "Look!" He shouts. "Somebody just caused us to put one of our own in the dirt. I want a name in 3 days.

I have $250,000 for the person or persons responsible for this. If Dirty Game wants it, then here we come." Cool Al cuts in, "I have $250,000 too."

"Everybody stay strapped and be ready for war."

Later that night...

DESTINY

"Yes, I asked you to dress casual, so yes, I am dressed casual," Destiny says. Her and Cash have been talking on the phone like high school kids ever since they exchanged numbers. Destiny likes to hear a positive young brother. She couldn't believe it when he told her his birthday. They were born on the same day, not the same hospital. If that ain't some E.T. stuff, they said, laughing. She's on her way to the house his parents gave him in Tampa Heights. Cash really stays at the other house in Lutz, but he doesn't want Destiny to go there yet, it ain't his anyways. Tonya and C-Money gave him the one in Tampa Heights. C-Money made a decision that they are gonna keep their home in Lutz. He reasoned that him and Tonya will travel back and forth a lot, because they still have a lot of family in Tampa.

"I'm pulling up to the address you gave me now." Cash steps out of the house. Debonair in a purple linen two-piece Cavalli suit with some black Ferragamo hard bottom shoes; a black Movado watch, with a diamond necklace tucked inside his shirt. He smells of Clinique Happy. "Whoa," Destiny says, admiring how good Cash looks. She gets out of her Altima to greet him, looking absolutely gorgeous in a Kate Spade all cream, long dress, with a split at the knees, in a pair of black Prada heels with a black Prada purse to match. A nice Michael Kors black watch. Her hair is done in a french bob, nails trimmed in cream; she smells like peaches and cream; Victoria Secret body spray. "Uuuum, you smell good," Cash says, "but looking so gorgeous." "Thank you," Destiny says, returning his hug.

"Come on, the show starts in 30 minutes," Destiny says, getting in the car.

"Where are we going?" Cash says, getting inside her car. He wishes he could have brought the Rolls Royce, as good as they're looking tonight. He already knows, with her being a cop, that could never happen. "To the Improv. Michael Epps is in town tonight and I have tickets to the show," she says, smiling. She knew he went to the funeral today and wanted to uplift him in some way. "Wow! This is my dude. I love all his movies," Cash says excitedly. "All about the Benjamins, and The Last Friday are two of my all-time favorite movies." "Mine too," Destiny replies after parking her car. Cash says, "you better not move," as he gets out of the car and goes around to open the door for her.

"Nice," she says. "You're my queen; that's my job." "Okay," smiles Destiny.

They are having a great time, eating shrimp, and drinking wine. Michael Epps is finally on stage after a few openers.

Hey, ya'll. How about I went for this job interview last week, and they told me I had to have a urinalysis test because you can't have drugs in your system for this job. I go in the room to get the results and the manager says, I'm sorry, you can't Get a job here. You had drugs in your system. I said, I haven't smoked all day. Give em back hell, Day Day says.

The crowd goes wild. Cash reaches over and grabs Destiny's hand. She grips his hand in return. She feels so safe with him. After the comedy show, they take photos with Mike Epps and a few of just them too. Then they head to Bigmouth to eat.

Later they stroll down 7th Avenue holding hands. "Thank you so much," Cash says. You're welcome. I really had a nice time," Destiny says. "I needed this," Cash responds, giving her a hug. Destiny drops him off at his house. Before he gets out of her car, he reaches over and gives her a nice passionate kiss. "Good night, pretty, call me when you get home." "Okay," Destiny shouts. As soon as Cash gets inside his door, he texts her; *I miss you already...Cashmere.*

CHAPTER 22

No Love For Me

CASH

"Son, we need for you to make us a promise," Tonya says. Her, Cash and C-Money are at their house sitting inside the kitchen. "A promise of what, ma?" "We just buried Fat Dre two days ago. We need you to promise us that you are not going to do nothing crazy like trying to kill someone." "Ma, I can't lie to you. If I find out who's responsible for killing Fat Dre, I've got to have them." C-Money says, "son me and your mama raised you in the game. We have both played our part in creating this lifestyle for you. We need to leave Florida knowing that you have your mind right." "I'm good, pop.

I'm not a renegade. Ya'll taught me how to use my mind, not just how to deal with anger and emotions. So ya'll can head off today, knowing I'm gonna do what I'm supposed to do." "Cash, we don't even know who killed Fat Dre. They could be after you too," Tonya says. "It's very true ma, and I don't doubt that that is why I need to get to the bottom of this and put them to rest." "I buried my sister. It would send me to an early grave to have to bury you. Please make sure you keep that in mind in all the decisions you make. We love you and want the best for you. We have money, you have money; just walk away and enjoy life," Tonya pleads. "I'm trying to ma. I start school next month. I'm also working with Uncle Jahiem to enhance my business and life skills." "I trust you son.

We are leaving today. Look out for your sister Camille, and my grand-kids and keep your head in the game until you decide to walk away." 'I love ya'll," Cash replies, giving both his parents a big hug. "We love you too," they say in unison.

DESTINY

"You what?" Destiny screams. Tiger just called her phone and told her he had some very good news for her. "I'm at Belmont Heights Park. How long will it take for you to get here?" Tiger says. "I'll be there in ten minutes. I'm on 40th and Highway 60."

Ten minutes later....

"Tell her what you told me," Tiger says to the lady he has in his back seat. She looks nervously at Destiny, then says, "I know who the guy is who shot and killed the man who ran the store on 26th and Nebraska." Destiny's heart goes to beating so fast; she has to step out of the car for a second to catch her breath.

Getting back her composure, she says, "why after 4 years, you are now saying something? And how do you know for sure?"

"I'm not trying to go to jail. I need to get high, and I had no reason until now, to share this info." "I caught her trying to break into a house, and she had all this stuff on her," Tiger says, lifting a sandwich bag in the air with a glass stem, a lighter, a pocketknife and 3 big rocks of crack cocaine. "I asked her what she had for me and she told me what she just told you," Tiger says. "I told her we would give her this stuff back and $100 if she leads us to this guy and $500 if she testifies against him. She claims she was in a room, tricking with him the night he went to do the robbery/murder." "Where is he now?" Destiny asks." "He just got out of prison last month. He's hanging out on 29th and Lake Ave.

Tiger sees Destiny shaking so bad; he says, "do you want me to handle it?" "No. Let her get in the car with me.

It's my personal car and I have tint. I'll ride by 29th so she can point him out." "I'm going with ya'll. Let me lock up my cruiser. I'll hop in the back seat."

5 minutes later......

29th is only 4 blocks up, Strawberry, (the smoker) shouts, "there he is right there!" Pointing inside the alley next to the package store. Tiger says, "that's Ice Man. I've arrested him over 6 times. Let's head back to my car. We'll get him after we get a team together and drop her off." "No! Before we give her her stuff back and the $100, she is gonna have to sign an affidavit, saying everything she just told me." Strawberry says, "when do I get my $500?" "I'm gonna give you my personal cell number.

You have my word once he cops out or goes to trial and you testify, I'm gonna hand you 5 $100 dollar bills." "Okay, can we please get this paperwork done? I'm ailing. I ain't smoked all day.

CASH

"What's this I hear about a half a million dollars C.M.F. has on the head of the person who killed Fat Dre?" Uncle Jahiem says heatedly. "It is what it is," Cash replies. They are at Jahiem's car lot, pulling some new cars off of a trailer Jahiem bought at the auction last night. "So, you being here giving you the legit game, going to school, getting out of the game was all smoke you were blowing up my ass." Cash has never seen his uncle so upset. "They blew my nigga brains out, Unc." "Sometimes some people have to die for other people to live. I love Fat Dre too and I'm upset about how his life was taken, but I've told you before... your strongest muscle is your brain. Cash, to be the best, to reach the highest pinnacle, requires self-denial, sacrifice, discipline, humility and preparation.

Sometimes you have to hurt yourself, scold yourself, analyze yourself; you have to recognize your weaknesses and try to eliminate them. Those weaknesses you can't eliminate, must be minimized. You must create a plan that highlights your strengths and hides your flaws. You have to do more than simply want to win. Hell, everybody wants to win. But only a few of us are willing to prepare to win. You may have to do things that are difficult, painful, and even unpleasant. You must be willing to do today what nobody else will do. So, you can accomplish what others can't. Do you understand me, nephew?" "Yes sir," Cash answers.

DESTINY

"Is everybody ready?" Shouts Sgt. Wilson. "Yes, sir." "Destiny let me have a word with you," he says, pulling her to the side. "Yes, sir?" Destiny replies. "I know the victim was your favorite uncle. Please don't let your emotions cause you to put your life or career on the line. I just put in a recommendation for you to be a detective. Please don't let me or yourself down." "Sir, I stand for justice. I just want this heartless criminal off the streets and in prison, where he belongs." "That's the spirit. Let's go," Sgt. Wilson says.

They attack 29th so fast and hard, Ice Man didn't even get a chance to run. "Hey, what the fuck is going on?" He screams, as Tiger body slams him to the concrete. "Man, I just got out! I haven't done nothing wrong!"

"How about armed robbery and 1st degree murder?" Destiny says, putting the handcuffs on him super tight. She wants to take her gun out so bad and pound his face while telling him what a wonderful man he took away from her. She has so much anger and rage, she can barely read him his rights. Tiger helps her. "You have every right to remain silent...."

30 minutes later....

"I'm not saying shit to ya'll. I ain't never killed nobody. I have been on 29th and Lake since I've been out. Destiny says, "does this man look familiar?" She says while showing him a photo of her Uncle Melvin. "Nope, never seen him," Ice Man says. "How about him?" Tony comes in, looks at him and walks out. Destiny then shows him a photo in her phone she had taken of Strawberry. "Why did you have to kill him?" Destiny shouts, walking outta the squad room.

CASH

"Hello?" "Yes, I'm here, Uncle Jahiem says. He's sitting up at his house in deep thought, as Cash calls him. "I'm sorry Unc. Putting that reward out was not a smart move. The streets will lead the cops right back to me. That is not the type of attention I need on myself. I made a decision based off of emotions. I know ain't no emotions from a king. The kidnapping of my mom, Cool Al getting shot, Fat Dre getting killed kinda took me off the edge. I've pulled the reward off. I've asked Cool Al to chill." "What good is that gonna do?" "I don't know. Lately he's really been on some nino stuff." "Yeah, I know," Uncle Jahiem says. "He gave me $300,000 tonight to specially order something." "What? I need you to sell my Rolls Royce for me." "Why are you selling your car?"

"It's too flashy and I'd rather sell it now while it's still in fair market value." "You mean so you won't lose too much money." "I won't lose anything. It was a gift from ya'll, remember?" "Well, I'm getting my 10% on the sale, so I'll get my lil money back," Uncle Jahiem laughs. "This police chic has really made an impression on you." "You have too," Cash says, before saying goodnight and disconnecting the call.

DESTINY

Goodnight, handsome... Your Destiny, she texts Cash before getting in the shower.

A minute later.

"Hello," she answers her phone. "My Destiny, huh?" Cash says. "I texted what was on my mind. I've had a really long day." She had told Cash about Uncle Melvin and how important he was to her. "I arrested the guy who murdered my Uncle Melvin today." "Wow! That is great news. What happened?" She tells him the story. She was honest with him about her whole life story, so he knows about Tiger, and gets kinda jealous that Tiger made some points with her. Not holding his tongue, Cash says, "Tiger is a good guy.

I love what he did, but make sure you go to bed knowing that you're my Destiny." Laughing, Destiny says, "oh you're jealous?" "Very much so," he agrees laughing. "There is no need. He is my past, and I'm your Destiny."

CHAPTER 23

Straight Stuntin'

MAD MAX

"That's what the fuck I'm talking about," yells Mad Max. He's in Miami at 305 Customs. Him and Lizanne came down to pick up his new car. "Bruh, I really appreciate this hook-up." "The more you look like money, the more of it you will get," Rondo says. "I'm proud of you, my dude. You and my lil brother are doing big thangs." "This is only the beginning," Mad Max says. "I'm about to open up two more traps when I get back to Tampa." "That's real," Rondo shouts. "You already know I'm with you all the way, as long as our creed stays the same. "Death by Dishonor." "Go ahead and give your new ride a spin," Rondo says, looking at his new 2001 Porsche 911 Turbo.

It's smoke gray with all chrome 22-inch Forged rims.

"Come on baby," Mad Max says to Lizanne, getting inside his whip. "Damn baby be careful. It says 230 on the speedo! After we hit up 183 street, and USA Flea Markets, copping us some jewels, I'm gonna try to do the whole 230 heading back to Tampa. No, you are not. Don't play Max." Lizanne says, terrified. "I want a customized tag on the front that says Dirty Game."
After handling their business, in Miami Mad Max and Lizanne head back to Tampa.

3 day later....

"I like the way this lay out looks. We are gonna use an apartment in the back," Mad Max says to Tear. They are standing inside the parking lot of Johnson and Kenneth Court Apartments. "What about the niggas that hustle around here?"

Tear says. "Let me show you how we are living from this day forward." Walking up to 5 niggas standing by the mailboxes. Mad Max says, "who has some weed for sale?" Two of the dudes say. "me. What's up?" Mad Max pulls out his .45 and shoots the one closest to him in the thigh, boom!! Damn near taking his thigh off. "Look here," he shouts. "This is Dirty Game. I'm opening a trap around here, starting tomorrow. I will be selling X, crack, and weed. If you want to get you some real money, holler at my lil brother right here and we'll put you on. You want beef, we're gonna kill you." Mad Max walks off and goes to his Ford Taurus crew car.

"Damn, big bruh! Let me do that in the other new spot. I'm feeling that. That is exactly what they do in the projects in Wimauma."

Friday night...

"You and the girls be on point in the back of us in your truck." Tear bought a 2001 Cadillac Escalade and put it on 24's two days ago. "We are about to show these pussies how to stunt." Driving down main street 2 hours later...

Mad Max is the star of the show in his Porsche. All eyes are on him. Everybody thinks it's a ball player stuntin this hard with so many niggas from Tampa in the pros in baseball. Tear is right behind him swerving. He's yelling, "Dirty Game" out of the window.

Lizanne is on the passenger side looking like money. They ride down the set twice before pulling off.

COOL AL

"Please tell me my whip is ready, Unc."
Yells Cool Al. Mad Max and the Dirty
Gam crew came through, stuntin and it
has Cool Al hot. It will be here by
Friday, Uncle Jahiem says. "I'll be there
bright and early to grab that. Do I owe
you any money?" "Naw, you good
nephew. Hold up. Cash wants to speak
with you," Jahiem says, handing Cash
his cellphone. "What's the deal, bro?"
Cool Al asks. "Working hard. I start
school tomorrow." "Which one are you
going to? I know it's gonna be some bad
lil honey's on deck." "I'm going to the
campus on Hillsborough. Past Dale
Mabry. I need to get at you." "Where do
you want to meet to eat a quick lunch?"
I'll meet you at Silver Ring in 30
minutes," Cool Al responds. "Okay
one," Cash says, disconnecting the call.

30 minutes later....

"Sup, bruh?" Cash says, giving Cool Al some dap. "Getting this money, my dude. What's good? I hear these dirty money cats are on some get down or lay down John Doe type of shit." "I heard," Cool Al says, like he could care less. "That is the type of shit that get niggas in prison. The crackers send the dope to us to sell. It keeps the economy flowing, but when violence and bodies go to coming up, they are forced to shut you down. I just wanted to let you know we are not gonna stoop to their level. We've been getting money since we were teenagers and neither one of us ain't never seen the backseat of a police car. My cuzzo Baby Doll made a mistake and it's costing her 7 long years. If it ain't mandatory, let's let them have the heat with that violence," Cash says. "Fuck them niggas.

I listened to you when I got shot. I listened to you and pulled the reward for the killing of Fat Dre. If them niggas step on my toes again, it's war. Simple as that," Cool Al says. "You ain't got to worry about it because you'll be at school. You gave me the throne; let me run my kingdom. You just sit back and keep getting your money. "I hear all that fly shit you speaking. In all of your favorite movies; Scarface, New Jack City, King of New York, it was greed and violence that caused their demise. Don't let it happen to us," Cash says.

Later that night....

"Yeah, big bro I'm up here with some of the team. I'm on my way," Cool Al says, disconnecting the call. "This is the life." Cool Al says to himself. He's riding down Columbus Drive about to turn in to Central Court Apartments in his 2001 Maybach coupe.

It's black with black 22 inches Diablo's; his tribute to Fat Dre. "I'm the king," Cool Al shouts, turning up the music. He's listening to 400 Degrees, by Juvenile. *If I ain't a hot boy, then what do you call that?* He raps along with the song. He cruises through the parking lot. Seeing its's empty, he heads towards Main Street.

When he pulls up on Main, he see's Black Isaac posted up in front of the Zanzi Bar. Every eye on the block is locked in on the Maybach. Most of them ain't never seen a car this exclusive up close. The dark tint has the identity of the driver hidden.

Cool Al parks on the sidewalk and steps out in an all-black Versace linen short set, with Versace black sandals, a black Girard Perregaux Opera $150,000 watch on one wrist, a diamond bracelet gleaming with stones on the other, and a long diamond necklace hanging to his dick with a medallion in diamonds that reads: King AL. "Oooh, shit!" Black Isaac yells over the music. Way of Life is playing on Cool Al's stereo system. He goes to rapping to the music: *cause you know it ain't trickin' if you got it.* "I'm a stunna, C.M.F.," he yells. "This is our city. This is what money looks like," pointing at him and his car. Tear is on fire. He is standing next to Shayla at the food truck. "I will put that pussy down right now," Tear says. "Fuck that nigga. We're getting money and doing us," Shayla says, trying to cool him down. Secretly her pussy is throbbing watching Cool Al show his ass. "Let's go," Tear says, walking off.

Cool Al sees them crossing the street and says out loud, "how much does this club cost? I may just buy this bitch tonight." He's smiling from ear to ear. All the hoes and niggas are on his dick.

MAD MAX

"Yeah! Oh, that pussy wanna act gangster and show out?" Mad Max screams. Him and Tear are standing in the condo him and Lizanne share in Apollo Beach. "Yeah, big bruh, the nigga copped a fucking Maybach. Popping that C.M.F. shit. They got money." "I'm gonna see if they have heart," hating ass Mad Max says. "Baby come here," he yells. "Yes, King?" Lizanne walks up looking stunning. Take the girls and go shopping. I want you looking like a million dollars tomorrow when we walk through the block party Wewee is throwing at River Front Park. I can't wait to see the look on that pussy nigga's face when he sees you with the Dirty Money crew.

The next day…

"Are all ya'll ready to go?" "Hell to the yeah, it's a couple of our crew already there. They say that bitch so thick, you can't even drive through no more." "You made sure everybody is strapped up, right?" "You already know, big bro." "Let's roll ya'll," Mad Max says to his crew.

20 minutes later….

Mad Max is rolling down the boulevard watching all the hoes and niggas crowd the park. Big whips, short shorts, shit is live, eyes are turning as he glides through in the Porsche. He turns into the park and begins to ride down the set. Tear, Shayla and Elise are right behind him and Lizanne.

When they get to the spot his Dirty Money crew has reserved, he pulls in and parks sideways.

He steps out looking like money in a grey and black Roca Wear short set. Some black and gray retro J's and an Oakland Raiders hat. A big Cuban Line bracelet on his wrist. A chain to match, with an iced-out medallion flushed with diamonds that reads "Dirty Game." Lizanne gets out after him in a black Zac Posen short set top and bottom, a pair of gray Guiseppe Zanotti pumps, with her neck, wrist, and ears glistening with diamonds. Her hair is flawless. She is clearly the baddest bitch at the park.

COOL AL

"Say no more," Cool Al says. "I'm on my way." "I'll save you a spot bruh. We have about 20 C.M.F. members here and you already know we're strapped up, Shorty," Black Isaac says. He's at the block party. "I'll see you in 20 minutes bruh," Cool Al says. Walking to his wall safe, he takes $200,000 and puts it in a duffel bag, grabs his jewels, and walks out the door. He pulls up to the park in his Maybach 20 minutes later. People are looking at his car like it's a ghost. Cool Al is smiling to himself. He knows he is killing the game. What he doesn't know or think about is all the snitch niggas and hoes at the park looking for something to tell.

Turning into the park, he's bopping to the beat of Mystical- The man right chea, when he sees her.

"That's that bitch," Cool Al says to himself. Mad Max is grilling him. Cool Al is so hot, he's about to pull his 9mm out and go to busting right out of his window. Breaking his train of thought, Black Isaac is knocking on his window. "Yeah, bruh," Cool Al says, opening his door. "We're over here," Black Isaac points by the DJ booth. He sees his crew waiting on him. I've got something for these poor ass fuck niggas." Cool Al says backing in. He jumps out, fresh to death full of Jewelry. Looking at Lizanne and the Dirty Money crew, he dumps the money that is in his black tote bag on his hood and yells, "CMF. The man right chea, while lying on the money on the hood. Tear ups his .45 and shoots in Cool Al's direction. Boom, Boom!! Its pandemonium. Everybody goes to running. Gunshots are ringing out; Cool Al and Mad Max are shooting too.

Shit is crazy. Somebody yells, "police!" Cool Al grabs his money and is stuffing it in his tote bag. He sees Fonda, a dike chic that runs their trap in Robles Park, on the ground bleeding. She's holding her arm. "Get in," Cool Al says, opening his passenger side door. Black Isaac says, "they're gone, big bruh. I think I got one of them hoes that was with them." "I hope so," Cool Al yells. "Have everybody on point.in the morning. You already know its war." "For show," replies Black Isaac. "Damn," Cool Al says to himself. He knows Cash is gonna be trippin, and he knows wars cost money. "Fuck that," Cool Al shouts. You're either prey or predator in this world...The art of war.

CHAPTER 24

Motivation

DESTINY

"How did it go?" Auntie Donna ask. "I did my best, it was easy. I think I aced it," Destiny replies. She's at Lee Davis visiting her aunt Donna. She just left from taking the last part of the test to become a detective. "Well, it's in God hands now. No, lets pray together Auntie, then we'll officially put it in God hands." "Bow your head," Aunt Donna says, as she begins a deep prayer. "Thank you," Destiny says. "I have been dreaming about this since I was 6 years old." "God knows your heart; he knows that you really have good intentions. You're gonna be ok." "I'm hungry. Take your Auntie to Gene Anthony's to grab some lunch."

"You must have read my mind. I can taste one of them devil crabs now," Destiny says, walking towards her car. "What's up with you and this young man Cashmere?" "What are you trying to kick me out?" Destiny says, smiling. "Stop it. You already know that it is our house. I was just wondering, because you've been mighty happy since you started talking to him." "He's so different. I mean, to be my age, he doesn't go to clubs, he's smart, he's ambitious, he started H.C.C. last week. He's a gentleman, he's compassionate, he has a great sense of humor and he's not a hustler. He works at his uncle's car lot. I really like him. I'm taking it slow because I don't want to get hurt again and we are both still finding ourselves. As far as career wise, I know I'm gonna be busy if I make detective, he wants to open a lot of businesses.

That's time consuming, so I'm just gonna continue to bond with him and push for the best." "A good man is hard to find, and opportunities are far and in between. If you feel it in your heart and ya'll make each other happy - go for it. Don't let the fear of failure stop you. Step out on faith. Have the courage to go at what you want. For what it's worth, I think he's a keeper.

CASH

"This is not as hard as I thought," Cash says to a white boy (Chris) who is in class with him. They are leaving school for the day. "Yeah, the professor seems to be cool. But remember, it's only our first week," Chris says. "I'm feeling that. Have a good day, main man. Hopefully, I'll see you tomorrow," Cash says, turning to get in his car. "Cash! Is that you?" Angela yells, walking up to him. "All day," Cash says, looking at his first love. She's looking great in a BeBe pants set and some red and white J's. Her hair is done nicely, and she smells very good. It's a fat gap between her legs. "Hey boy, give me a hug," she says, hugging him tightly. "What are you doing here?" "I started school here this week," Cash says, returning the hug. He gives her fat ass a little squeeze. "That's good. I'm a semester away from getting my degree. I'm going to be a dental hygienist.

"That's great. I'm glad to hear that. How is your family?" "Everybody is good." "How is Ms..T and C-Money?" "They're good. They just moved to California." "What?" She yells, "what's up with you? Last I heard the hood gossip, you were the Kingpin, riding around in a Rolls Royce." "It wasn't the life for me. You see where I'm at. Getting this Business Administration degree is my goal, so I can take off in the business world." "You always had big dreams. I'm proud of you. You need to talk to your BFF. Yesterday they tore Riverfront Park up with all that shooting." "Who?" Cash replies. "Cool Al and the C.M.F. crew went at it with the Dirty Money crew. I heard a few people got shot. I was there with my home girl, but as soon as we heard shots, we took off running. Later that night, she texted me that her baby daddy told her all about it." "Damn," Cash responds. "Hey, I've got to go. I'm gonna holler at you." "Hold up, I want to talk to you about something else I seen." "Call me," Cash says, shouting out his cellphone number. Getting in his car, he sends Cool Al a text, saying:

what's the deal, main man?

I'm good. Getting ready to go to war, Cool Al responds.

Meet me at my house in Tampa Heights in 20 minutes, Cash texts back.
Tru, Cool Al responds.

DESTINY

"You know I'm proud of you, right?" Destiny says, "I know." "I want to thank you because if it wasn't from your motivation, I wouldn't be about to cut this ribbon," Cherell says. They are standing on 22nd across from the Florida Sentinel building. Cherell has a building where Gene's Bar used to be. She's about to open her day care center. They're entire family is there to support her.

"Cut the ribbon, big sis. You're gonna do a great job. You know we're all gonna be right here with all the support you need." Destiny and Cherell are both crying. "Hello," Destiny says answering her phone. "Yes sir. I'm two minutes away from you sir. Okay, I'm on my way.

That was my sergeant. It's an emergency. I have to go. I'll be right back. He's at the substation next to Lee

Davis." "Okay, I love you too," Destiny says getting into her car. "I'll call y'all in a few," Destiny waves to auntie Fee and Donna.

A couple of minutes later...

"Sit down. I'll be with you in a minute," Sgt. Wilson says. What's going on? Destiny thinks nervously. Tiger walks into the room and says hello but keeps walking. "Come in," Sgt. Wilson says, asking Destiny to come into his office. "Yes, sir." "I'm sorry to have to do this," he says with a serious face, "but I'm going to have to ask you to give me your badge, and all of your uniforms." Stunned, Destiny yells, "why, sir? What did I do?"

Smiling, Sgt. Wilson says, "congratulations, you made detective." "Oooh, my God," Destiny screams. Tiger and the Quad squad come in the office clapping. She hugs Tiger. "Thank you so much," she yells. "Thank all of you." She goes around hugging everyone, then she goes back to Tiger and says, "thank you again. No matter what we've went through, I never would have achieved this goal without you." She's crying. "You're welcome. Nobody deserves it more than you. You're a great person. It has been a pleasure working with you. Good luck on your next journey." "You're to report at 9:00 am to Sgt Graham at the police station on Tampa Street," says Sgt. Wilson. "Thank you, sir," Destiny replies. Destiny sends a text to all the numbers in her phone. I just made detective...even Cash.

CASH

"We just talked about this a couple days ago," Cash says. "Bruh, these Dirty Game niggas are some grimy, hating niggas. They wanna stunt, but when I turn up and show them whose team is really winning, they want to bust they're guns. They had that bitch who set me up to get robbed and shot with them I believe they robbed and killed Fat Dre, and kidnapped auntie Tonya," Cool Al says. "Fonda got shot and I have two bullet holes in my Maybach." "Is Fonda ok?" Cash asks. "Yeah, she was hit in the arm. She was back to work getting money this morning." "You know this heat is gonna slow down the money," Cash says. "I'm bringing in some guns from outta town. I want these chump's dead." "That hoe Sensation, or whatever her name and the one who shot me.

He's also who started bussing yesterday. "A natural mistake is to get so caught up in your situation that you fail to analyze the motives, maneuvers, and talents of your opponents," Cash says. "We have to put our minds together to make a plan where we win." "You worry about school. By the time you finish, I'm gonna give you 2 million of my money to invest too. I've got this war under control." "Are you sure? Because if you're sure these are the people that did us all harm, my gun busts too." "I got this bruh," Cool Al says, giving Cash a hug. "Learn to stay 3 moves ahead of your enemies, bruh", Cash says, hugging him back.

MAD MAX

"That was some stupid shit you did, lil bro," Mad Max screams at Tear. "It wasn't more stupid than you having Lizanne step out at the block party. You pretty much said fuck you, Cool Al. I shot and robbed you," Tear screams back. He's hot and he's hurt. His big brother chastised him in front of the women. Anybody else in the world would have come at Mad Max like Tear just did would have been dead. He loves Tear more than he loves himself, so he says, "I'm sorry lil bro. You're right. Fuck them pussies. How are we gonna kill these pussies? We need to have somebody pick Shayla up from the hospital before the detectives get to her." "I know. How is she?" Asks Mad Max. "She's good. In a hell of a lot of pain. The bullet went in and out of her shoulder."

"Fuck that! When are we gonna touch these nigga's? They have my home girl in pain. I want some blood," Elise shouts. "Friday will be a hump day. We are gonna hit their trap in Robles Park. Every week were gonna hit one of their traps until we close them all down. Wherever Cash or Cool Al show their faces, we're gonna leave," Mad Max says. "That nigga Cash has been real low key," Tear says. "I ain't seen him since Fat Dre got killed." "Just like with a snake, you kill the head and the body falls. That pussy was hiding behind Fat Dre's muscle," Mad Max laughs.

CASH

"Who is this?" Cash answers his phone, not recognizing the number. "It's me, Angela. Damn. You don't remember my voice?" "What's good, ma?" "Can you come by my house," She says. "Where do you stay?" "In my old house. My mom gave it to me." "What time you want me to come through?" Cash asks. "About 9:30 pm" "I'll be there," Cash says disconnecting the call. Cash dials Destiny's number...

"Hello, Mr. Cashmere," she answers, sounding super-sexy. "I wanted to congratulate you on making detective. I'm very proud of you." "Oooh, thank you," Destiny responds. "Your strength motivates me." "When are you gonna rub some of that good luck off on me?" "You are already doing the right thing, putting yourself in position to win is better than luck, my uncle Melvin taught me. It's a poor hunter who waits for the game to come to them. Stay in attack mode." "That's why I like you," Cash says laughing. "When do you start your new job?" "9:00 in the morning. I'm so excited. I'm gonna be narcotics detective. I've always dreamed of this day. Now I can begin to really make a difference." "You already have done that. You have captivated me." "Whatever young man. I'm sure you've had your share of women." "None as special or beautiful as you," Cash responds. Destiny instantly gets wet at the complement. She hasn't had sex in 5 months, since Tiger. "Am I gonna see you this weekend?" She asks. "If you aren't too busy chasing bad guys. I'd like to take you somewhere nice." "One thing I always said I was gonna do, is take the time out to enjoy life.

My job will not be my life. I want to be a wife and a mother one day." "That's funny," Cash says, "because I plan on being a good husband and a great father." "Prove it," Destiny says. "Keep living," Cash replies, laughing. "Goodnight handsome."
"Goodnight beautiful."

One hour later....

"Come on in," Angela says opening the door. She has on a red lace Victoria's Secret nightgown. It's see-through. He can see her fat pussy cleanly shaved through it. His dick instantly gets hard. She has candles burning and the stereo playing Silk, I wanna freak you. Trying to play cool, Cash says, "what's on your mind?"

Grabbing his erect penis, she says, "this." Dropping to her knees, she quickly pulls out his dick and engulfs him. Cash is immediately paralyzed in ecstasy as she skillfully pleasures him. "Oooh, shit," Cash moans. He ain't had no pussy in a couple of months. Angela smiles up at him as she increases her motion. "The fuck am I doing," Cash thinks to himself. His mind goes to Destiny. He feels like he's betraying her. Her words from earlier tonight come to his mind, prove it. He pulls his dick out of Angela's mouth and quickly zips up his pants and runs out of the door. "Cash, wait!" Angela yells. Cash gets in his car and pulls off. Only the strong survive!

CHAPTER 25

Love and War

DESTINY

"Good morning sir," Destiny says while shaking Sgt. Graham's hand. She's at the Tampa Police Department headquarters on Tampa Street. "Have a seat," he says. "I am not a mean man, but I do expect results from my detectives. You're the only black female detective on the force. Because I'm a black man, I will not show you favoritism. I will show you respect and lead by example, are we clear?" "Yes sir, I am ready to get to work sir. Making detective has been my dream since I was 6 years old. Mentally, and physically I've prepared myself for this opportunity since high school. You will receive my all every single day I have this badge." "That's the spirit. You will be partnering with Detective Von Miller.

He's from around the East Tampa area and he's a good young detective. I hate to put so much on ya'll right off the bat, but the drug rate is off the hook in Tampa and the Mayor is starting to ask if we are earning our salary. So, get with Von and ya'll get to work. Ya'll have a report on my desk in 3 days as to what ya'll are gonna do to put some drug dealers in jail." "Yes sir," Destiny says, walking out of his office in search of Detective Miller.

CASH

"Do you know why I asked to see you?"
Mr. Carlos asked. "No, sir!" Replies
Cash. Him and Mr. Carlos are standing
in the back yard of his house in Ybor
City. "I've been living in Tampa since
I982. I swam to Miami into the Keys
from Cuba in 1980. I have never seen the
inside of a jail or prison cell. You know
why?" "No, sir," Cash replies. "Because
I don't be seen. I've never owned a
Mercedes, BMW or a Porsche. My home
is built in the woods in Wimauma. I
never clubbed. I don't have many
friends. I love you like a son, but I can't
allow you to send me to prison. Either
you take back over your team, or you
need to retire. This friend of yours, Cool
AI is too flashy and wild. I know you're
wondering how I know everything that
I know. Just know that sometimes our
friends become our enemies and
sometimes our enemies become our
friends. Wisdom...

MAD MAX

"Ok, this is the plan," Mad Max says. "We're going to hit them in broad daylight. The element of surprise is gonna catch them off guard. Tear, Lizanne, Elise and Mad Max are inside the back of a Astro minivan. They are all in black and strapped with big guns. "Shayla is gonna drive. Once we get in front of their trap, we are just gonna start bussing. Ya"ll ready?" Mad Max asks. "Let's do it," Tear yells. "Ladies, there ain't no turning back. We are shooting to kill. This war is officially on," Mad Max says. "I'm your queen baby," Lizanne shouts. "I'm about this life," Elise says. "Let's roll out then." "Let's go wake Shayla up and get this party started.

20 minutes later....

They turn Robles Park into a firework show. Fonda gets shot again; this time twice; once in the leg and once on her ass cheek. Three other people get shot, but nobody dies. Pulling off, Tear screams, "Dirty Game, bitch!"

COOL AL

"Cuzzo, I want you all in Tampa in 30 minutes." Cool Al says to Rolo and Ike. "What's up, big cuz?" Rolo replies "I'll tell you when ya'll get here. Bring your heat." "We are on our way." "These nigga's think it's a game," Cool Al shouts. He's livid! He has to shut down his spot in Robles Park on a money coming Friday. Two C.M.F. members got shot and two customers. Him and Black Isaac are at the spot by Central Court, standing in the back yard.

"I know a lil young nigga who is fucking the bitch Elise," Black Isaac says. "Kill the hoe. I'll give you a brick and 5 pounds." "I'm on it, big bro. I will have the hoe by Sunday." "To turn up the heat, I'm about to light up their spot in Oak Village right now.

Them niggas need to know, if they play with my money, I'm gonna play with theirs. Ain't no rules in war, main man."

An hour later…

Rolo and Ike shoot up Oak Village apartments. Shooting two people. One dirty money runner and an innocent bystander.

DESTINY

"Hey there, partner," Detective Miller says to Destiny. She's in the break room, getting a pack of Starburst out of the vending machine. "I've got everything set up. We're about to have a detectives meeting." Destiny worked with Miller a couple of times when she was doing undercover sting operations. They clicked well, both being from the hood, and energetic.

Walking into the room full of detectives, Miller takes the podium. "This is a rough draft of the two crews we need to take down. They are not only flooding our city with drugs, but they are violent and have no regards for public safety. Just this past weekend they had a shootout at a local park where kids and all were in attendance. They are ruthless, and their pushing major weight in crack, ecstasy pills, and high-grade marijuana. The sources that I have, pegged the names of the crews as C.M.F., which stands for Cash Money Family and Dirty Game. The dirty game supposedly plays by their own rules. We need to get on all of our snitches and make some arrests. Put some pressure on the low-level workers so we can put these violent criminals in prison. Now I've broken down some sections where they are supposed to have spots. We need to get on top of this ASAP. Today we had two shootings and five people wounded at the minimum."

Sergeant Graham stands up and says, "ya'll get to work, its Friday night. By Tuesday, I expect to know who's with these crews." "Yes Sir," all the detectives shout in union. Walking off, Von says, "let's take a ride, Destiny. I have a C.I I need to go see.

"I'm with ya partner," Destiny says, following him to their car. Twenty minutes later, they arrive at the Dominoes spot. "Good I'm outside." "Walk down 21st, I'm gonna pick you up." "The fuck you want man?" "Get your ass out here," Miller says, hanging up. Arthur Raye climbs in the back seat of the Ford Taurus.

5 minutes later....

"Listen to me. I know you want a get out of jail free card. I'm giving you a one-time offer to get one. As long as it's not a capital felony you commit, you'll be able to call me or my new partner and we'll make sure you're set free." "What's up? I call that! Arthur Raye responds. "What's the deal with C.M.F. and Dirty Game crews?" "They are beefing about some who's the king shit. Mad Max,

The leader of the D.G. crew came out two weeks go with a 911 Porsche. The next week, Cool Al, the king of the streets, and the leader of the C.M.F. shuts the game down in a motherfucking Maybach." Police-ass Arthur Raye is all dramatic telling on these crews. "So, who are all the other main players? I don't know them dudes like that. I know this dude Mad Max just got out of prison recently. He has a brother that likes to shoot up shit and they have two hoes that sell a lot of the dope for them." "Where are these spots?" "Dirty Game has two. I know of one in Oak Village and one in Johnson and Kenneth Court apartments. Now C.M.F., they have been getting money for years there outta Tampa Heights, but they got traps all over the place, Robles Park, Oakhurst.

I think they have one in Palm River. They have hoes running all they're spots. That's all I know." Can I get her number?" He says, pointing at Destiny. I may need my pass at any time. "Yeah, and you also may have some more info for us," Destiny says. "That's my kinda news. What's your number? Arthur Raye says, pulling out his phone.

CASH

"I guess we're gonna have to cancel," Cash says. "Yes, I'm sorry," Destiny says. Her and Cash are sitting inside her car outside of his house. I just got this big case tonight and it's gonna be hectic, but for the safety of everyone. These monsters need to be off of the streets. I don't condone no criminal activity but people shooting and putting innocent lives in danger really gets me upset. And it's all about who's car is the nicest or who's the biggest drug dealer. They are destroying our community. On Sunday I'm gonna be off, what about then? Destiny asks. "Call me at 10:00 am. I'll be waiting," Cash says. I'm about to finish this book I'm reading called, The 14 Laws of Success. Russell Simmons wrote it. Call me and let me know you made it home safely." "

"Okay handsome." Destiny reaches over and kisses him softly on the lips. He gently grabs her face and kisses her back. Ten minutes later before they unlock their tongues and break their embrace, electricity shoots through Cash. She has never had sex in a car but at this very moment, she's so hot and motivated to do so. "I'll call you in a few minutes," Cash says, getting out of Destiny's car before he loses control.

ELISE

"Hey hon, what time are you coming to get me?" Elise asked. She's talking to Smoke. This young nigga she met at the trap one day, coming to cop with his homie. Smoke is a jet black, 5'11, 190 lbs., pretty boy. He has long dreads down to the middle of his back. He hustles in Port Tampa to buy clothes and shoes. Elise has spoiled him. She bought him a Camaro on 24's, and some jewelry. All he has to do is keep the dick in her life. He has no idea running his mouth is about to cost him and Elise their lives. Black Isaac has been following him since he left Port Tampa. "I'm on my way babe, you ready?"

"Yes, I'm at the spot in Johnson Court."

"I'll be there in 20 minutes," Smoke says.

Hanging up the phone, he turns up his two 12' square kickers. He's listening to Shine by Lil Wayne.

20 minutes later....

"Alright, ya'll I'm gone, Elise says to Tear and Shayla. "Tell that young nigga don't be playing that music all loud when he comes here. Ok?" Elise says. She thinks Tear is the biggest hater in the world. He's mad she ain't never gave him no pussy. Hell, he keeps the music in his truck on blast. "Alright bitch!" Shayla screams. I'll call you chic," Elise says, walking out the door.

Black Isaac has creeped out of his stolen car and is behind the stairs, waiting on Elise. As she opens the door to get inside the Camaro, he comes up busting; boom, boom, boom, boom, boom!!

He's letting his .40 caliber bark. He runs up to her and hits her two more times before he runs off. Boom, boom!! He shoots Smoke twice in the process.

TEAR

"The fuck!" He yells, hearing gunshots. He grabs his .45 and runs out of the door. It's too late. By the time he reaches the Camaro, all he sees is blood. The music is still playing. Go DJ is now playing by Lil Wayne. He must have the Carter CD on. "Oooh, shit"! He yells looking at what's left of Elise. "Fuuuck!" He screams. He ain't love Elise like that, he's just mad that a person got one over on his team like that. Shayla comes running up. When she sees Elise, she passes out.

Sunday…

CASH

"You heard about the young couple who were killed last night in Johnson Court?" Destiny says. "Yes, that is so sad." "I hear the young man was 20 and was the only child, and the woman was 26. She wasn't from here. She was from Memphis, Tennessee." It's sad to see our people killing one another like that," Cash says. "I went to the scene. It was horrible," Destiny says. I'm gonna get the person responsible. Anyways, so what do my handsome future hubby have planned for us." "Well, I thought you may need a little relaxation, so we are going to Lithia Springs park to have us an old school picnic." "OMG! I've never been on a picnic." "Me neither," Cash replies. "So, I hope I have everything right.

"It will be okay as long as I'm with you we'll enjoy ourselves." Cash takes out the comforter and places it on the sand. He bought fresh fruit, strawberries, pineapples, and grapes. He has all kinds of lunch meat. A loaf of bread, two wine glasses, a bottle of Chardonnay wine, and for dessert he has a Red Velvet cake he got this morning from Publix. He even has a small CD player with R. Kelly vs. Jahiem CD. He makes them a small fruit salad and feeds Destiny. They drink and eat the sandwiches while watching kids play in the water. Cash picks her up and runs her towards the water. 'Stop! Wait!' She yells. 'Nope. Our phones are over there.' Cash dives into the spring with Destiny in his arms. The water is so cold at first; they play and fight and have a good time. Then back to laying on the comforter, eating red velvet cake.

A few hours later, Cash says, "I'm crazy about you." "Prove it, "Destiny says. Cash locks his lips onto hers and puts his tongue in her mouth. They are in a zone. It's like they are the only two people in the world. "Come on," Cash says, pulling her up. They pack up their picnic stuff and get inside Cash's Intrepid. Still kinda damp, Cash takes her to Crabby Tom's seafood in Brandon. After they eat, tell jokes, kiss and talk, Cash takes her home and says his goodbyes. "I have school tomorrow and you have to catch some bad guys." "Thank you so much for a great day," Destiny says, hugging him and giving him a nice sloppy kiss. "The pleasure was all mine," Cash replies. (Love?)

CHAPTER 26

Kept It Too Real

MAD MAX

"I am not gonna sleep until one of them nigga's is dead!" Mad Max yells. "They killed my baby," Lizanne says, crying. "We've been friends since grade school." "We're gonna get them nigga's back," Mad Max says, giving her a hug. "That won't bring Elise back!" She shouts. "God! She's gone! Oh my God, she's gone!" Shayla is boohoo crying also. They all grew up together in Memphis, Tennessee. "Baby, after we put these niggas to sleep, we need to open up something legit and fall back." "Me and Shayla know how to do nails and hair. Let's open a full- scale beauty salon, hire a masseuse, do it big." "I like that ma." "Me and Tear can run the barber shop side and push weight to only a few nigga's that's really eating. That nigga Black Isaac is their muscle. He likes to go out. We're gonna snatch his bitch-ass up if he goes to the Zanzi bar tonight. Ain't nobody but him is the one who put Elise to sleep." "Say no more," Tear says. Ready to put somebody in the ground.

COOL AL

"Baby, are you ready?" Cool Al shouts. "Yes king," answers Seleena.

Her and Cool Al are at the condo he bought for them in New Tampa. "I need to make a quick run and we're going to enjoy a good week of fun in the sun. They're going to Miami for a week to let the heat die down off him and to do some shopping for her birthday present. Cool Al promised her a new car. He's going to Dade to do it because he doesn't want to go through Uncle Jahiem. They are in her BMW.

Ten minutes later they are heading to Tampa Heights. "Come outside," Cool Al says into his phone. "For show," Black Isaac says walking out of the trap by Central Court apartments.

Cool Al is already out of the door. "Sup, my dude?" He says, giving him some dap. "Cooling," responds Black Isaac. "You did your thang with that bitch; I dig that." "All day, you know if I tell you it's a hit, that's what it is." "Listen main man, I'm headed on a lil vacation. We have 11 bricks and 23 pounds of weed on deck. Keep you one of the bricks and 1O pounds of the weed for your great work. The other 1O B's and remainder of the pounds, spread them out to our traps in Palm River and the two over here in the Heights. Take $150,000 to Cash once you get it. I should be back by then. I want you to chill until I get back. Hell, go to Orlando with a bitch or something. "Here," Cool Al says, handing him the keys to his Bentley coupe. "It's at my mom's house. I'll call you on Saturday."

"Love my nigga," Black Isaac says walking off.

Getting back in the car, Cool Al says, "let's go baby."

BLACK ISAAC

"Yesss," he screams walking back into the trap. He's been down with C.M.F. for years and has made his share of money, gambling, clubbing and fucking hoes has kept him at a $100,000 dollar nigga. He's worth more than that with his jewels and 3 whips; he has a Chrysler 300 on 24's, a Dodge Magnum also on 24's and a Dodge Ram truck he just put 26's on. Tonight, is Friday. He has a free brick and 10 pounds. He's going to pick up the yellow Bentley coupe and head to University Mall and going to 112 til about 2:00 am, then the thug in him has to go on Main Street to stop by the Zanzi Bar to show his ass. "I'm fucking some exclusive shit tonight," he says to himself.

Later that night...

Black Isaac is super drunk leaving Club 112. He's on his way to the Zanzi Bar on Main Street. He's only gonna go show his face and act silly in the Bentley. He's on a mission; he caught a dime-piece from Clearwater in 112. She was in line waiting to go inside when he pulled up in the Bentley.

He's so fresh tonight in an all-black Ferragamo linen suit with the Ferragamo hard bottom gators to match, big chain and a bracelet full of diamonds, with his black Jacob's the Jeweler iced out watch.

"Hello," he says, answering his phone as he's stepping out on Main Street in front of the Food Caboose. "What's up King Black?" That was the name Black Isaac gave all the hoes he met tonight. "You baby. What's good?" King Black responds.

"You coming to my place in Clearwater or do you want me to stay over here in Tampa with you?" Chrissy says sexily. "We're gonna get a suite here at the Marriot downtown. As a matter of fact, you can meet me there in..."

That was all King Black got out before someone hit him across his head with a .45 magnum. Talking with his head down, slipping is about to cause him his life...

MAD MAX

"Open the trunk," Mad Max says. People are looking at him and Tear. They are in all black and masked up, so he doesn't care. Tear wanted to go bare face to make a statement. Mad Max promised him they were going to make a statement with what they are about to do to dude. Lizanne pops the trunk. Her and Shayla are driving the Intrepid. "Come on let's go," Mad Max says, as him and Tear jump into the backseat. Go to our condo. We should be good this time of night.

30 minutes later....

Tear and Mad Max has Black Isaac tied to a workout bench in the garage of Lizanne and Mad Max's condo. "Bitch ass nigga, you ready to die?" Mad Max says, slapping the spit out of

Black Isaac's mouth. "I was born to die pussy!" Black Isaac replies. "Let me handle this nigga Memphis style babe." Lizanne says, stepping up. "Bitch ass nigga! Since you killed my homegirl I'm gonna turn you into one," she says opening his pants. "Come on Shayla, let's give him a makeover." They cut his dick off, arched his eyebrows, and put lipstick on his lips. Then all four of them took turns pissing on him. Tear ends his life by cutting his throat. "Now for the grand finale, babe. See if you got a dress big enough to fit on this pussy. We are gonna tie him to a pole outside of the Zanzi Bar." "It's a dirty game!" Shouts Lizanne smiling.

COOL AL

"You fancy, huh?" Cool Al says. "You mutha fucking right," Seleena shouts. They are leaving 305 Customs in Miami. Cool Al just traded in her 740 BMW for a fire-engine red Aston Martin DB7. "This is how your queen is supposed to ride," Seleena says while gunning the car to 90 miles per hour. "All day," Cool Al says. "Let's go shopping on South Beach and head to our suite so I can make love to your pretty dick first," Seleena says. "I want you to fuck me in the ass and spank me." Cool Al's dick flies to attention.

20 minutes later....

Seleena skillfully wraps her mouth around Cool Al's dick. "Uuuummmm, shit baby," moans Cool Al. Seleena is slurping, gagging, and bobbing her head like a woman possessed.

She's swallowing Cool Al's 8 inches like she's sucking her thumb. Cool Al's eyes are rolling into the back of his head. "Fuck!" He yells spinning around. Seleena screams, "now punish this ass!" Grabbing a bottle of hot lubricant from under her pillow, she reaches back and squeezes some down her ass crack. "Now fuck this tight little ass until you make me cry," she yells. "Wait! Pull my hair and smack my ass cheeks first. I love it rough." Cool Al yanks her hair and slides his dick roughly into her asshole. "Ooohhh, shit daddy! Get your ass," screams Seleena in pain and pleasure, which has Cool Al in a zone. "Goddamn Chic, you're trying to run me crazy," Cool Al yells. He ain't never had an experience so wild. "You make me like this," she replies. "Baby, I'm tired of hiding. I want to enjoy my queen status." "It's almost time baby," Cool Al responds.

It's a process. I'm on phase 3 now."
"Phase 3?" "Yes. Who do you think had
Mrs. T kidnapped?" "What?" Yells
Seleena. "Or Fat Dre killed? To be the
king sometimes you have to rule like
they did in the Old Testament." "What
about Cash's bitch ass?" Seleena
questions. She's still bitter about how he
up and left her. "Soon as I get me
another connect, he's gone." "That's
why I love you," Seleena says giving his
dick a kiss.

CASH

"Where are you, pretty boy?" "What are you the police?" Cool Al says playfully. Heatedly, Cash says, "no the police is putting Black Isaac in a body bag as we speak!" "Oh shit," Cool Al screams. "What the hell happened?" "Maybe you should tell me. Your Bentley is parked 15 feet away from his body, which he has on a Dolce Gabbana dress." "The fuck?" Yells Cool Al. "Our nigga wasn't gay!" "Duh!" Cash responds. "Some of our people say 5 minutes after he pulled up on Main in your car, somebody kidnapped him. They found him this morning tied to a pole, eyes arched, with lipstick and the dress on." "I told him to go out of town," Cool Al yells. "Damn, damn, damn. Fat Dre, now Black Isaac," Cool Al yells. "Dirty Game retaliation is what this is. The police are gonna be trippin. You need to shut down shop until shit cools down," Cash says. "I'm in Miami, bro." "Okay, I'll swing by and shut down all the spots. You stay in Miami for a couple of weeks. I'll have your car towed to your mom's house. We can't be seen at the wake or the funeral. But I'll make sure he goes out in style." Cool Al is quiet. Black Isaac was his dude. He feels responsible. Snapping back, he says, "it's casualties in war. I love ya bro." "I love ya more," Cash responds disconnecting the call.

DESTINY

"This is the second homicide scene in two weeks. Ain't that Bentley the one they say Cool Al drives?" Destiny says, pointing at the Bentley. "Yellow with chrome and yellow rims." Detective Miller confirms. "Why is it just sitting here?" "I don't know but I don't believe in coincidences." "Me either," Destiny says. "And look at this body. This shows anger. A slit throat, penis cut off, put in a dress; like saying you killed our girl." "It's a message. We have to bring some pressure to these dudes before this bloodbath continues," Detective Miller says. "Yeah, Sgt. Graham is gonna be on our asses come Monday morning."

CHAPTER 27

Stop Being Greedy

DESTINY

2 Months later...

"It's like these dudes just disappeared," Destiny says to Detective Miller. They have been doing small stings, made a few nice arrests but nothing on neither the CMF or Dirty Money. "Give them another week or so. They are too greedy. They won't keep their spots closed for too much longer and we'll be on their asses. All the people we've arrested the past 2 months; I've broken nine that can't wait to do some CI (Confidential Informant) work." "Yeah, I've broken four myself," Destiny says with a smile.

"We have been living on the job. I'm going out of town this weekend. I'll be back on Monday. Hey, ride with me really quick," Destiny says. "I'm your partner," Von replies laughing.

"Smartass, this is a personal mission," Destiny laughs back. Ten minutes later they are parking their Ford Taurus in the parking lot of Fee's beauty salon on Louisiana and 34th. Going inside, Destiny is in awe. Fee's shop is very nice. Fee comes running up to her. Grabbing her in a bear hug, Fee starts to cry. "Thank you soooo much," Destiny Fee yells. "Destiny gave her $2,000 and helped her get a loan through Bank of America, along with the money she's saved. She was able to open her own shop. "This is my auntie Fee, "Destiny says to Det. Von. "Hello," he says checking Fee out. Fee is fine as hell. She still doesn't have any kids and works out 3 to 4 times a week. "Nice to meet you," Fee says, catching him checking her out.

"He's cute," she thinks to herself.
"Come on, let me show you around."
Fee kept everybody, including Destiny
out of the shop until today, which is her
grand opening. She wanted to surprise
her, and she wanted no opinions, as far
as decorating. She had this all done in
her mind before she left prison. "Auntie,
it's so nice in here! You did a great job.
That's what I do," Fee says smiling.

CASH

"Boy, stop all that complaining," Cash says. "Fuck you," shooting his big sister a bird. She is getting married to Pale and wanted Cash to be there. "We are at the courthouse and you wanted me to dress casual? Ma and pop begged you to let them throw you a nice big wedding and you declined." "Yes, I did. I'd rather have the money. I want to open a Super T's in St. Pete next month and I'm trying to buy a new house." "Since when has money been an issue with the Jones's?" Cash replies. "My husband wants us to have something for ourselves. So, I figure I'll take our wedding money as a wedding gift and invest it. So here we are, young man." Camille says, messing with her little brother. "We're gonna renew our vows in a year and have a big wedding and reception.

Pale didn't want to bring our child into the world with unwed parents; he's on this spiritual thing," Camille laughs. "He's right," Cash replies. "How many months are you ugly?" "I look like your daddy," she teases. Cash laughs.

DESTINY

"I'm on my way to your house," Destiny says. "Okay beautiful. I'm packed and waiting on you."

Ten minutes later, Destiny gets out of her car and greets Cash with a big hug and a kiss on the lips. "Damn, I've missed you so much," she says. "Not as much as I've missed you," Cash replies. The past two months they have only talked on the phone and hug here and there due to Destiny going so hard at work and Cash going to school, working at the car lot and shutting down all the spots.

They're now on their way to Orlando for the weekend. Cash has a suite reserved at the West Chase resort and a 3-day pass for them to go to Universal Studios, Disney World, or Island of Adventure. "I'm so excited," Destiny screams.

She has never been to Universal Studios, Disney World or Island of Adventure. Cash has been to all three over 5 times, but he's excited too because this is the first time he'll be sleeping in a bed with Destiny and he's also happy to be making a dream of hers become a reality. "Well, let's get going baby," Cash says, taking Destiny's tote bags out of her car and putting them inside the Yukon he rented. "This is so nice," Destiny says while leaning her seat back.

Looking at the scenery as they head down I-4, "You look tired. Go on ahead and get you a lil nap in. We have about an hour drive." "Thank you, baby," Destiny says, turning down the CD, "Ask of You" by Rafael Saddid is on. Cash is feeling guilty as he's watching Destiny sleep.

Here he is in the car with a narcotics detective; a woman that has endured so much hurt in her young life, grew up so rough, and defeated the odds. He gets so much energy and motivation from her. Seeing her sleeping peacefully, he vows to love and protect her until his dying day. She's beautiful. Her skin is so smooth. He can't wait to make love to her.

"Dedicated" by R. Kelly comes on. Cash starts singing to the music:
"You have given me the best f you and you have made my dreams come true and after all the things that you have done…"

Destiny is not asleep; she keeps her eyes close and enjoys Cash trying to sing. She feels like he is really the one. He's so sensitive when dealing with her. His heart is genuine, he knows how to treat a woman.

He's sexy, handsome face, he's ambitious, smart. All that I ever dreamed of in a man. I'm going to give him some tonight. I hope he passes that test and is not a selfish lover or has a tiny dick. She laughs at that thought. As "Butta Love" by Next comes on, Cash gently rubs her thigh. "Beautiful, we are here." Looking at his watch he says, "it's 2:25 pm. How about we go to Disney World first? We can go to Universal Studios, which is my favorite, tomorrow, so we can get there early. I want to take you on so many rides there." "Okay baby. Don't you think we should take our stuff and check in to our room first?" "Yeah, that makes sense," Cash says getting off the interstate.

After taking their bags up to their resort, they head to Disney World and have a great time. They ride Space Mountain. Cash wins her a few teddy bears.

They eat giant turkey legs, milk shakes, take photos and buy souvenirs for their nieces and nephews. After they leave there, Cash takes Destiny to the Crab House. They bring her shrimp to the table and cook them in front of her. She's so giddy. Cash even plays a joke on her by telling the staff it was her birthday. All of the staff come to their table singing Happy Birthday to her. She punches Cash in the arm. She's so embarrassed. She doesn't even tell the people it's not her birthday. They share a bottle of Dom Perignon, which has them both tipsy because neither of them a drinker.

Upon entering their suite, Destiny is in awe. She thought the suite Tiger took her to was nice, but this resort is on another level. It has a 60' Plasma TV hanging across the king-size bed, separate walk-in closets, a huge 6-seat garden tub with a separate enclosed stand-up shower. His and her sinks and a nice balcony overlooking downtown Orlando. Grabbing her tote bag, Destiny goes into the gigantic bathroom. "I'll be back, sweetie." After taking a hot bubble bath, Destiny emerges from the bathroom in a sexy lace purple Victoria Secret lingerie set. Cash eyes damn near pop out of his head. He's so stunned while looking at Destiny's beautiful, sexy and toned body. He's already taken a shower and is in a pair of white Polo boxers and a Polo tank top. "Come here," he says pulling her towards him.

Cash begins to softly kiss her lips. Destiny wraps her arms around his neck and returns his loving kiss. As they are kissing, Cash slowly relieves her of the sexy lingerie. She begins to tremble as his hands and lips caress every inch of her soft body.

He is watching her eyes as he's paying attention to her most feminine areas. His body is throbbing and he' s so excited. He dips his head and disappears between her thighs. "Aaahhh," Destiny moans from the intense pleasure. Her moans and whimpers increase but Cash shows no signs of slowing down. Destiny begins to beg for mercy as she crimps the sheets, turning her head from side to side in ecstasy. "Oooh God Cash," she yells. Cash is on a mission; he wants her to reach the ultimate peak of satisfaction. She has to succumb to the undeniable pleasure he had dreamed of giving her. He's enjoying the moment as much as she is. "Ooohhh baby, you taste so good," Cash moans. That makes Destiny say things she has never said. "Ooooh fuck Cashmere, I love you," she yells.

Hearing exactly what he already knew, motivates him to torture her a little more, until she screams. Cash is speechless. He takes great pleasure seeing his Destiny satisfied. He quickly moves between her legs, all the passion between them comes with explosive forces as he pushes into her super tight wet pussy. Savoring her body and soul all at once, he makes lover to her with such fervor, position after position. "Yesss Cashmere, get it baby," Destiny screams. "Is this my pussy, baby?" "All yours, baby. I'm your Destiny. No other man will ever get it again." "I love you Destiny," Cash shouts. "Oohh God I'm cumming," yells Destiny. "Me too baby," Cash screams letting his seeds of passion release inside of her. Cash trails kisses down to her navel and back up to her lips. "You're the woman for me and I'm never going to let you go," Cash says.

"I love you Cashmere. Please stay committed to us as I promise I always will." "All my life," Cash responds. They fall asleep half tangled in each other's arms.

They have a great day the next day at Universal Studios. Cash rides all his favorite rides with her; Jaws, E.T., Back to the Future and Terminator 3. They ride Earthquake, eat at the Hard Rock, bought more souvenir's and call it a day. They make love all Saturday night.

CHAPTER 28

Power vs. Money

MAD MAX

"We are leaving in the morning, so you can call Shayla and tell her to get off my main man's dick and be ready." "Fuck Rondo, every nigga is sweating my girl." Rondo and Shayla have been an item the past 3 weeks. They have been in Miami. Tear chose to stay in Tampa, to keep his eyes on the streets. It's his phone call that has Mad Max ready to get back to Tampa and put their traps back pumping. Tear explains that with C.M.F. in hiding, the streets were dry. "I'm ready, baby. Just remember what I said," Lizanne says, reminding him about them getting something legit to fall back on. "I got you baby. Give us six months of pumping all 3 spots and we can retire."

"I'm with you, daddy. Let's get it."
"Let's go get Shayla and pick up the work. We can be back in Tampa by 6:30 pm and the spots can be rocking by 8:30. Tear already has the team up and hungry." "Dirty Game baby!" Lizanne shouts.

COOL AL

"Bro, I need you to go see Papi," Cool Al says. Him and Cash are at Ryan's Steak House on 78th street having dinner. "I'm only making a few more runs, Pretty Boy. I'm 10 months away from finishing school. Baby Doll gets out in 11 months. I'm taking off as soon as she's free. The first thing I'm opening is a Hungry Howie's. In a few months, I'm buying a few houses to flip. If you want in, let me know," Cash says. "I may but right now I need to get these traps back up and jumping. I talked to the team. Everybody ain't got millions put up. They are starving." "If they stop spending their money on stupid shit, they'll have some money put up," Cash says, looking Cool Al in the eyes, letting him know he caught his flip ass psychology.

"Yeah, you right," Cool Al says. In his mind he's saying, why am I arguing with a dead man? "I'm only gonna open up one of the spots in Tampa Heights. The other 3 is a go though. I just want to cut down on the traffic." "Do as you choose," Cash responds. "I want 50 stacks for making the play. I ain't dealing with none of the other shit." "That's cool," Cool Al replies. He's hot that Cash is talking to him like he's still the king. "When are you gonna be on point?" Cool Al asks. "I'll call you," Cash says, getting up. "I love you bro," Cool Al says. "I love you more," Cash says, leaving the restaurant.

DESTINY

One Week Later...

"We are moving today, not tomorrow, but today," Sgt. Graham shouts. Destiny and Detective Von have people that says the crews C.M.F. and Dirty Money are back in business. "I want them in Orient Road Jail by 8:00 pm tonight. Do I make myself clear?" "Yes, sir!" All the detectives yell. "Detective Destiny and Von will head the raids. Ya'll put a plan together, call TPD for assistance and get to moving." "Listen ya'll," Destiny yells; "We are gonna have two 13 person crews. I want to attack two of their traps at a time. Today we're gonna hit two of the C.M.F. crew spots. The one in Oakhurst in West Tampa and the one in Robles Park at 10:00 am in the morning. We're gonna hit Dirty Game in Oak Village and Johnson Court.

Does anybody have any questions?"

The raid goes well, 16 members of C.M.F. are arrested. Over 25 pounds of weed, 3 kilos of crack cocaine are found, along with $26,000 in cash; no weapons were recovered. The next day they get 10 Dirty Game members, 15 pounds of weed, 200 ecstasy pills, two½ kilos of crack cocaine and seize over $21,000 in cash. They have been questioning the workers and they have broken 3 on one side and 2 on the other. They now know all about Cool Al and all his top lieutenants. Cash was lucky he was only mentioned once and by the name Cash. That snitch was a new person; he was telling something he heard. He doesn't know nothing about this Cash he mentioned, so they don't pursue the Cash angle. The detective's biggest things are the information they got on Cool Al.

The cars he drives, places he hangs out. Same with Dirty Money. They told on Tear and Shayla. They didn't have nothing on Lizanne, but they told Mad Max is the king pin and about the Porsche.

"Good job," yells Sgt. Graham. "Now all we gotta do is build a case on these lieutenants and Cool Al. They will give up their connects. Same with Dirty Money. Get Shayla and this Tear person and we get Mad Max." "They are brothers," Destiny shouts. "I've already gotten their names. The oldest is Maxwell Roberts and the little brother Terrell Roberts, is Tear. Maxwell just got out of prison a little over 2 years ago. He did 11 years for attempted murder. "I want these monsters in prison," Sgt. Graham says, walking off.

CASH

Beep Beep! "Who is this?" Cash says looking into the fire red Aston Martin DB7. He's coming out of 7-11 on Skipper Rd. Somebody has blown their horn at him. The dark tint makes it hard to see inside. He sees a chrome tag on the front that reads, QUEEN. To his surprise, Seleena opens the driver's door. "Hey handsome," she says, looking even more beautiful than the last time he saw her. "What's good, Seleena?" He says as she's getting out. Seleena looks stunning in a tight red Givenchy dress hugging her sexy body. Her long jet -black hair is hanging down to her ass, which is poking out the back of the dress. She knows she's all that. She has on a white gold diamond necklace with the earrings, bracelet, and engagement ring to match.

The iced-out Chanel watch is glistening on her wrist. She gives him a hug. Seleena says, "how have you been?" "I've been cooling. I finish college in a few months. After that, I'm taking off on the business tip. How did you know I was in the store?" Cash says. "I saw you getting out of that," Seleena says, pointing at his Intrepid. "I was with you for 4 years. I can spot you from a 100-yards out." "Looks like you're on top of the world," Cash says stroking her ego. "Yes, the king takes care of his queen," she replies. "I see," Cash says. "You're looking great." "Thank you. You know can't nobody take your place; I miss you so much," Seleena says, really meaning the part about missing him. He used to treat her like a woman, not just a show piece. Curious to see who her king is, Cash is goes along with her game.

What if she is sleeping with the enemy? He thinks. Because ain't but so many niggas can afford to spend like she's looking. "Give me your number so we can chat from time to time," Seleena says. Cash has two phones. He gives her his burn out number. "I must be going," she says. "I need to stock up my condo. I'll be calling," she says getting inside of her car before pulling off. Cash notices something as she pulls off, she never said who the king was. Knowing Seleena, had she been with a Buccaneer player, big-time rapper, or an actor, she would have loved to rub it in his face. She showed in her emotions that she is still bitter towards him.

CHAPTER 29

It's Levels to This Shit

DESTINY

"So you are telling me you can get me a one on one with Tear?" "Yes, I can! Take you with me to cop. You have to promise me your gonna arrest him and protect me," Malcom says. He's one of the guys she arrested at the trap in Oak Village. He is on probation for getting caught with a pistol. He promised to work for Destiny if she could get him out. He knows a trafficking charge on top of the violation would be at least 6 years with 3 minimum mandatory because of the gun. He ain't never been to prison and ain't trying to go. He's 22 and has 2 kids on the way. Destiny did her thing and got him released. Now he has to work his case off.

Him and her are at one of his baby momma's apartments across from King High School.

"So, tell me the plan," Destiny says. Detective Von is with her listening. "He only sells weight and he's making people drive out to the trap they have out in Wimauma. I'll call him. Tell him I need a 125 (street code for 125 grams). I'll take you with me like you are one of my hoes giving me a ride." "You're smart. That could work. Why don't you young brothers use ya'll brilliant minds to think of positive plans to stay out of prison?" Destiny asks him. "You have two kids on the way. They are gonna need a father. Someone to love, support, and protect them. After we get this done, I'm gonna help you get in school or find a job. How would you like that?"

"I could try." "Trying is lying. You have to do it." "Okay, I will." "Be ready in two days," Destiny says walking towards the door to leave. "Yes Ma'am.

CASH

"What? Dad, please tell me you are not serious," Cash yells. "He's gone, son. I'm sitting here trying to console your mom. Her and Mr. Carlos had a unique bond. She's crying like a baby." C-Money just told Cash that Mr. Carlos died of a heart attack earlier today. "I'm blowed. When Alvinia, his wife of 61 years, called me... I knew something was not right. She said he was in their garden with her and next thing you know, he grabs his heart and that was it. He was dead when the ambulance got there." "I'm done pop. I've found the woman of my dreams. I made love to her for the first-time last week pop, and I felt the magic. That look and feeling you described

When you first seen ma. I felt this with her." "Well, you need to bring her out here and let me and your mother meet her." "You've already seen her, pop." "The young woman at your school, Cash?" "That's her pop. I told you I felt something that day we bumped into each other." "That's good, son. A true man needs a cause, an adventure, and a good woman to love, cherish, protect and rescue. I thank god every day for your lovely momma," C-Money says. "She's all that, pop. I'm going to see if I can get her to fix her busy schedule for us to come soon. She's a narcotics detective." "What?" Yells C- Money. Laughing, Cash says, "fate is something else ain't it? How I was born on the same day and in the same hospital as her?" "Get the fuck outta here!" C-Money states.

"What do I need to do? I owe Mr. C a couple dollars." "I'll get back with your mom, we'll get it to Alvinia. I'll get back at you soon." "Ok, pop. Tell my mother I love and miss her." "What about me?" C- Money says. "You already know old man." "We love and miss you too."

DESTINY

"I really needed this," Destiny says. Her, Meme and Auntie Donna are at Gold Ring in Ybor City having lunch. "I miss ya'll," Destiny says all excited. "Ooohh boy. Cashmere has laid the D down," Meme says smiling. "Um huh!" Auntie Donna laughs. "You should have seen how she was floating when she came back last Sunday." "Whatever," Destiny says. "Let me go first," Auntie Donna says, surprising them. "You know I've been going to Charlie T's to get my eyes arched since I was young, well the week before last, while I was in there waiting to get in the chair when this sexy, tall, brown-skin brother comes in, dressed all nice, in a linen suit. I'm watching him, he's watching me. Next thing I know he sits next to me and asks me my name and tells me I'm the most beautiful woman he's seen since he moved to Tampa.

He's from Texas. His job transferred him down here. He's a professor at USF. His name is Draymond. Dr. Williams to y'all. He's 46, has one adult daughter, has never been married and fine as wine. We have been on two dates so far. He took me to the museum and to Channel side for bowling. We're going out to dinner tonight." "Yaaaah," Destiny shouts. "I'm so happy for you." "That's great, Auntie." Meme says. "Me and Rick got engaged over the weekend," Meme says flashing her skinny diamond ring. "I'm loving my new job. My mother-in-law and I are getting really close. She's like a second mother to me. The kids love Rick. We are trying to have our own child." "That's so good Meme. I'm so proud of you." "Me too," Auntie says. "I'm in love," Destiny sings. "Cashmere is the one. He texted me on the way here saying he wants to take me to L.A. to meet his parents next month. I am so alive around him. I feel like I've been waiting my whole life for him. He asked me to move in with him. After I give him some more time, I'm gonna go for it." "Okay!" Meme yells. "I like Cashmere and he was crazy about you from the day he saw you," Meme says. "As long as you're happy Destiny. You know I am. From all I hear this is a real good young man." "He is," Meme and Destiny say in union.

CASH

"I'm on my way now," Cash says. He's on the phone with Cool Al. Cool Al asked him to meet him in Central Court Apartments. Damn, Cash thinks to himself as he's riding down Central Avenue, deep in thought. The game has been good to him, he has over 1.6 mil. put up since the sale of the Rolls Royce. He's met the woman of his dreams. He's a couple semesters away from having a college degree, never been arrested, shot or robbed. As of now, Kuske advised him he's not on any federal or state radar. Right at the age of 25, a black male couldn't ask for more.

"I'm done," he shouts to himself-hyping himself up for the conversation that's bound to turn into a confrontation with Cool Al.

As he turns into Central Court apartments, "less is more," he says to himself. "I'm gonna tell him about Mr. Carlos and let him know I'm done. I don't need to explain myself." Pulling in he sees Cool Al leaning up against his Maybach, with a neck full of diamonds. "I'm not about to be seen with this hot-ass idiot," Cash says. Rolling down his window, he tells Cool Al to get in. "Sup, bro?" Cool Al says, giving him dap. "I'm cooling," Cash replies pulling off. He's going to Regan Park so he and Cool Al can talk. "Bro, I need you to go and see Mr. C," Cool Al responds. "He's dead," Cash responds. "Fuck you mean he's dead?" "Just what I said. He had a heart attack a couple of days ago." "And I'm just hearing about this?" Cool Al shouts, heatedly. Cash just shrugs. "So, what are we gonna do now?" Cool Al asks. "I'm not sure what you're gonna do, but I'm done.

Mr. C. was our pops only connect the whole time they were getting money. I'm not about to step out of that circle." "What about his cousin, brothers? Shit, he ain't got no kids?" Cool Al yells. 'I don't know and I'm not trying to find out. I'm done bro. Game over. I'm onto some other thoughts." "So, fuck me and the crew huh?" "Ya'll are all grown and can make ya'll own choices. I told you, you can eat with me on the legit business tip. The same energy and resources we put into doing dirt, we can use to become legit millionaires. And what crew?" Cash shouts. "Two spots were just hit a couple of weeks ago. You trying to go to prison? Or let a hater kill you? The Dirty Game crew is going to hell real soon." "I have a tip on where the nigga Mad Max and that bitch that robbed me lays their heads," Cool Al says. "So what?" Cash responds.

"In a month, another crew will form and what about the nigga Tear? He's gonna go mad, when something happens to his brother, a lot more blood will shed."

"Fuck them pussies. I'm gonna respect your mind bro because I love you," Cool Al shouts. But I'm not done. There is no such thing as quitting. You rest, you sleep, you pout, you can even cry. You can get mad and sad, but you can't quit. You're allowed to step down, but not quit. You know what stop means to a survivor? Sit, think, observe, and plan. Quitting is dying. And I'm the surviving kind, not the dying kind. Kings don't resign. They either die or remain King. Fuck them crackers and fuck the haters. Kings can't be humiliated. If you're weak, you're weak. You ain't got no business with the throne. Tear is next to die. Blood is the coin of power. All through history, no conqueror has made his mark without shedding blood. Napo1eon, Alexander the Great, Julies Caesar, Attila The Hun, Hitler, Nino, Scarface; need I name more?" Cool Al says. "When things look simple, they usually are not. Good or bad are in the eyes of the definer. Good luck, pretty boy. I'll always love you." Cash responds pulling back up to Central Court. Before Cool Al steps out he says, "nothing hurts more deeper than betrayal not even death because I can perceive death. Love is an action word." Cash is crushed. Him and Cool Al have been best friends their whole lives but as his pop told him, you don't really have friends, just enemies and people who could become your enemy. Betrayals start with lies hidden in the shadows of silence. Cash has a lasting thought as Cool Al is headed towards his car... he didn't say he loved me back.

DESTINY

Destiny is excited. She's riding in a Chevy Camaro convertible rental car on her way to Wimauma to make a buy from Tear. Malcom is driving. Detective Miller and two more detectives are trailing them in unmarked cars. She has been up since 5:30 in the morning rehearsing her part. This will be a major break in the case against the Dirty Money crew. They are not going to make the arrest today. She just wants to secure a transaction. They will then get a search warrant and come back next week and bust the spot.

"You ready?" Malcolm says pulling into a rundown house on a corner lot in Wimauma. "Let's go," Destiny says grabbing her purse.

"Yeah," Tear screams coming to the door. "I called you 20 minutes ago," Malcolm says.

"What's up Slim?" Tear says allowing Malcolm to enter the trap. "Who is lil momma right here?" Tear says, eyeing Destiny lustfully. "My new chic," Malcolm replies getting off by slapping Destiny on her butt. Destiny is looking super sexy in a BeBe tight fitting short set and a pair of Mark Jacob heels. "You got you one there," Tear laughs. Destiny takes control; she's already peeped the trap. It has 5 monitors on a big nightstand, so camera's must be hidden outside. It's a girl standing in the kitchen putting weed into sandwich bags. It's a scale on the table, a guy is on the couch, counting money. "I'm ready to go," Destiny shouts. "Is he," she says, pointing at Tear, "going to do this for us or not?" "What is she talking about?" Tear asks Malcom. "I told her I was gonna flip her money for her. She thinks I'm on some fuckery with the prices and the profit, so I told her I would show her the whole process, every step of the way. A 125 is how much?" Malcom says. "$3,000," Tear replies. Pulling out a wad of cash from her purse, Destiny says, "and how much should I make?" Tear says, "depending on how he sells it, if he breaks it all down to singles, you will make about $7,000 selling 5's, 10's, and 20-dollar rocks. But if he wants a quick flip, he can sell each ounce for $900 and the half for $450." "That's a little over $4,000," Destiny finishes for him. "The single sales will take how long to complete?" "Maybe a little over a week if money is coming," Malcom replies. "The flip I could do in 3 days tops." "Here," she says handing Tear the $3,000. "We'll be seeing you in a week. I like the sound of that $7,000." Destiny says, smiling. Tear goes to the kitchen goes into a cabinet over the sink and grabs a sandwich bag filled with crack.

He gets the scale from the chic, clears it, and sets the bag on top. It reads 126 grams. He says, "it's all there lil momma," handing the bag to Destiny. "If you need to ever come solo, my number is 813-293-5419," he says walking them to the door. He wants to fuck Destiny. As she's walking off, she puts on a lil show, slinging her ass. "Damn," Tear yells loud so she can hear him. "I'll pay for it," he says smiling. Getting into the rental car, Destiny says, "touch my ass again," punching Malcom hard in his ribs. Laughing, he says, "I had to make it look good." "Whatever," she says smiling.

CASH

5 days later...

"I'm so glad you could make it on such short notice. My uncle had the place on reserve for him and his special friend, but a bad argument last week made it available to us," Cash says. Him and Destiny are in first class on an airplane headed to Hawaii. Destiny is in awe. She's never been on a plane, let alone out of the country. "This is a dream come true," she comments. "Since I was a small child watching Hawaii 5-0, I've always wanted to come to this place." Cash remembered her telling him this one night, when they had stayed up one night talking on the phone. He vowed he was gonna make it happen asap. He is smiling. He loves to put a smile on Destiny's face. "I've always wanted to come here too," Cash says.

Which is true. C-Money and Tonya offered to take him. He declined. He said he wanted to go one day with the woman of his dreams. "We are staying on this big island they have," Cash says. "As long as I'm with you, it could be the small island, I'd be happy," Destiny replies. Damn, I've got a good queen Cash thinks, savoring her comment.

The next day...

With their hoolas (lays) on their necks, they are in swim gear walking around the island having the time of their lives. "Thank you sooo much," Destiny says. "Baby, I'm so happy being here with you. I owe you, thanks for this joy. Come on," Destiny says, pulling him toward their suite.

"Let's take a hot shower," she says pulling him towards the standup shower. They disrobe quickly and are nude in the shower under the hot water.

Destiny takes a sponge, put some shower gel on it and begins to bathe Cash. She gently cleans his entire body. As the warm water is rinsing him off, Destiny drops to her knees. She grabs Cash's semi-erect penis and puts the head into her mouth. "Oooh shit," Cash yells. Destiny has watched 5 porn flicks and Googled how to suck dick. She's trying to make this moment a joy to Cash. Cash has his eyes closed. He feels like he's died and is now gone to heaven while feeling Destiny's warm mouth on his manhood.

She tells him that she has never tried this before. "Damn baby," he moans. As Cash's dick began to pulsate in her mouth, Destiny slightly grips his manhood with her hand, relaxing her jaws.

She pulls away, letting her tongue massage his tip. Looking up at his face, she hears low moans of pleasure corning from his mouth. Destiny says,

"don't pick at me. It's my first time."
Destiny begins to kiss, lick, and suck all
over Cash's 9-inch pole. "Damn, that
feels good baby," Cash moans. Destiny
stands up and starts planting soft kisses
down Cash's neck before whispering in
his ear, "don't think about nothing.
Please give me my dick." She turns
around and bends over.

Cash slides inside her warm juices with
pleasure. "Ooh God," she yells out in
ecstasy as Cash is bringing a sensation
of pleasure that she's never felt. "Yesss
daddy!" Destiny screams. Her screams
turn into a soft cry as Cash keeps
stroking her wet tight walls at a steady
pace. She's meeting him stroke for
stroke. "I'm cummin," Destiny yells. "I
love you," Destiny cries out, totally

obviously to anything but how much
pleasure Cash is giving her. "Oooh god,
this pussy is so good," Cash shouts.

"I'm about to cum again," yells Destiny. Cash could no longer hold back. He cums so hard. Every muscle in his body seems to collapse. "I love you," he screams. Laying down on the bamboo canopy bed 5 minutes later, Cash says, "I'm sorry." "For what?" Destiny questions. "I saw you crying. I thought for some reason you were upset." "How can I be upset? When I'm at this sexy island with you, our hotel room is sitting on top of a cliff with views of the big island, there's a tiered swimming pool connected by waterfalls. This place is so beautiful. I've never been out of Florida," Destiny says. "It's not even close to as breathtaking as you," Cash replies. "I love you Destiny and I want to spend the rest of my life with you."

"My tears were of joy, Cash. I want to grow old with you." "Move in with me when we get back." "Okay, baby. I love you."

CHAPTER 30

I'm going in...

DESTINY

"This guy is dangerous. I saw guns in this place so everybody make sure they have on their bulletproof vests," Destiny shouts. Her, 1O detectives and 10 quad squad members are gearing up to go and bust the spot where Tear and some of the Dirty Money crew is located. "I'm gonna go inside and try to put them off high alert. Once I push the panic button, ya'll need to come in at full force," Destiny says. "I need you to be extremely careful," Sgt. Graham says. "Remember, these guys are not only drug dealers, but are killers." Let's get it popping," shouts. Destiny, she is hyped up.

CASH

"Damn Cuzzo you looking good," Cash shouts, as he's giving Baby Doll a hug. She's getting out of Camille's SUV. Cash was not going to Coleman to pick her up. The feds could have been watching, so he sent Camille. He waited at Camille's house, playing the game (Xbox) with his nephew (Supreme). "Glad to be free, Cuzzo. Ready to take off on this business shit." "Look at you," Cash says seeing Baby Doll dressed like a woman for the first time in his life. Camille bought her coming home clothes. Baby Doll is tall, almost 5'9, light brown skin. Her hair is in dreads, they are hanging damn near to her ass. She has a sexy, slim shape, but a fat round ass to go with it. She is looking like a dime piece in the Gucci tight fitting dress with a pair of Robert Cavalli boots, some gold and diamond accessories on her neck, wrist and in her ears. "If I'm gonna take over the corporate world with you, I gotta look like money, right?" Baby Doll says. "Think like a success, act like a success, and be rich," Cash responds. "I've got all of your bread for you. You had $296,000. I put $54,000 with it. In your safe there is $350,000. You already know my mom and pop paid your condo off, so you're good. I bought you an Audi A4. It's in your driveway. Here," he says, handing her the keys. "Camille furnished your condo, it's nice." "Thank ya'll so much Cuzzo." Baby Doll is in tears. "I miss my mama so much. I don't know how I'm going to go forward without her." "You have us and you gonna go hard on the promises you made to your momma before she passed," Cash responds.

The urn is on your dresser, in your bedroom. Come on," Cash says walking her towards his Dodge Intrepid. Let's go cruise the city and get you some real food. Today is Thursday. Cool Al is throwing you a party at Club 112 tomorrow night. By Monday we need to be at the lab putting us a plan together. I want us to open our first business together by the end of next month." "That's what's up Cuzzo. What's up with this chic you were telling me about on the phone?" "I'm fucked up about her, Cuzzo. Her name is Destiny. She's a narcotics detective." "What?" Yells Baby Doll. Does she know about our family business?" "Hell, to the no! Let sleeping dogs lie. If it ain't broke don't fix it. Why poke the cat when its smiling in its sleep?" Cash replies, laughing. "I feel you, Cuzzo. I'm glad to see you happy."

"Yeah, I'm ready to pop the question."
"Get the fuck outta here," Baby Doll says, laughing. "Real shit, Cuzzo. I want kids. I like to travel. She makes me happy and she's truly a good person."
"I'm right behind you as soon as I find one of these dudes that are not with the bullshit. You said Cool Al is throwing me a party? You ain't coming through?"
"Naw, Cuzzo, I'm gonna put something together with Camille for you on Sunday. I'm chillin on the club scene."
"I feel you Cuzzo."

Cash takes her shopping. They hang out visiting family and friends from the hood.

DESTINY

"What's up, pretty?" Tear says while opening the door to the trap. "I came to holler at you about something," Destiny says. "What's the deal, ma?" "Malcom has given me $5,000 of the money he made for me. What can you give me for it? I ain't mean to be disrespectful and just pop up. I'm just trying to get me some money." Destiny has on a Pepe tight-fitting jean outfit, with a big Gucci knock-off bag, but it says Gucci. "It's okay lil momma. Come over here," Tear says guiding her towards the kitchen. "I'll put you something together where you can make you a nice flip." He goes to the cabinet over the stove and pulls out two big zip-lock bags filled with cookies of crack. When he reaches for the scale, Destiny pushes the panic button.

Twenty seconds later the girl watching the monitors screams, "oh shit! The crackers are coming about 30 deep!" "Fuck that! I ain't dying in prison!" Tear says reaching for a tommy-gun laying on the kitchen table. Grabbing her 9 mm glock out of her purse, Destiny screams, "don't do it!" Pointing at Tear. The sound of the door being kicked in temporarily throws Destiny off. Tear grabs the gun and busts off a round at Destiny. Boom! She quickly dives to the ground and returns fire. Boom! Boom! Boom! Hitting Tear in the arm and shoulder. He falls down and drops the gun. Det. Von has his .40 caliber in Tear's face, screaming, "don't move!" The girl and two other guys that were in the spot are arrested. "Are you ok?" Sgt. Graham says, helping Destiny off the ground. "Yes Sir, I'm good. This monster tried to kill me."

Tear in pain says, "you police-ass bitch! I wish I would have knocked your head off." Pushing him roughly on the ground, Detective Von says into his radio, "we need an ambulance. We have a suspect shot." Tear is bleeding badly. Destiny takes some towels and a first-aid kit and tries to stop the bleeding. She says, "I don't want you to die here. I need you to do 40 years in prison. Growing old, missing your freedom, then dying of AIDS, because you will be a sissy." "Fuck You," Tear grimaces. "Good job ya'll. We found 1,700 grams of crack, 6 pounds of weed, 157 pills and recovered 4 weapons and $31,000 in cash that was confiscated." Von whispers in Destiny's ear, "the young lady we arrested is already willing to cooperate." The ambulance comes to get Tear. "He's gonna make it. The arm wound was a flesh wound and the shoulder shot went straight through.

It's a Dirty Game.

CASH

"I think this will be a great spot," Cash says pulling up to the comer of Hillsborough Ave. and 21st. Him and Baby Doll are together in his car. They have decided to open a Rent a Roll shop selling rims and tires. Their gonna paint cars and install music systems. "I've talked to the guy who owns the building, he wants $1,800 a month. That's reasonable. We'll get in touch with a nice distributor who will wholesale us rims and tires. We will get an account with Bose to get the music systems wholesale. I've got two guys who can paint and do bodywork," Cash says. "We are pretty much set. We have to get cards made, get in touch with the radio station Wild 95.7 and the Florida Sentinel. We're gonna use them along with word of mouth for advertising."

"Let's do it Cuzzo," Baby Doll says.

In 3 weeks, Baby Doll and Cash has a one stop shop up and running. Customers are pulling in, spending money like crazy. "We did it Cuzzo," Baby Doll says, giving Cash a hug. "This is just the beginning, Cuzzo. I see the building across the road open. Let's buy it and open a Dairy Queen." "All day," Baby Doll says.

"Hello," Cash says answering his phone. "Hello handsome, what are you doing?" "Outside, thinking about you," Cash replies. "I'm at the spot. Our grand opening is today, remember?" "Of course, darling. I'm pulling up now," Destiny says smiling as she is pulling up in her car. She sees him standing in front talking to Baby Doll. "Come here beautiful," Cash says. Opening the door for her.

He gives her a great big hug and kiss. "This" he says pointing at Destiny, "is the love of my life." "Nice to finally meet you," Baby Doll says shaking Destiny's hand. "I'm his cousin Veronica." "I know," Destiny says. "I've heard so much about you. I'm proud of both of you. It's nice to meet you." "Come here," Cash says taking Destiny on a tour of the shop. "This is nice babe," Destiny says, looking at how nice Cash and Baby Doll have the shop looking. "I'm looking at the building across the street. I'm thinking of opening a Dairy Queen or a Hungry Howie's." "That will be great babe. I got to go. I have the meeting today with Internal Affairs about the shooting. Anytime a detective or police officer is involved in a shooting, they are on paid leave until an investigation is done."

"Okay. Good luck, Sweetheart." "I'll be home at 9:00," Cash says. "Okay baby. I love you." "I love you 10 times more," Cash replies.

They have been living together in Cash's house in Tampa Heights since they came back from Hawaii and they both have loved every day of it.

They are so happy.

MAD MAX

"Bro, the lawyer says he may be able to beat the whole case because they never showed ya'll a search warrant. The only thing that you may have to cop out to is the attempted murder of a police detective, which no bodily harm was involved. So, he's gonna try to get you 12 years." "12 years!" Shouts Tear. "Bro, I'd rather be dead!" "Lil bro, this game comes with consequences. I did 11 years to the door for shooting that pussy nigga we had for a stepdad. You will do about 10 years with this 85% shit. You're still young. You will get out stronger and wiser. You already know I'm gonna keep you strapped. Keep hoes coming to see you. Bringing you weed and shit. I got you 1il bro. That prison shit ain't nothing." "It is what it is big bro. Just please hold ma down." "I've got you lil bro. I'm leaving $5,000 on your books when I leave here."

"I miss you lil bro," Lizanne says. "Shayla says what's up? And she misses you too. We are headed to Miami for a few weeks. When I get back, I'm gonna put them C.M.F. niggas to sleep." "I love you big bro," Tear says getting up. "I love you too bro," Mad Max says. He's furious. It's like a part of him is gone without his 1 lil brother. He leaves Orient Road jail in a daze. "Call Shayla and Rondo and tell them we will be there in the morning," Mad Max says. "Ok daddy," Lizanne says pulling her phone out.

COOL AL

"Why ain't these people dead?? Cool Al shouts. He's at him and Seleena's condo outside on the balcony talking to Ike and Rolo. "Cuzzo, that nigga Mad Max ain't no slouch. The nigga has camera's all over the place and whenever they go anywhere, he has the bitch driving so he can be on point with the fire. We are on him. Trust me Cuzzo. The day he slips, him and that bitch are dead. We have been living in Tampa waiting on this pussy." "I need him dead by Friday," Cool Al says. "Hey what's up with the nigga you say got them bricks over there for the low?" "Lil Cot is his name. I'll introduce you to him this weekend after we kill dude." "Okay bet," Cool Al says. "I'm ready to get shit poppin. I've got a Mexican outta Wimauma that's gonna give me all the weed I want for the low.

If your dude ain't got good numbers on this coke, I'm gonna holler at them about some coke too." "Alright cuz, let us go so we can catch this pussy slipping." All day," Cool Al says.

MAD MAX

"What do I need to pack babe?" Yells Lizanne. "Bring $200,000. We're gonna stay down there for a couple of weeks. So how much clothes we will need. Put me something together too. When we get back, babe, I'm opening back up the spot in Oak Village. It's been a while since the crackers raided it. This time we ain't doing no hand to hand. We're gonna sell weight in weed and coke. Fuck the pills and crack. Once we get to a mil, we're moving to Atlanta. Me, you and my mom. We will open up something or do real estate." "I like that babe. I'm ready to leave when you say. I already had us a couple of weeks' worth of stuff packed. I'm putting the money together now." "In ten minutes, we can pull out. I have to take a shit real quick.

30 minutes later...

"Let's go baby," Mad Max says grabbing two big tote bags. "You grab that one babe." He says pointing at the smaller Gucci tote with the money inside it. Mad Max is putting the bags in the backseat of the Porsche while Lizanne is sitting in the driver's seat turning on the car. They don't see the two guys run up to the car with their guns drawn. Bloca! Bloca! Bloca! Boom! Boom! Boom!

Rolo and Ike let off round after round, shooting Mad Max first. He can't even react because half his body is leaned into the backseat. Lizanne screams but they are cut short quickly as Rolo shoots her 3 times in the face. Bloca! Bloca! Bloca! "Grab them bags bro and let's go!" Shouts Rolo.

They leave a bloody scene. It's a Dirty Game!

CHAPTER 31

California Love

CASH

"Baby, are you ready?" Cash shouts. "Yes, baby. I'm all set." "Pull the car up and I'll help you with our stuff." "Okay, our plane leaves in 2 hours." Cash and Destiny are about to head to California for a week. They are going to meet his parents, go to Disneyland and she promised Chrishonna they would attend a showing of her play.

"I'm excited baby," Cash says 3 hours later as they are in the air on a nonstop flight to California. "Me too," Destiny says. "I have not met your mom and only seen your dad once. And my girl Chrishonna, I haven't seen her since we graduated from college."

"I've never been to Cali," Cash says. "I want to visit the Staples Center. Disneyland has always been on my wish list. The walk of fame where all the stars are. We should have a lot of fun sweetheart. Grabbing Cash's hand, Destiny says, "as long as I have you, I'm happy." "Gimme kiss pretty," Cash says puckering up.

Later that day....

"LAX is sooo big! Where are they?" Cash says looking for his parents. "There is your pop over there with that sign," Destiny shouts. Spotting her son, Tonya runs towards him, "heey," she shouts grabbing Cash in a big bear hug. C-Money hugs Destiny at the same time. "Oh, I've missed you baby," Tonya yells. She lets go of Cash and hugs Destiny. C- Money hugs Cash.

"Ma and pop, this is Destiny." "Hello ya'll." "The pleasure is all ours. You have transformed our son and he's so happy. You're all he talks about." Destiny smiles and says, "he does the same about ya'll." "Come on everyone," C-Money says picking up some of the luggage with Cash. They head out to C-Money's Escalade. "Pop, I know ya'll want us to stay with ya'll, and I respect that and will do so tonight, but we are staying the rest of the week at a place we have both dreamed of since we looked it up on the internet. It's a 6 Star hotel called The Alastair on Burton Way." "Okay, son. I know where it's at. Me and your mom stayed there when we first ever came out here. It is nice. Right now, we're headed to our house to party and have a good time. Your mom prepared a feast for ya'll." "That's real," Cash shouts.

DESTINY

"Hey chic, I'm here!" Destiny yells into her phone. "OMG, are you serious? Where are ya'll staying?" Chrishonna says. "The Alastair on Burton Way." "Wow excuse me big baller," Chrishonna says laughing. "I'm on my way to come and get you so we can do some shopping and catching up." "That's good because Cash's dad and mom probably want a lil alone time with their only son." "Give me a couple of hours. I'll be there by 2:00 pm." Okay, I'll be ready. We are in suite 602." "Bye chic." "Get off my phone," Destiny says hanging up. Destiny looks over at Cash. He's asleep in his boxers. Watching his body, she gets horny. She starts licking in his ear. "Ooh," he moans. Destiny turns him flat on his back and starts to kiss all over his chest, licking down to his navel.

"Ooohh shit babe," Cash moans. Destiny is slowly stroking his pipe to a full erection. Destiny begins to make love to Cashmere's cock with her lips and tongue. "Ooohh God," moans Cash loudly. Cash's hard dick is standing up like a flagpole. Destiny straddles him. Putting his hard dick inside her hot wet pussy and begins to move up and down. "Damn Cashmere," she yells while feeling his dick deep inside her. Cash groans, exhaling some indescribable words. Destiny is in a zone, rocking up and down on Cash's dick. He leans back and is meeting her stroke for stroke. "Is it good babe?" Moans Destiny, working herself to a climax. "It's so good ma. I fucking love you," Cash yells, shooting off a hot load of cum inside of Destiny. "Wow," Destiny yells getting off of Cash and head to the shower.

Her and Cash take turns bathing each other.

1 0 minutes later....

"What are you going to do today?" Asks Cash. "Well, I talked to Chrishonna about an hour ago. She wants to do a lil girls day out and spend a lil time with me. I figured I'd let you get a lil quality time in with your parents while her and I hang out a little bit." "Ain't the play tonight?" Cash responds. "Yes." "Here," Cash says, grabbing his pants, he hands Destiny $3,000. "Have fun and grab us something to wear tonight." He gives her his sizes. "I'm a detective," she smiles. "You don't think I already know your sizes?" "Is that enough money?" Cash asks. "If not, I got us sweetie," replies Destiny.

"So, what are you gonna do?" She asks. "Probably let my parents drag me all over this place and do a lil sightseeing. About what time do we need to be back here?" "The play starts at 9:30 pm. It's 20 minutes from here, so I'd say we need to be here by 8:00 pm to shower and get ready," Cash says. "I hope I just got you pregnant." Destiny is startled. She would love to start a family with Cash, but she hasn't thought about the idea like that. "Me too," she replies, giving him a passionate kiss.

Later that night....

"Thank ya'll for coming, Mr. and Mrs. Jones, this really means a lot to me. This is my best friend I met in college, Chrishonna. It's her first play. She wrote and produced it," Destiny says.

Her, Cashmere and his parents arc in C-Money's Cadillac Escalade pulling up to view Chrishonna's play, why do-good girls like bad guys."

"We needed to get out and we are loving being in the company of our son and his future wife," C-Money says. "I'm also all for supporting positive black people." "This is special," Tonya says. "I hope we get to meet this wonderful young lady." "Yes Ma'am. After the show she's invited us to the after party." "Good," Tonya says.

They are all dressed to the 9's in casual clothes. Destiny knows Cashmere's parents are rich, but she really admires how down to earth and laid back they are. She sees why Cashmere is so respectful and good hearted.

They have a ball. The play is a big success. Afterwards, Cashmere meets Chrishonna. Mrs. Tonya and Chrishonna exchange numbers and promise to do lunch. Her, Destiny and Chrishonna have a lady talk.

By 2:00 am they are all tired and end up staying at C-Money and Tonya's mini-mansion.

COOL AL

"This is my cousin main man. I trust him with my life," Rolo says to Lil Cot. Him, Ike, Cool Al and Lil Cot are in St. Pete at the racetrack. Lil Cot has a 1100 High booster bike he brings here to race for money. "It's nice to meet you," Lil Cot says while shaking Cool Al's hand. "Same here." "What's good? The last time I seen you I was in Tampa at a block party. You were stunting in your Maybach before getting into a shootout with some nigga's." Cool Al is blowed because he doesn't know Cot, but he knows it's a small world. "Yeah, I'm the king of C.M.F," brags Cool Al. "Shit has been crazy. My plug literally has a heart attack." "For real," Lil Cot says. "Real shit bro." "Well, I ain't gone waste too much of your time. I get them h's for 14 from my peoples.

I know you're used to way better numbers so I'm not sure what we can do," says Lil Cot. "I'll grab 10 at a time if you can work with me and I'm talking like every week," Cool Al says. "Let me see what I can put together. I'll give you a call later on today." "That's the peace," Cool Al says shaking Lil Cot's hand. "I'll get with you, main man," Cool Al says, heading towards his car.

"What do you think, Cuzzo?" Rolo says as they are pulling off. "I've got more money than him. He's a middleman. He's gonna find a way to meet me in the middle. We'll go through him until I can put something better together for us.

LIL COT

"Hello?" "Yes, this is me, Cotney." "What do you have for me?" Agent Filmore asked. "A guy they call Cool Al out of Tampa, he wants to buy 10 kilos, asap." "What?" Agent Filmore yells into his phone excitedly. He's glad he followed his 1st mind and allowed Cot to cooperate after catching him with a half kilo 2 months ago. "When can we make this happen, Cotney?" "He's ready now. I can call him and tell him I'll let him get them for 14.5 and he'll be ready asap." Barely able to control his excitement, Agent Filmore says, "let me make some calls. You tell Cool Al you're ready and I'll get back with you in a couple of hours." "This should clear me, right?" Lil Cot asked. "If all goes well, hell to the yes," Agent Filmore replies knowing this bust will be a career builder for him. "Okay I'm on it," Lil Cot says disconnecting the call.

4 hours later....

"What's the deal main man?" Lil Cot says. "What it do?" Cool Al replies answering his call. "If you wanna bet 14 on the race, I call that." "I'm really losing, but I feel like I'm gonna win the race," Lil Cot says, talking in code. "I call that," Cool Al says. "When you gone be on point?" "Tomorrow." "Call me when you're on your way," Lil Cot replies. "That's the business," Cool Al says hanging up.

DESTINY

"Babe, this is so nice."

Her and Cashmere are at Disneyland walking hand in hand, enjoying the theme park. "Yes, it is," Cash responds. "I can't wait until the day we'll be bringing Cashmere Jr. and Cashina." "Who said you were naming both of our kids, Mr. Cashmere?" Destiny says laughing. "You're right, baby. You can name our daughter," he laughs because our first son has to be a junior. "The way you were moaning and running today we'll probably have our son 1st," Destiny says messing with Cash. Speaking on the saying about if they woman does all the work it will be a boy. Smiling, Cash says, "oh you're bragging?" "Naw, babe. I was just kidding." "Naw I got you, we will see who's who tonight," Cash smiles.

"Whatever. I ain't scared of you," Destiny replies grabbing him in a big hug while putting her tongue in his mouth. "I'm in love with you," Cash says after she lets him go. "I know," she says running. Cash chases her down and goes to tickling her. They enjoy the rest of the day and the next few going all over L.A.

They visit the Staples Center, the college campus of U.S.C. and Berkley. They have a great time on the beaches. After saying their goodbyes to Chrishonna, C-Money and M.rs T, they head back to Tampa with big smiles on their faces.

SHAYLA

"I can't believe they are gone," Shayla says crying.

A homicide detective answered Lizanne's phone telling her what happened. "I got you baby," Rondo says holding Shayla in his arms. "Thank you," she replies crying. "It's just so crazy how the game is. One minute we're all together stuntin' on top of the world and 3 months later... Lizanne, Mad Max and Elise are dead. Tear is in jail and I'm here in Miami, broke." Shayla cries. All she can think in her mind is it's a Dirty Game.

COOL AL

"Hello?" "You moving around my dude?" Cool Al asks. "The money don't stop," Lil Cot replies. "I'll be in your town in a couple hours. I'm ready to race that slow ass bike you got." "Meet me at the track. I'll be there with this high booster." "One," Cool Al yells hanging up his phone. "Let me see what's up with Cash," Cool Al says to himself, while dialing Cash's number. "Sup main man?" Cash says. "Just cooling bruh." Cool Al replies. "Bruh, how about we make one more run for the road?" "Where are you?" Cash interrupts Cool Al. "On the Interstate headed to my parent's house." "I'll meet you there," Cash says hanging up. Cool Al looks at his phone like I know this nigga ain't just hang up on me.

15 minutes later...

CASH

"What's up with you bruh?" Cash shouts at Cool Al. "Fuck you mean?" "You talking crazy on the phone. You already know ain't no crazy talking supposed to be done over no phone. The past two years you have been on this movie shit. Nigga, we are not Nino and G-Money and this ain't New Jack City. This shit is real life," Cash yells. "I heard you're in love with a narcotics detective," Cool Al says. "So what? Yes, I am. I'm actually going to ask her to marry me next month." Cool Al has a smirk on his face. "I guess that's why I haven't met her huh?" "My parents just met her a couple of days ago. We came back from Cali a couple days ago." Cash does feel a little guilty. "It must be nice." Cool Al shouts. Tired of the bullshit, Cash says, "so what's up?"

"Bruh I need you. I want to make one last 6 month run." "Give me one good reason why I should consider this?" Cash replies. "With Dirty Money out of business, it's so much money to be made." "There is no way you can tell me you're not a millionaire," Cash says. "And where would we get work from?" "I got that under control on the work tip. I met a nigga through my cousin from St. Pete that is gonna let me get 10 B's for $140,000 and I have a Mexican in Wimauma who will sell us all the weed we need. And so what if I got a mil or so? That ain't no money." "You're crazy," Cash says shaking his head. "Who is the nigga in St. Pete? Have you had him checked out? The Mexican too. They snitch? With Dirty Money out of the way who do you think the police will be focusing on?"

"You have the detective girlfriend. You tell me," Cool Al replies smiling. Cash swings a wild haymaker that catches Cool Al square on the jaw. Stumbling back, Cool Al ups a 9 mm handgun from his waist and points it at Cash. "What? You gonna kill me?" Cash shouts. He's beyond hot. Cool Al came at him like he did. "Naw. I ain't gonna kill you," Cool Al says putting the gun back in his waist. "You're already dead, he says as he walks towards his parent's front door.

"Fuck," Cash yells. He's lost his last best friend. He badly wants to follow Cool Al and apologize. He knows he was dead wrong for putting his hands on him. A tear escapes his eyes as he pulls out his phone.

He texts Cool Al: *I'm sorry, bro. I was dead wrong for putting my hands on you. I love you bro. Cash.*

Cash gets into his car and speeds off as he pushes send. Cool Al doesn't respond.

DESTINY

"So, who's left?" Destiny says to Det. Von. They are at the morgue looking at the bodies of Mad Max and Lizanne; well, what's left of them. "It's another girl and a few loyal workers but I think Cool Al sent this hit." Destiny explains. "More than likely yes. From what I hear about this guy," Det. Von points at Mad Max's body, "he made a lot of enemies." "I will not rest until I see Cool Al behind bars and C.M.F. shut down." Destiny says looking at Lizanne's body. "How old was she?" "26." Detective Von answers. "Now that Dirty Money is out of the way, C.M.F. is gonna tum up and we will be right there to put them away." "Yeah, I have Fonda Tompkins, one of the top lieutenants, about ready to break. Once they offer her some prison time for all the stuff they found when we hit that spot in Oakhurst.

She'll be ready to lead us to Cool Al."
"That's what I'm talking about,"
Destiny yells, getting excited. "Come on
let's get out of here. Looking at these
dead bodies, these young African-
Americans, not even the age of 30 makes
me sad." "Me too," Det. Von says.

COOL AL

"I'm on my way Cuzzo. I will call you once I handle the B.I. with main man," Cool Al says. "You want us to roll with you?" Rolo asks. "Naw I have my baby with me." Cool Al replies talking about his 9mm. "Well, we'll be at the spot just come through." "All day," Cool Al says hanging up.

He's on his way to St. Pete in his Denali with $140,000 in a Finish Line bag. *I'm 25 minutes away from you,* Cool Al text Lil Cot. *I'm waiting on you my dude, Lil Cot texts back.* "I should have killed that chump," Cool Al says to himself. He's still upset he allowed Cash to put his hands on him. He has a better plan. That is why he didn't kill him. He knows Cash has over a million dollars. He wants it and knows how to get it. He smiles to himself before screaming, "who fucking put this shit together?"

'Me, that's who." A quote from the movie Scarface.

Ten minutes later...

"Sup, main man," Cot says shaking Cool Al's hand. They're standing in the parking lot of the Racetrack. "Ready to rock and roll," Cool Al replies pulling the bag out of the passenger's side of his Denali. "$140,000?" Cot says walking over to an all-black XLT Cadillac truck with black 26" Diablos. He opens the door and hands Cool Al a big duffel bag with 10 kilos of fish scale cocaine. "This is that fish scale here." Lil Cot says opening the bag. "I'm gone holla at you." Cool Al says heading towards his Denali. As soon as he closes his door his whole world changes. "Freeze!" Yells agent Filmore as him and 15 Federal agents 9mm converge on Cool Al with their guns drawn.

"Oh shit!" Yells Cool Al blowed as fuck. He's so blowed his mind locks up. "Put your hands where I can see them!" Yells agent Filmore. He has his glock 9mm pointed at Cool Al. Another agent opens the door of the Denali and pulls Cool Al out. He still has the 9mm in his waistband when they throw him on the ground. "Damn," Cool Al yells to himself. Saying this police ass nigga has fucked me up. Agent Filmore frisks him and finds the gun and screams, "look what we have here!" Cool Al also has $7000 in his pocket. "You're a big boy, huh?" Agent Filmore asks. "I ain't trying to talk cracker." Cool Al shouts. Grabbing the duffel bag out of the Denali, agent Filmore says, "trafficking and conspiracy? Oooh wee. I'd say you're looking at life in federal prison." "Fuck you, cracker," shouts Cool Al.

As Cool Al is being placed into the back of the Ford Taurus, he sees agent Filmore getting the bag of money from the passenger seat of Lil Cot's Escalade truck. They say a few words and Lil Cot drives off. "Bitch ass nigga," Cool Al says to himself. His mind goes to the conversation him and Cash had a little over a couple hours ago. "Did you check him out?" He thinks of his money, his whips, Seleena, he's already plotting in his mind…

CHAPTER 32

Matrimony

DESTINY

"Good morning, Mr. Cashmere," Destiny yells full of glee. Her and Cash are lying in bed together at his house. "Hey sweetheart," Cash replies smacking her on her butt lightly. "Alright now," Destiny smirks.

She has on a pair of light blue, sexy lace Victoria Secret panties with no bra. "Alright now, what?" Cash shouts grabbing her. "Stop!" She yells as they begin to wrestle on the king size bed. Destiny breaks free and hits him with a big pillow; Pow, right on the top of his head and she runs. Cash takes off behind her and catches her in the living room. Cash spins her around and takes a moment to savor her beauty.

Destiny starts blushing from ear to ear as Cash admires her every curve and her sexy legs. Cash turns her towards the sofa s that she will be facing him. Destiny pulls her panties to the side and places the head of Cashmere's dick right where it needs to be. "Ah....Ah. Omg!" Destiny yells as she slides down. She arches her back, giving it a C shape and grips Cashmere like a seasoned vet, working her pussy muscles. "Ride your dick baby," Cash moans. "Ooohh Shit. It feels sooo good baby." Cash palms both of Destiny's ass cheeks and helps guide her up and down on his hard pole. Destiny is biting her lip and rubbing her breasts. "Um, um. Damn Cash I love you so much," she yells as she reaches back and removes Cashmere's hands. She wants to be in total control.

"Cashmere?" Destiny says. "Yes, baby!" "Are you all mine?" "Only and all," Cash moans feeling pressure building up. He feels Destiny's walls contracting, he screams. I'm cumming baby." Destiny continues to throw her pussy hard at him while jerking violently and screaming, "meee toooo." Cash and Destiny are both out of breath. Cash's now limp dick is still inside her. She turns around and says, "baby I'm in love with you." She begins to kiss all over his neck and chest. "Baby, we need to go to the mall and get us something nice to wear," she breaks their embrace. "You know my dad is having a family cookout at Rowlett Park later on today as a matter of fact. You're gonna have to shop for the both of us because I have to go help him get everything set up." "You know I got us sweetie," Cashmere replies.

"I'm still kinda nervous about meeting your family members. The only person I really know is Meme, with her crazy butt," Cash laughs. "You'll be alright. My family members are real down-to-earth black people." "I can't wait to tell your parents how glad I am they made you," Cash says. "Let me go," Destiny says, "before I attack you again." "Okay baby. I'll meet you back here so we can shower and dress at 3:30pm." "Love you," Destiny says heading towards the shower. "I know," Cash says hitting her with the pillow and running towards their bedroom.

COOL AL

"Baby listen to me carefully," Cool Al says. "Go take Paul Stavrou $20,000 and tell him I'm in jail in St. Pete." "What?" Yells Seleena. "I can't talk on this phone, baby." "When were you arrested?" Cool Al responds, "baby please. Do what I asked you to do. I'll be out soon." "Okay. I'm gonna borrow the money from my dad and go handle that right now." Glad Seleena is on point, Cool Al says, "I love you baby." "I love you too." Seleena says hanging up.

CASH

"Yes, sir!" "That will be $17,000," the clerk at Zales jewelry in University Mall tells Cash.

Cash just bought a 2-karat engagement ring for Destiny. He's gonna propose to her at her family's get together today. "Do you want it gift wrapped sir?" The clerk asks handing Cash back his American Express card. "No thank you," Cash says. I need to find me and my baby something nice, Cash says to himself. Walking out of the jewelry store, he goes to Dillard's and buys them both a nice Polo short set, with the Polo boots to match. Leaving out of Dillard's, Cash calls his pop. "Hello," answers C-Money. "What's the deal old man?" "Only thing I have that's old is money," C-Money replies laughing.

"Is my mother around?" Cash asks. "Yes, she's right here laying in my arms. We are watching Family Feud." "Good. Put your phone on speaker please." "Hey beautiful," Cash yells. "Hey Son," Tonya replies happily. "How did you all like Destiny?" Asks Cash. Tonya goes first and says, "I think she's a good girl; she's really pretty, has a good heart, very down-to-earth and most of all she really loves you." "I can feel a real woman's strength." C-Money says. "I love her for you son. She is truly genuine in her ways. I see a lot of your momma in her. She's fine, pretty, smart and like your mom says... really cares for you." "Thank you both. I'm going to her family's get together today to meet them. I'm going to ask her to marry me." "Wow. That's great, son." C-Money says.

Tonya screams, "I'm so proud of you son. I'm gonna plan the wedding reception. Tell me when ya'll pick a date and we'll come to Florida for a month." "Dad, I have one more favor. I want to buy us a nice house." "Okay," C- Money says. "I'm gonna need you and ma to buy it for me like it's a gift from ya'll." "Why, son?" "Pop, I don't want her to know about my past." Cutting in, Mrs. T says, "Cash, that girl loves you. Everybody has a past. I'm sure she's not perfect. I think she would respect you more if you told her the truth." C- Money says, "at least partially the truth. Son remember what I told you. Betrayal starts with lies hidden in the shadows of silence, and some things once destroyed can't be rebuilt. So, if you don't give her the truth and allow her the opportunity to accept it or not, if she ever finds out the truth on her own, she could feel betrayed and lose trust.

Sad as it may be sometimes, the ugliest of truth is better than the prettiest of lies," C-Money says. "Ya'll are right. Thank ya'll so much. I'm still going to propose to her today, but I promise before we even set a wedding date, I'm gonna give her a little history about me." "A little talk is good," C-Money says. "Sometimes less is more," Mrs. T says laughing. They are basically telling Cash he doesn't have to go too deep and get them all indicted. Telling her stuff that's old and not her business, but to at least say hey at one time I used to hustle or run with C.M.F. "I love you both," Cash says. "We love you too," they shout in union.

SELEENA

"Can I see you? It's really important," asks Seleena. "I'm leaving University Mall. Where do I need to come to?" Cash replies. "I live in New Tampa in the condo's off Bruce B. Downs." "Okay, I'll be there in 20 minutes," Cash says disconnecting the call. Rushing to jump in the shower, Seleena heads to her stand up shower. Taking off her Prada dress she wore to meet Cool Al lawyer. Seleena shakes under the pressure of the hot water. "Damn," she says to herself. Remembering the conversation, she had with Cool Al's lawyer. "Ma'am, this doesn't look good. They have him on audio discussing a meeting to purchase a large quantity of cocaine. Then he was arrested with a firearm on him. In possession of 10 kilograms of cocaine, over $147,000 in cash was recovered.

This $20,000 will get me started. A case of this magnitude will be in excess of $150,000 if there is a trial," Mr. Stavrou told her. "Is he gonna get out?" She had asked. "I'm gonna try. It may be a couple of days and will be at least a half million dollars." Right then, Seleena made up her mind the $640,000 that Cool Al had at they're condo, she was keeping, and she was gonna put the double cross down on him by telling Cash about Cool Al's betrayal. She's hoping to seduce him in the process and get back in his life. Breaking her train of thought, Seleena exits her bathroom naked, running to her bedroom. She quickly dries off, grabs her Apple Cinnamon Victoria Secret lotion and goes to applying lotion on her beautiful body. She throws on a pair of sexy gray Victoria Secret panties and a tank top to take it to the next level.

She puts on a pair of white Prada high heels. She checks in the mirror to make sure her hair and makeup is flawless then she runs to the kitchen and to start making a chicken salad. Grabbing her phone, she excitedly says hello. "I'm at the gate," Cash says. "What's the code?? "883 pound," she replies. "I stay all the way in the back. Park next to my car and come to apartment 83." "One!" Cash says disconnecting the call.

5 minutes later....

Seleena opens her door, looking like a Victoria Secret supermodel. Not being able to help himself, Cash says, "damn" after seeing her beauty and camel toe. "Come on," she says pulling him towards the kitchen. Cash looks around and sees all the exclusive things inside the condo. Imported furniture to expensive art covering the walls. "This place is nice," Cash says. "Thank you. I was just making a salad and about to chase it with some wine. You want some?" Seleena asks. "I'm good ma. Actually, I'm in a rush. I have a BBQ I have to attend." Disappointed, Seleena hands him a glass of wine and turns up the charm by walking super sexy up to him. "Come on, let's go to my room so we can talk. Her smell is mesmerizing Cash. The panties look like they were made for her body. Her nipples are poking up erect through the tank top. Walking behind her up the stairs, Cash can't help but see her neatly shaved sexy crotch and huge gap between her legs. He wouldn't be a man if his dick didn't instantly get brick hard. As they are walking inside Seleena's gigantic bedroom, she smiles as she sees the bulge in Cash's pants. I got him; she thinks. "What's the deal?" Cash says.

Seleena begins her show by starting to cry. "Cash, this is so painful," she says. "I guess I should start off by saying I'm so sorry Cash. I swear I never meant to hurt you. I really made a selfish decision." "Talk to me," Cash says. "I slept with Cool Al and we have been a couple the past 15 months," Seleena yells. Cash is so blowed. He can't even respond. Going on, Seleena says, "he's the one who bought me this place. We actually live here together. He brought me the Aston Martin too. We've been basically living as king and queen." Cash is torn. His heart is past broken. He could care less about Seleena. His hurt is all from Cool Al. "Why are you telling me now?" He calmly says. "When he took me to buy my car in Miami, he admitted to me that he was the one behind your mother getting kidnapped and he had Fat Dre killed."

Cash becomes dizzy and almost passes out. He has to sit down on Seleena's beautiful canopy bed. "OMG," he yells. "He hates you," Cash. "He was gonna have you killed if your connect would not have died. He wants to be you. That's why he came and found me and told me he would love me, spoil me, and make me his queen," she lies. Seleena tries to grab Cash's dick. Temporarily because he so stunned, he allows her to. She pulls out his dick and is about to engulf him before... SWAP! Cash slaps her hard across her face. "I'm still in love with you Cash," she yells. "Why would you betray me?" He yells back. "When you left me, I was so torn. I may not have shown you how you wanted me to, but I was in love with you. I felt like you ditched me for someone else, so I accepted Cool Al's proposal to get back at you.

I'm so sorry," she sobs uncontrollably. "Where is Cool Al?" Cash asks. "He's in jail." "Jail?" Cash yells. He just seen Cool Al yesterday. "Yes. The feds caught him yesterday in St. Pete. He was trying to buy 10 kilos. He had a gun on him too. I took Paul Stavrou $20,000 this afternoon. He says things look bad, but he may be able to get him a bond of a half a million in a couple of days." "Do you have the money to get him out?" Cash asks. "No," Seleena lies. "I have to go," Cash says getting up. He's in a daze. "Please don't leave me," Cash. "If I didn't love you, I wouldn't have told you this stuff. I loved Fat Dre and you know Mrs. T and I was tight. I swear I didn't know nothing about none of this crazy stuff until my b-day weekend when he bought me that car. We can get past this. I'll help you set him up. Give me a chance, please." Seleena begs.

"I will call you in a couple of days." "Maybe we can go out of town for the weekend." "Let me go. I need to clear my head," Cash says lying. "Okay baby," Seleena says hugging him tight. Love changes, things change, and close friends become strangers... life!!!

DESTINY

"What's up partner?" Destiny says laughing.

She's at home about to get dressed, talking to Det. Von on her cellphone. "Got some good news. Our boy Cool Al aka Albert Conley is in custody." "What?" Yells Destiny! "Unfortunately, the feds got to him before us. He bought 10 kilos from a federal informant in St. Petersburg and he had a 9mm on him during the arrest." "Yes!" Destiny shouts. "I hope he gets life." "Hopefully, he will somehow get tied to these murders and some of this drug dealing he did here in Tampa." "We'll see if we can get a crack at him on Monday morning. As of now he has lawyered up and ain't talking." "Okay, I'll see you first thing Monday," Destiny says disconnecting the call. "What are you so excited about?" Cash says walking into their bedroom

Destiny usually doesn't bring her work home, but every now and then she mentions cases to Cashmere. "This monster I was chasing has been arrested by the feds in St. Pete. I'm hoping to get a chance to tie him to some cases here in Tampa. He's responsible for a lot of murders and drug dealing the past couple of years in Tampa. Anyways handsome are you ready to go? Because we are just about late." "Yes, I am sweetie," Cashmere says kissing her softly on her lips. "Let's go," Destiny says getting wet. "Before we never make it," Cash smiles walking her towards the door.

25 minutes later...

"Just be yourself. I'm a detective. I can tell you're tense." If only she knew Cash thinks while getting out of her car.

"Auntie Destiny," D3 and Terrance Jr. scream while running up to Destiny. The party is in full swing. Destiny's whole family is there. "Hey ya'll," Destiny yells, giving the boys a hug. "We're going to play," they yell then run off. "Come on," Destiny says grabbing Cash's hand. They walk towards the pavilion where all the food and adults are. "I want you to meet my parents first." "Hey baby girl," Desean screams before they can make it all the way to the pavilion. "Hey daddy," Destiny says, giving him a hug. "Daddy, this is Cashmere," Destiny says, introducing Cashmere to her pop. "Hey there son," Desean says, giving Cash a firm handshake. "Nice to finally meet the man who created this beautiful woman," Cash says pointing at Destiny. "I like him already," Desean says smiling. Drena comes up yelling,

"Hey, ya'll," giving Cash and Destiny a hug. Destiny introduces Cash. Cash says, "Ma'am, you and your husband created a beautiful woman and I see where she gets her beauty from." Blushing, Drena says, "Thank you."

The party is in full swing. Everybody is eating, dancing, or playing dominoes. Destiny introduces Cash to both of her Aunties, Fee and Donna. Her brother and sister Meme is there with Rick, Cashmere and Meme share a few jokes. Auntie Donna has her lil friend Doctor Williams there too. DJ's, baby mamma, Veda, even Auntie Fee. Cash fits right in. He's playing dominoes with the men when Step in the name of love comes on by R. Kelly. Everybody goes to cutting up, kids and all. Destiny is having so much fun. She grabs Cash and goes to dancing with him. Cash is shocked to see that Destiny can dance so good.

As the song goes off, Cash walks over to the stereo and push's pause. "Excuse me," he yells. "I'm sorry to slow down the fun. I have an announcement to make. First off, thank you all for a great time. It's been great meeting you all." He pulls Destiny to him before kneeling down in front of her. He pulls the ring box out of his cargo shorts and says, "Destiny Jackson, the day I laid my eyes on you, you captured my heart and thoughts. You're all I've ever dreamed of in a woman. The joy you bring to my life is immeasurable. Would you please be my wife? And allow me to love and spoil you until my dying day?" "OMG!" Yells Destiny. "Yes, Cashmere! I love you," she shouts, and Cash puts the ring on her finger. Everybody is clapping; her mom, both aunts and Meme are crying. Destiny is crying also.

30 minutes later....

"Baby, can you please drop me off to my cousin Veronica's place?" Cash asks. "Okay, baby. Do you need me to wait on you? Or are you gonna have her drop you off home after ya'll finish handling ya'll business?" "I'm good. I need you to head home, get in the shower and be ready for us to celebrate our engagement," Cash says smiling. "Okay daddy. I got you. Gimme a kiss," Destiny says pulling up to Veronica's condo. Cashmere gives her a deep passionate tongue kiss before exiting the car. "I love you beautiful," he shouts closing the passenger door. "I love you better," Destiny yells pulling off.

CASH

"This is a pleasant surprise," Baby Doll says opening her door. Cash grabs her and breaks down crying. "Cuzzo, he killed Fat Dre and set ma up to get kidnapped," he sobs. "Who?" Baby Doll yells instantly furious. "Cool Al," Cash replies. Thinking she heard wrong, Baby Doll yells, "who?!" "Cool Al, Cuzzo. I talked to Seleena today. Her and Cool Al have been living together for the past year and a half." "What"? Baby Doll shouts. "They have been living out this king and queen fairy tale relationship. He was gonna kill me too if Mr. Carlos had not died. He was on some takeover shit." "He had to have some help to do this." "I know," Cash replies. "I pray it wasn't Black Isaac or Trigger." "It had to be somebody because Auntie Tonya said two guys kidnapped her," Baby Doll says. "Yeah, Cool Al was with me, pop, and Fat Dre when the kidnappers had ma." "You think this bitch could be lying?" Asks Baby Doll. "Naw, Cuzzo. How would she know about the kidnapping? And Mr. C dying?" "Why now after all this time would this slimeball bitch tell you all this? Oooh! I'm gonna get that hoe," Baby Doll shouts while pacing her floor. "Cool Al got arrested by the feds yesterday buying 10 kilos from a C.I. in St. Pete, with a pistol on him," Cash says. "Woooh," Baby Doll replies. "So now she wants to tell you this to get in your good graces. Like she's on your team. This bitch is scandalous as fuck!" Baby Doll shouts. "Yes Cuzzo, the bitch even offered to set Cool Al up for me if he gets out. She said she took Paul Stavrou $20,000 today to start on his case and get him a bond and she said Paul stated that would be at least a half a million dollars. How about the slick bitch tells me she doesn't have the money," Cash laughs. "We both know Cool Al has 3 times that and it's most likely right there in the crib with her. That bougie bitch is trying to put the double cross down so she can cuff all that paper, "Baby Doll shouts. "Over my dead body will that bitch get that lucky after she partnered with this deceitful, lowdown, conniving ass nigga, kidnapped my Auntie and killed my big homie Fat Dre. Naw Cuzzo, Fat Dre is who put that pussy Pancho to sleep for me. I ain't going for it." "This shit hurts Cuzzo. I had no idea he was so jealous hearted towards me. I gave him the keys and told him, you're the king, my dude. And he was still gonna kill me? He stole Fat Dre's money, got my pops for $500,000." Cash is so hot he's about to cry again. Baby Doll grabs him in a big bear hug.

"Cuzzo, you're one of the smartest people I know. We have enough problems. We need to come up with a solution." "You're right Cuzzo. I'm sorry," Cash says. This is what were gonna do...

CHAPTER 33

1st 48... What does the cigarette do?

DESTINY

"How you pulled this off?" "I don't know but I'm glad we're gonna get our shot at this loser," Destiny says. "Me too and it wasn't me. Sgt. Graham pulled a rabbit out of his hat and got us this chance to break this chump through the feds," Det. Von replies.

Destiny and Det. Von are on their way to St. Pete to the Federal Holding Facility to have an interview with Cool Al. For two days, Agent Filmore hasn't been able to get nothing out of him. They figure his lawyer will get him out on bond and he will bond out soon, so the last resort was to allow the T.P.D. to step in and see if they can get him to cooperate.

COOL AL

"Get Agent Filmore in here!" He screams at his lawyer. "Why? Are you willing to cooperate?" Mr. Stavrou says. "Yes, but I only want to deal with Agent Filmore." Agent Filmore advised Cool Al a couple of hours ago that two narcotics detectives from Tampa were coming to see him today if he was willing to hear them out. He said yes but after his lawyer just told him Destiny was one of the detectives, he's screaming, there is no way he's gonna tell her anything, knowing she's Cash's girlfriend. He feels terrible about what he's about to do, but after hearing his options from Mr. Stavrou, he's left with no other choice. It's casualties in war he thinks to himself. He can't let it end like this. He's the king. "Go," Cool Al shouts to his lawyer.

"And if the detectives show up from Tampa, tell them I said fuck them. I only asked them to come so I j they can waste time, gas and to kiss my ass!" He laughs

Ten minutes later....

"I don't have time for your bullshit," Agent Filmore shouts, now knowing he's broke Cool Al and the upper hand is his. "I'm gonna let this pussy get off," Cool Al thinks to himself. "How about this," Cool Al says. "I will hand deliver you two cold blooded killers, a double murder, some assault rifles, drugs and a couple hundred grand. I want in return to be released immediately and this case forgotten about." "I'm good," Agent Filmore says bluffing. "Okay and I will make a few more busts for you once I get back on my feet. And you will work for me until I say its sufficient. Are we on the same page?" Agent Filmore says.

"Yes sir. One more thing. You cannot allow T.P.D. to know I'm working for you because it's a guy that's a heavy hitter, I want to bring down, has ties to one of those detectives," Cool Al lies. "Okay, done. I don't give two shits about T.P.D. What's the deal with the murders, drugs and weapons?"

Cool Al goes on to tell Agent Filmore about the murders of Lizanne and Mad Max and how he can get Ike and his own cousin Rolo on tape admitting it. When he goes to arrest them, how the money drugs and guns will be inside their spot. Excited, Agent Filmore rushes out of the room to put all the paperwork together to get Cool Al released.

DESTINY

"Yes, we would like to speak to Agent Filmore," Destiny says. Her and Det. Von are in the lobby of the Federal Holding Facility. "Hold on ma'am. Here he comes now." Rushing up, Agent Filmore introduces himself and shakes Destiny's and Det. Von's hands. "I'm sorry," he says. "This guy is a real asshole. His lawyer just notified me that he doesn't want to talk to ya'll. That he actually stated to tell ya'll that he never had intentions to speak to you all. He wanted to waste ya'lls time and gas. H also said for ya'll to kiss his ass. Stunned, Destiny rarely curses but she's so pissed she can't help it. She yells, "this little creep ass fuck boy thinks this is a game, huh?"

"Apparently so," Agent Filmore lies. "Sorry again. If something changes, I'll get in touch with you all," "Sgt. Thank you," Det. Von says grabbing Destiny before she gets them into trouble. "That chump," Destiny says walking towards their cruiser. "I'm gonna put his ass away, I promise. Let's go back and get to work." "We never went and talked to Terrell aka Tear. With his brother being killed he may have something to say," Det. Von says.

CASH

"Pop, I need for you and ma to make that month long trip to Florida now. I need some help taking care of some things." "What's up, son?" C-Money says. "I want to play a couple of games of chess old man," he is telling C-Money in code. This is serious business that can't be discussed over the phone. "Give us a couple of days. We will be there in less than 48 hours." "Okay pop. Tell my mother I said I love her." "Boy, I'm getting tired of your shit," laughs C-Money. "You know I love you too old man," Cash says laughing. "We love you too. How did the proposal go?" "Great, she said yes. Her family is a group of real down to earth people. I had a great time." "That's good. Tell my daughter in law I said hello, and we send our love." "For show old man," Cash says disconnecting the call.

COOL AL

This shit is crazy he thinks to himself. He's standing outside of the Federal impound waiting on Agent Filmore to bring him his Denali.

"What part of the game is this?" He shouts. "I've sold my soul to the devil." He knows his life will never be the same. He actually loves his lil cousin Rolo and has mad love for Ike. "Fuccck," he yells seeing his truck pull up. Getting out, Agent Filmore says, "let me show you something. All you have to do is push this button I had installed under your steering wheel and a recorder will pick up all of your conversation. Make sure you tum the music off before you get them to talking. Get them to admit the location of the crime, how it took place and what they did afterwards.

You're gonna have to get at least one of them to say their government name. If you can find out what they did with the murder weapon, that will be all the better. You have 3 days to get back to me. If I have to come and find you, you're not going to like it." "The fuck ever, let me go. Crazy as it may sound, I'm a man of my word," Cool Al says getting inside his truck. "Here is your cell phone. My number is programmed in it as Angie," Agent Filmore says giving Cool Al a wink. "Gay ass cracker," Cool Al says pulling off.

Ten minutes later Cool Al is on the Skyway bridge on his way to Tampa. He wanted to get as far as can be from St. Pete. Picking up his phone he calls Rolo. "Sup, Cuzzo?" Rolo answers. "I've been trying to call you all day and half of yesterday," Rolo says. "I saw the text. I had to put everything together," he lies.

"Ya'll ready to get this money?" Cool Al asks. "You already know. Ike is right here with me. We have 3 fine-ass white hoes over here. They are from Pinellas Park. You wanna come and get all the pussy and head you can stand?" "Naw, I'm gonna pass on this round. I'm on my way to my condo to beat up in super head Seleena's deep ass throat," Cool Al laughs. "That's the bizzness," Rolo shouts laughing.

DESTINY

"Bitch, I ain't got nothing to say to you," Tear shouts.

Destiny and Det. Von are at Orient Road Jail in the interview room with Tear. "Watch the way you talk to a woman," Det. Von says. "Fuck you too," yells Tear. Destiny calmly says, "we are here to help you. I personally went to the morgue to see your brother and the young lady Lizanne Wilson. It was not a pretty sight. I want the people responsible punished." "They'll get punished," Tear says with an evil look in his eyes. "My brother was my best friend and all I had to depend on to make sure my mother is safe." "For what it's worth, I'm sorry," Destiny says. "What do ya'll want?" Tear asks. "Tell us who killed your brother and his girlfriend." "I was in here thanks to you," Tear yells.

"And I'm not a snitch. If that's all you wish to speak about. Please call the guard to return me to my cell." "If you want us to put in a good word when you go to court, give us your connect or some good info on how to shut down the C.M.F. crew." Det. Von says. "Officer!" Tear yells loudly. "I ain't no snitch! Officer!" He yells again.

COOL AL

"Damn I'm tired." Cool Al says to himself while getting out of his Denali in front of him and Seleena's condo. He sees her Aston Martin in her space and smiles. Walking into his door he hears the stereo blasting Seleena Johnson's hit song, Heard it all before. Cool Al creeps around the condo until he sees Seleena laying naked on their king size canopy bed. "Hey queen!" He shouts scaring her damn near half to death. "Oh my God! You scared me boy!" She screams grabbing her chest. "You miss me?" Cool Al asks coming out of his clothes. Putting on a show, Seleena jumps up and jumps on Cool Al like she's so excited to see him. "Hey daddy," she yells grabbing him in a big bear hug. "I'm so glad you're out. I was so scared. When did you get out?" "You already know I came straight home to my queen.

I had my parents put up their house to get me out," he lies. He doesn't want nobody to know he's working for the feds. He feels so bad about doing so. "Come on daddy. Let me give you a hot bath. I'm so horny," she moans. "Me too," Cool Al says, heading towards the restroom.

One hour later....

"Ooooh shit," baby Cool Al moans. Him and Seleena are in the 69 position. "Oh, oh, yes that's it," Seleena shouts, having her first series of a powerful orgasm. "Eat it. Lick my cunt. Make love to your pussy. Cum, cuming I'm....cuming," she yells as her body begins to convulse uncontrollably. Grabbing Cool Al's dick as she opens her mouth to engulf his entire shaft. She begins to suck with earnestness. "Umm... Umm. You like that daddy?"

She moans with a mouthful of dick. "Oooh yes, baby eat your dick," shouts Cool Al. Seleena grabs his ass and buries his dick into her warm mouth. With one hand, Seleena grasps Cool Al's dick around the base and begins to jack it in time to meet her bobbing head. With the other hand, she cradles his balls and begins to squeeze them. "Oooh fuck," Cool Al stifles a cry, and he erupts in her adorable mouth, sending jet after powerful jet of hot semen slashing against the back of her throat. Freaky to the core, Seleena continues to keep sucking and swallowing until Cool Al goes limp in her mouth and releases with a pop. Looking up at Cool Al for approval, Cool Al notices a few droplets of sperm at the corner of her mouth which she promptly licks off. "Fan-fucking-tastic," Cool Al yells.

CASH

"We are at the airport now. Are you close by?" C-Money asks. "I'm pulling up, pop. Ya'll can walk outside. I'll be parked in front." "That's the business C-Money says.

Ten minutes later....

"Hey son," Tonya says hugging Cash. "You beautiful lady," Cash says hugging her back. "What's good, slim?" C-Money asks giving his son a big hug. "Money, power, respect," Cash says. returning the hug. "Ya'll miss Florida?" Cash asks. "No!" They reply laughing. "You better believe it," C-Money says smiling. "I need to see my crazy daughter and my grand babies." "Me too," Tonya says. "You know we're 813 all day. Let's go," she says getting into the passenger side of Cash's SUV.

Cash tells them the bad news. Tonya starts crying and says, "little Albert had that done to me? And had Andre killed? Why?" "Greed baby," C-Money replies. "Jealousy and envy. Don't leave that out pop." "Those guys shot my friend. What would they have done to me had you not given him the money?" Tonya cries. "He's got to go," C-Money yells. "No, we are not gonna kill him," Ms. Tonya shouts. "What?" Cash yells. "We're not gonna kill him I say. You say the feds have him. Let that be his punishment. I don't want any more bloodshed. I want you both to look at me and promise me ya'll won't kill him or have him killed." Cash says, "okay ma." C-Money says, "I ain't promising shit! He kidnapped my queen, took my $500,000 and had my best friend son killed." "I'll give you your money back," Tonya yells. "Can you give me Fat Dre back?

What about my guilt? I will only promise that I won't touch him while he's in prison or jail. If I see him, I don't care what I may do." "Please talk to him Cash," Ms. Tonya shouts. "I'm his dad, ain't nothing to say," C-Money shouts. He's past upset. "Take me to the house in Lutz," Mrs. Tonya shouts. "I feel ill." "I'm sorry baby," C-Money says. "I'll go to the house with you and calm down. Cash, call your big sister and ask her to bring my grandkids to the house."

DESTINY

"Well partner, I guess we have to accept that these two crews are over."

Destiny is at the police precinct, sitting at her cubicle talking to Det. Von. "Cheer up. We took them down. Most of them are in jail. Unfortunately, the rest are in the graveyard." Det. Von responds. "I know it. Feels like we didn't win. Nobody is being held responsible for the murders." "Maybe they will. We're narcotics detectives. Let the homicide department do their jobs." "You're right partner. I'm sorry. Let's hit the streets and see what's popping now that C.M.F. and Dirty Money are done. One thing I know, people are not gonna stop doing or selling drugs because two crews were shut down." "That's my partner," Det. Von yells patting Destiny on her back. "Come on. Let's ride.

SELEENA

"I'm glad his ass is asleep," Seleena thinks to herself as she watches Cool Al sleep like a baby. She creeps out of the bed and grabs her phone. She sends Cash a quick text. *He's out. He came here about 5:00 pm today. I miss you and love you. Seleena.* She then erases the text and goes to the kitchen to fix her a glass of wine and wait for a reply. It comes a few seconds later. *You bonded him out?* Cash text. *No! He say his parents put their house up to get him out.* Seleena responds back. *So what's the deal? You still with me?* Cash texts. *Of course. This is why I'm sneaking to text you now. You're the only man I've ever truly loved. Okay this is how we are gonna handle this.* Cash texts.

CHAPTER 34

I know you love this life....

DESTINY

"Baby what do you want to eat?" Destiny asks. "It doesn't matter baby. I've been at the spot all day. Me and Veronica have both been running like crazy. You know its income tax time so everybody has money. I personally sold 7 pairs of rims, set up two paint jobs and 4 music hook-ups." "Why don't we just order a pizza? I'll meet you at the house by 8:30 pm." Cash says, "ok sweetie. Do you need anything out of Walgreens? I need to stop by there to grab a few things." Destiny responds, "no baby I'm good." "I love you, beautiful." "Not more than I love you," Destiny replies.

Two hours later....

"Stop teasing me," Cash moans. "Finger licking good," Destiny says smacking her lips as she begins teasing Cash's dick again with her lovely mouth. "Oooh yes baby," Cash moans in pure joy. Destiny is licking from the base to the tip of Cash's dick as if it's a popsicle. "Do you love your fiance?" "Sooo much," Cash moans.

The past 3 months Destiny has turned into a straight freak with Cash.

Her head finally goes down on his 9' dick. She almost makes the whole thing disappear into the depths of her warm-mouth. Cash sighs in ecstasy, building intense waves of pleasure. He's almost at the brink of a climactic explosion. Destiny abruptly stops and grins. "Oh, hell naw," Cashmere yells. "You wanna play?"

Cash flips Destiny on her back and begins to lick her inner thighs, tantalizing but not yet touching her labia lips. He works up and around teasing and taunting Destiny with his tongue. "Oooh shit," Destiny moans as Cash returns to her impatient sweet-smelling cunt. The entrance to her pleasure purse opens slightly revealing a bright pink interior that glistens with love honey. Cashmere plunges his tongue deep inside Destiny. He's determined to lick and suck her dry. "Oh God, that's it!" Destiny screams rocking to the rhythm of Cash's oral probing. Cash withdraws from Destiny, not wanting her to climax. "Ooh you think this is a game?" Shouts Destiny. Cash smiles saying, "you still wanna play?" "Whatever," Destiny yells as she takes Cash's erection in her hands.

She raises herself to her knees and poised her dripping pussy over Cash's trembling dick. "Uuummm," Destiny slowly impales herself on his dick. "Ooooh baby it feels so good," Destiny moans. "This pussy feels sooo good!" Yells Cash. Destiny goes wild, humping up and down, round and around. Faster and faster, she pumps Cash's dick with her pussy. "I can't take it baby," Cash yells. "I'm cumin," Cash spews his milky load in a violent series of eruptions at the same time Destiny is trembling in throes of her own convulsive climax. Her body arches and stiffens as she cries out in ecstasy. "Omg!! I'm so in love with you," Destiny yells. "I love you more," Cash replies.

Ten minutes later....

"Baby look at what I bought," Destiny says holding up a home pregnancy test. Cash smiles. Destiny's period ain't been on in almost 2 months. "Come on," she yells pulling him towards the bathroom. "We'll do this together.

Five minutes later...

"Omg, Cashmere, it's pink! I'm pregnant!" Cash screams, "I'm about to be a father!!" He's ecstatic. The feeling of having a family with the love of his life overwhelms him so much, tears are coming out of his eyes. He grabs Destiny and shouts, "baby I'm gonna be the best father and husband in the world. Set up an appointment to see a doctor as soon as possible, so we can make sure you're both in the best of health and care. "Oh baby, I love you," shouts Destiny. "God is soooo good."

TEAR

"What the fuck you want cracker?" Tear yells. "Get dressed. You have court today." "Man, it says I don't have a court date for 2 more months on the kiosk machine." "I don't give two shits about what's on the kiosk machine. You're on the court docket for today. You have 10 minutes to be dressed and downstairs by the officer station," yells the burly bad bodied detention deputy.

3 hours later...

"Man, I don't know what the fuck is going on," Tear says talking to a nigga named Toot out of West Tampa. They are sitting in a holding cell at Hillsborough County Courthouse on Twiggs Street. "Terrell Roberts!" Shouts a bailiff. "Let's go. They're ready for you.

Walking into the crowded courtroom in his freshly pressed orange jumpsuit, Tear immediately spots his mother sitting next to Shayla. Shayla is looking like a super model in a yellow Versace pantsuit. "Yes, your honor. I'm attorney Charles Lohen. I'm representing Mr. Roberts. We have two motions to run by you today. One being a motion to suppress all the evidence and throw out the charges against my client. The officers never said T.P.D. and no search warrant was issued prior to the raid on the residence my client was a visitor of. "What says the state?" "Judge Bienke, your honor, I just got this motion two days ago. I have not had time to interview T.P.D. or look over this motion. T.P.D. is not available today. Can you please give me a couple of weeks to look over this motion?" "I'll grant you 3 weeks to have T.P.D. here in my courtroom with a valid search warrant," Judge Bienke says.

"Now this other motion is?" "It's for a bond your honor. My client has never been arrested in his life and has plenty of support. His mother, fiancé' Shayla along with plenty of other people he's never seen in his life stand up. "WTF," Tear thinks. State Judge Bienke says, "your honor, this violent man attempted to murder a police officer. He's a menace to society. He's been connected to numerous murders and suspected of being a major drug dealer. I request he remains without bond. I would think that T.P.D. would be available to see a monster who shot at them." "Seeing they're not, I'm granting this motion and setting Mr. Robert's bond at $75,000. I want you all back here in 3 weeks to hear this motion to suppress. Next case. Bailiff, you may take Mr. Roberts back to the holding cell." "I need 5 minutes with my client your honor." "Granted. Next case."

"Terrell, your fiancé' Shayla hired me. She said to tell you she is posting your bond now. She has to head to Miami for a few days. Your mother has $10,000. She'll see you soon and never forget it's a Dirty Game." "Thank you, main man." Tear says shaking Mr. Lohen's hand. Walking back to the holding cell, Tear has one thing on his mind, revenge, "I'm going to kill everyone affiliated with C.M.F. and that detective bitch Destiny Jenkins for shooting me and causing me to not be able to protect my brother...

THE END

END OF BOOK QUESTIONS

1. Who is your favorite character?

2. What happens with Chrishonna?

3. Is Auntie Donna going to stay with the Doctor?

4. Will Drena and D ever change?

5. How does the fairy-tale end for Meme?

6. Does it end happily-ever-after for Camille - or in disaster?

7. Is Lil' Cot gonna get away with setting up Cool Al?

8. Is Cool Al really gonna set up Rolo and Ike?

9. Is the Dirty Game and CMF crews over?

10. Does Destiny and Cash ever get married?

11. Is Baby Doll going to fulfill her promise she made to her dying mom, Roxy?

12. Will C-Money listen to his wife and let Cool Al live?

13. Do you think Destiny will ever find out Cash was the head of CMF?

14. What happens with Shayla?

15. Does Cash need to get revenge for his moms kidnapping? Fat Dre's murder?

16. Would Destiny allow her love for Cash to hinder her from arresting him?

17. Should Cash tell Destiny the full truth about his past life?

18. Is Fonda gonna break and start snitching?

19. What does Destiny have? A boy or a girl?

20. Does Tear complete his mission?

THESE QUESTIONS (and more) WILL
BE ANSWERED IN PART II

Made in United States
Orlando, FL
18 October 2022

23579207R10320